EMPTY BETWEEN THE STARS

- Book 1 in the Songs of Old Sol series. -

by Stephen Hunt

EMPTY BETWEEN THE STARS

Copyright © 2018 by Stephen Hunt

First published in 2018 by Green Nebula Press.

Typeset and designed by Green Nebula Press. The right of Stephen Hunt to be identified as the author of this work has been asserted by him in accordance with the Copyright, Designs and Patents Act 1988.

All rights reserved. No part of this publication may be reproduced or distributed in any form or by any means, or stored in a database or retrieval system, without the prior written permission of the publisher. Any person who does any unauthorised act in relation to this publication may be liable to criminal prosecution and civil claims for damages. Cover illustration by Grand Failure (via Deposit Photos, Inc).

This book is sold subject to the conditions that it shall not, by way of trade or otherwise, be lent, re-sold, hired out or otherwise circulated without the publisher's prior consent in any form of binding or cover other than that in which it is published and without a similar condition including this condition being imposed on a subsequent purchaser.

ISBN: 9781983183980

www.StephenHunt.net

Twitter: @s_hunt_author
www.facebook.com/SciFi.Fantasy

First Edition

Printed in the U.S.A & United Kingdom

"The world of the future will be an ever more demanding struggle against the limitations of our own intelligence, not a comfortable hammock in which we can lie down to be waited upon by our robot slaves."
- Norbert Wiener, cybernetics pioneer. Carbon Age (1894–1964).

"Any sufficiently advanced technology is indistinguishable from magic."
- Arthur C. Clarke, author. Carbon Age (1917–2008).

To receive an automatic notification by e-mail when Stephen's new books are available for download (and get a free e-book), use the sign-up form at http://www.StephenHunt.net/alerts.php

To help report any typos, errors and similar in this work, use the form at http://www.stephenhunt.net/typo/typoform.php

Also by Stephen Hunt

SLIDING VOID
Sliding Void
Transference Station
Red Sun Bleeding
Void All the Way Down (Omnibus #1,2,3)
Anomalous Thrust
Hell Fleet (coming soon)

THE FAR-CALLED SERIES
In Dark Service
Foul Tide's Turning
The Stealers' War

THE JACKELIAN SERIES
The Court of the Air
The Kingdom Beyond the Waves
Rise of the Iron Moon
Secrets of the Fire Sea
Jack Cloudie
From the Deep of the Dark
Mission to Mightadore

THE AGATHA WITCHLEY MYSTERIES
In the Company of Ghosts
The Plato Club
The Moon Man's Tale
Secrets of the Moon (Omnibus #1,2,3)

STANDALONE BOOKS
Six Against the Stars
For the Crown and the Dragon
The Fortress in the Frost
Hell Sent
Empty Between The Stars

- 1 -
Epi-Log. As prologue.

I moaned. It wasn't easy being crucified. Certainly not at my age. Even a few centuries ago I would have been better prepared to survive this horrifying ordeal. Blood soaked my arms underneath the tight orange restraining suit binding me. I had just started coughing part of my lungs over my chest, too. I didn't need to have trained as a surgeon to know that wasn't a good sign.

I tried to recall how I had reached this desperate point. There had been a moon and a hard, thankless task. The kind I often find myself lumbered with. Death, treachery, murder. The usual.

Dying. My turn, this time, at long last.

Then I remembered. *Everything*!

= 2 =
Difficult. Arrivings.

Like so much of my life, arriving at Hexator was a harder process than it should have been – a journey of three parts, nested like a Russian doll. *Poor William Roxley. Never the easy path for Sweet William.* First, departing the foldship carrying visitors to this tidally-locked moon. My departure was entirely necessary, of course. The thirty-mile-long black dart of artificial diamond-hull composing our monstrous foldship had never been designed to land on any world. Not even a world-sized moon, one of many orbiting the ferocious crimson gas giant below. The name the foldship had chosen for herself was *You Can't Prove It Was Us*. An appropriate appellation for Madame Monster. Her massive bulk would stay hugging orbit until after the auctions had concluded below.

Thousands of mile-long tendrils quivered behind the foldship's stern, giving her the look of a cathedral half-swallowed by a squid. A sailor on board the vessel had told me her tendrils were designed to squeeze the universe so tight the universe begged the foldship to release it; passage across the vast gulf between stars being the tribute—or extortion, depending on your viewpoint—struck between craft and universe. *Hah*. Sailors never run short of their superstitions. Well, our foldship had squeezed space-time to beneficial effect. Here we were, now, only two months relative time-lapse out of Arius. You couldn't do much better than 2RTL reaching this forgotten corner of the galaxy.

Second, my own craft, the *Expected Ambush*, cut her mooring lines and drifted away from the mothership on controlled thrusts of air, her sleek lines trumpeting my true origins a little too loudly. I was enormously proud of *Exy*'s capabilities, don't doubt that. Her speed, her ability to soak up and dish out punishment second-to-none. I have even grown fond of her over-familiar manners. But as far as Hexator's inhabitants were concerned, possession of the *Expected Ambush* would be like dragging a sack of treasure into a tavern owned by outlaws. In the unlikely event I was permitted to land her on Hexator, my prize vessel would draw unwanted attention to her owner. Only the gods knew how many imbeciles I would need to slay to keep her as my property.

I had a more pressing problem to deal with: a rotting corpse to eject towards Hexator. A cadaver encased using a rock-like spray, all the better to burn up during re-entry while doing a fine impression of a meteoroid. I never discovered the woman's name or indeed much else about her. Except she hadn't anticipated my checking hand-move during the brief knife fight which ensued when she tried to fillet me on board the foldship. I suppose I could have teased out her identity, career highlights and who hired her to kill me. But the truth is I no longer cared enough to take would-be assassins alive. Like coping with toddlers throwing tantrums, I had grown tired of constantly being expected to be mother. "Oh dear, my little love. What have I done to upset you? What can I dangle before you to make you sweet again?" Mother was weary. No, I simply couldn't muster the requisite enthusiasm to sound like a detective in a bad piece of theater. "Who sent you? What do they want?" Better to slap that screeching brat down and shut it up. Motives are irrelevant. Intentions everything.

Irritated with humanity at large, I watched my identityless would-be executioner flare like a firework as her fake rock-covered coffin tumbled down towards the moon. I would have whispered a prayer for her if I knew what god she favoured; as pointless as such communion would have been. There weren't any gods in this system. But they were certainly coming. Sooner or later.

The *Expected Ambush* was one of a hundred smaller ships hitching a ride in the foldship's hangars or clinging limpet-like to her hull. Hexator's traffic control system operated as primitively as the planet itself, but even so, I didn't want to give the locals a fair chance at tracking me among the separating swarm of visitors. I had already positioned myself in a battered ferry loaded inside the *Expected Ambush*'s starboard launch tube – for my arrival's third act. The most notable thing about this previously owned ferry was that she had actually visited Hexator on several occasions – her transponder on record as a known quantity with the port authorities. The ferry didn't come with a name in the flea-market where I purchased her. Only a code, the CF-57D, registered out of Rigel. That and the logo of a heel with wings engraved on her saucer section. Mercury, perhaps? From an age where gods were imagined rather than manufactured. I had named the rickety ferry the *Pleiad's Daughter*. A twang from the rail and we launched. My ferry spun down towards the moon as the *Expected Ambush* started to fold gravity around herself like a cloak. Optical camouflage made her shimmer and vanish to the naked eye while she withdrew to a safe distance. The only trace of her presence from now on — even to me — would be tiny streaks of micrometeorites burning up in Hexator's thin atmosphere. In actuality, disposable communications packages. It was comforting to know I possessed a guardian angel circling in outer orbit. More immediate than praying to the many gods, in my experience. *Good.* I could do with the reassurance. I was a regular visitor to dark places. There were few darker than Hexator.

It went without saying that Hexator was about to become important. I wouldn't be visiting this arse-dirt clinging to the bottom cheeks of the galaxy if that wasn't the case. The first danger to survive was re-entry. Inside my ferry, the ancient composites of her construction whistled and creaked as the hull expanded in a blaze of heat. Shaking like a vindictive amusement park ride designed by professional sadists. I caught an eye-full of fiery hell from her bridge, a pitted pod atop the saucer-shaped cargo section. Unlike the *Expected Ambush* — which settled and rose where she pleased — my ferry relied on a friendly reception at port. I knew precisely when the harbour's landing beams locked onto the saucer's iron skirt. Perfumed lemon gel inside my acceleration couch hardened, vibrations increasing to a crescendo, the small trading vessel's iron skeleton flexed and squeezed. We slowed fast from that point. Man and saucer both. I smiled despite my concerns. The 50th millennium of man and here I was arriving at Hexator like some bug-eyed alien from a mid-twentieth century paranoia dream ... an invader from Mars or Venus.

It took twenty minutes from atmospheric interface to landing. Another five before I found my gravity legs inside the port proper. Initially, my ferry wouldn't allow me to leave due to the high radiation readings outside. I over-rode the craft's warning system. The moon's port was powered by a portable nuclear reactor, imported as a black box unit and left to its own devices as far as maintenance was concerned. A little like buying a ground vehicle and throwing it away after it ran out of its first battery charge.

Local gravity matched Earth-standard. About the moon's only similarity to our ancestral home, having studied Hexator's almanac listing at leisure. My suitcase struggled behind me, metal legs buckling as it acclimatized to the world. Our welcome was surprisingly sophisticated. It didn't matter how backward the planet. Where off-world trade was permitted, the local grandees ran as advanced a screening program as could reasonably be mustered. A series of sealed scrubbing locks, followed by scanning tunnels with clouds of medical and security nano. Imperceptibly sampling and poking, ensuring I wasn't nurturing a pandemic which would infect half the locals before a cure could be distributed. After the medical probes, a security tunnel manned by human port soldiers. Male, as far as I could tell under their light hex-plate amour.

They opened my suitcase and spread my clothes and possessions across a glowing table, little icons and trails of text floating above the surface indicating the origin and composition of my property. Prayer box. Oak. Universal configuration for multi-deity worship. Spare trousers. Seventy percent cotton, thirty percent polymer. A small bundle of yarrows for the *i-Ching*. Three bars of chocolate, eighty percent cocoa. My possessions, apart from the chocolate, did little to excite the soldiers' interest. This brute squad were Hexatorian locals, if the albino-white skin of the wrists I glimpsed between gloves and amour was any guide.

One of them leaned menacingly towards me. 'You are Doctor William Roxley?'

'I am,' I agreed pleasantly. Butter wouldn't melt in my mouth. Hah. Butter. Did they still have cows here?

'Purpose of visit to Hexator?' growled a soldier with rank markings on his shoulder plate. I obviously wasn't important enough to receive a polite reception. *Marvelous, truly.* If they began acting courteously towards me, I'd need to be seriously suspicious.

'spore-spice trading,' I answered. I noted the patina of text and images scrolling across his visor. Judging my papers, passport and visa details.

One of the soldiers held up a small linen bag where a brass mouthpiece was visible poking out of the sack. 'What is this?'

'A flute,' I replied. I saw he didn't have a clue about what I was talking about. 'A musical instrument,' I explained.

'The table told us that, but how can you play the thing when there're no strings on it?'

I drew the flute out of the bag, pressed it to my lips and blew a short piece from the *Flight of the Bumblebee*. 'You've never seen a flute before?'

'Clearly not,' said the soldier.

'You play well for a trader,' growled one of his comrades. It was good to be suspicious and you could never be too mistrustful of Sweet William.

'Traders spend a lot of time between the stars,' I said. 'It's nice to carry something of home with you. When I play, I dream of my family far away.' That might have been true, once. These days I played only to forget.

The senior officer tapped my bars of chocolate. Expensive even for the world of Thun, a place of quiet luxuries where master chocolatiers were treated like royalty. 'Foodstuffs aren't allowed on Hexator without an import license.'

I shrugged. 'I don't possess a license. They are intended as gifts for my contacts here. Could I not keep them?'

'Without a license they are confiscated.' The soldier scooped the bars off the table, carefully dropping them into a basket behind the table. All government is a form of robbery; shit-holes like Hexator were just less subtle about it.

I managed to look pained, but that was the point of those

bars. Better they steal the chocolate than my flute. Refined sugar was unknown on Hexator. A sweet tooth, though, was still almost universal among the human race. On dry worlds I carried whiskey with me. On orthodox worlds, a chip of the filthiest simcore. On sugarless worlds, chocolate. Bribing without offering hard currency is an effortless form of corruption.

'Your auction fees have been paid, your credit line recognized by the banking guild.'

I nodded eagerly. I'd have purchased their entire dirty world-sized moon if it would have helped matters. If it was for sale. But it wouldn't and it wasn't. Never the easy path for William Roxley. I am sure that is a universal constant baked into the physics of existence from the first quantum firing. If there is an easy path, let it be denied to Sweet William. I might have considered it character building if I hadn't lived for so long. Such nuisances are only character building for the first couple of centuries. After that, botherations are well-and-truly character-vexing.

'The spore-spice auctions begin in a couple of weeks,' said the soldier. 'Keep out of trouble until then.'

'Odd's fish, m'dears, of course,' I lied, keeping a straight face as I fibbed. How could these doltish armoured spear carriers actually believe me? Trouble was my business. My song. My raison d'être. The fingers that rubbed my rhubarb. I repacked my baggage, dropped it to the ground, and watched it regrow three legs on either side, all the better to scuttle after me. I was yet to catch my first proper glimpse of the moon's surface. The *Pleiad's Daughter* had settled on a repulser beam tower where I exited directly into the port's visitor decontamination system. On I went. The port's corridors and rooms were also windowless and brightly lit. They could have belonged to pettifogging bureaucracies in any number of locations – hospitals, police stations, tax offices. Like their expensive scanning equipment, the whole affair had been constructed by an off-world infrastructure outfit specializing in airlifting pre-built structures into alien locales. I took a single-direction airlock to exit the security zone and the true nature of the moon began to reveal itself. The port's interior a vast entrance hall of polished wood – one of many local fungal timbers. Port workers idled among groups of merchants, visitors coming and going. Panhandlers hollered slogans for services and wares. I approached a deck polisher in overalls on his knees, busy rubbing wax into the floor, his bucket nearby. He looked an ancient seventy. In this place that was probably his actual age.

'Local guides?' I asked, hopefully.

He glanced up wearily from his labours. Almost reluctantly, as though the floor was the most important thing in his life. 'Expensive or cheap?'

'Cheap, most surely.'

'In the far corner, moneyass.' Moneyass was local slang for offworlder. I smiled to myself. I didn't feel much like a walking wallet, but that was what I was to almost everyone here. Hexator wasn't so much Third World as Twelfth World. The cleaner pointed toward an assemblage of young urchins wearing cloth trousers and laced shirts in the local style. From the way they gathered it was obvious they weren't a gang – rather, a group of competing free agents. I passed Master Polisher a small coin by way of thanks which he accepted gratefully. It was the currency of the foldship above; its rarity here making it far more valuable than the local currency I carried.

The urchins' eyes flicked nervously towards patrolling soldiers from the city watch. No advanced hex-amour on these brutes. Just swagger, black-and-crimson leather uniforms and a holstered sawn-off shotgun belted to the right leg. *Excellent.* So, the urchins' presence was barely tolerated inside the port. Unlikely to have spies set to watch for the likes of me. Unlikely – but not, of course, impossible. Secret police and their informers were like crotch-itch; the scuzzers infiltrated the most unexpected places. The ragamuffins stood straighter as I approached, attempting to project a health and vigour I doubt any of them felt. My eyes darted across the group. I let my m-brain process their faces and builds, feeding me suggestions as a barely conscious hunch. The canny little bio-computer augment, curled tight inside my skull like a watchful fox, rarely let me down.

'You,' I said, pointing to a thin gawky stick of a boy at the rear. He appeared as surprised at being selected as his competitors. Delta dog in a beta pack. A few tuts and clenched jaw-lines among his chalk-skinned peers told me I had chosen exactly as intended. The lad didn't dare push through the others, but sidled around the back to join me by my side. He attempted to reach down to take my case. I smiled as I stopped him.

'Don't bother. It has six perfectly good legs and needs its exercise.'

'Is it alive or a machine, sir?' asked the boy, nervously.

'I don't doubt it's a little bit of both. What's your name, laddie?'

'Simenon, sir.'

'I am William Roxley, Simenon. You have no family name, no house name?'

'An orphan,' mumbled the boy. 'Simenon Wrongman.'

Old ways, here. A bastard. A thing of shame. A Wrongman. Bottom rung of society, with all the other steps pulled far out of his reach. Defined by birth, fixed from birth. Not everywhere was like Hexator, but far too many places were. Especially this far out from the Humanitum Core. "The Empty", sneered those born to civilization. But this border area wasn't really empty. If it had been, my life would be a lot less troubled. "The Contested" was a better description of this stretch of the galaxy. I glanced at my newly hired guide with his distinctive shambling gait. Simenon's face appeared pallid and gaunt, even for a native of Hexator. A sharp nose and curly black hair like someone had given a ball of string electro-shock therapy, then glued it down at random across the lad's scalp.

A strange bird. But then I could hardly talk. I appeared middle-aged even though I wasn't. Handsome enough – or vain enough to think myself still so. Take your pick. Sweet William's dark hair might be fading to silver, but his green eyes still twinkled with mischief. Six feet tall and never humbled. And you can take that to the bank.

We left the port complex through a high arched doorway and I caught my first sight of the real Hexator outside. The world's capital, Frente. Tidally locked to its monstrous gas giant, Li, this world-moon was a planetlet of two halves. Its habitable hemisphere lay in perpetual twilight, facing away from the storms and radiation spikes of the gas giant. The local star was way too distant for any significant night or day cycle here. Daylight on Hexator was murk. Nighttime was Stygian murk. By contrast, the half of the moon permanently facing Li existed as a burning hell-scape, seared so fiercely even the shadows had been chased away. Gravity compression of the moon's core kept the dark side of the moon warm enough to support life. It was a tribute to humanity's fecundity and love of making feet for children's stockings, shaking the sheets, biting the pillow and generally playing nug-a-nug that Hexator had seemed like a good bet to some settlers in the dim and distant past. Mankind had screwed its merry way across the galaxy and we'd seen no good reason to stop when we'd arrived *here* ten-thousand-years earlier. A world of always-night. No wonder Simenon and his cohorts were albinos.

Fungi were the dominant vegetation form on Hexator. Mushrooms and toadstool analogues in seemingly infinite varieties. The smallest as tiny as thumbnails, the largest as high as twenty-storey buildings. In the early days, the newly established Hexatorians – the ever-interloping *us* – had tried clearing the local biome to make way for a more comfortable Earth-standard ecosystem. Right up until humanity's colonists realized that the fungi absorbed the worst excesses of Li's energy storms. And you really *didn't* want to try to survive on Hexator without a forest of perfectly adapted lightning conductors nestled around you. I believe that opening period of Hexatorian history was still referred to as the Great Burning. A pertinent warning to any axe-wielding arse-hat tempted to lay around with gay abandon.

With the port complex sitting behind me, my guide and I overlooked a stone-paved plaza designed to overwhelm visiting villagers. Less grand to me, given the desperate clots of beggars lacking limbs, sight, and luck, rattling wooden cups for alms towards every visitor. Opposite the plaza, streets were laid out narrow and low for protection from the heavens. Given Mother Li's rages, everything on Hexator was built low. No building more than three storeys high – most just a couple of floors – and all nestled among towering mushrooms. Human structures were largely constructed from wood-analogue harvested from hardier fungi. Many of the fungi-forms radiated a gentle bio-luminance. The largest mushroom I had encountered to date was the Chanterelle-variety sitting on a plate. The effect here was as though someone had constructed a toy Tudor town among a giant mushroom wonderland. Perhaps as a reaction to living in permanent darkness, the locals lit their city like old Hong Kong. Lampposts around the plaza broke the perpetual night, strings of lanterns dangling from shopfronts and residences. Chinese lantern-style business signage. The world-moon was comfortably warm, an unwavering seventeen degrees. Clothes were mainly for social differentiation markers, here. I could have strolled around naked if it wasn't for the constant winds whipping around Hexator. Far too strong to endure comfortably. Gusts and darkness, those were the two abiding memories visitors left Hexator with. If they made it out alive.

Wagons and carriages rattled across the plaza, pulled by Terran horses. I felt a twinge of pity for the creatures. Their ancestors hadn't volunteered to be dragged to distant realms inside a clone bank. Nearby, a woman cried her wares. She pushed a mobile book cart, dogeared paper tomes pressed tight on its shelves. Cheaper to rent than to buy, apparently. A flock from a local winged species sat on the cap of a nearby mushroom. Creatures that looked eighty-percent insect and twenty-percent lizard, singing not unpleasantly with gossamer wings clutched around them like a vampire's cape.

Simenon fixed me with a neutral gaze. 'What sort of lodgings do you require, Master Roxley?'

'Not so cheap I will get fleas or mugged, but not much more expensive than that.'

'Mugged...?'

'Set upon by thieves, footpads and highwaymen, Simenon.'

The local idiomatic still tasted like magnesium on my tongue. I had downloaded the Hexatorian language the final night before departing the foldship. I briefly regretted I hadn't allowed my m-brain to fully marinate in the language over a couple of months or more. But on reflection, it was probably better I spoke like a machine-taught rube. Native fluency with linguistic subtleties would have marked me out from travelers with honest business on the moon.

'Ah, *rolled*,' said Simeon. 'Not much danger of that, sir. The city of Frente is heavily patrolled by the Watch as well as the Four's soldiers during auction season.'

'And which are the Four Families ruling Hexator presently?'

'The Derechors, The Trabbs, the Seltins, and the Blez, sir.'

He had correctly named the houses in order of precedence – by how much of the moon and its scant resources they controlled. Clever lad. And every scrap of knowledge he gained had been learned the hard way; the school of hard knocks. No m-brain downloads for this child. Not even a blackboard, wax tablet and old-fashioned stylus. Beyond apprenticeships little better than slavery, academic education in this realm was the preserve of the well-monied. Simenon spoke well, given his background – he had picked up on the vocabulary of those he toiled for. No gang argot or street speak. *Fake it till you make it,* I told myself.

Simeon continued, 'The *Sparrow's Rest* is clean and reasonably priced, sir, although it does back onto a canal.'

Which meant the tavern reeked; but you didn't get to my age without learning how to hold your nose – both literally and figuratively. Fine, it would be largely free of foreign traders and off-world travelers, which was my real requirement.

'And are there many sparrows on Hexator?'

The lad pointed to the flock of bug-parrot-lizards humming away on the fungi cap.

'Well, I can only trust my trading opportunities are prettier than your idea of sparrows.'

The *Sparrow's Rest* proved to be a coaching inn, nestled

between towering clumps of cactus-shaped basidiomycota. The tavern stood two storeys-tall with a gray slated tile roof. An archway led onto its central courtyard and stables. Stacks of kindling sat piled in front of the building as smoke coiled from kitchen chimneys into a dark star-scattered sky. Upon entering, I discovered the building actually had four levels –two of them basements. In an inversion of the usual state of affairs, the most expensive rooms were rented lower down. I took a pair of connecting loft rooms at the back of the inn on the top floor. Hopefully, the *Expected Ambush* would transmit word of out-of-season storms with enough warning for me to scurry towards a rock-shielded burrow. I paid my landlady, one Mistress Miggs, with native coinage; my Hexatorian currency so ancient it still carried sigil codes for digital counterparts on a blockchain that no longer existed. Hexator had lost the last vestiges of its mass consumer culture by the seventh century of the land's colonization. Now, my new landlady merely bit into the coin's rare metal to prove its providence instead of scanning my payment to ensure it hadn't been forged by my ship's printer. I would have to load up on the local currency at some point. Each of the Four Families now issued its own script, as did a few of the larger local banking houses. Backed by spore-spice and bad intentions. My accommodation offered a view over a herb garden at the rear, and beyond that, a rock wall and the promised canal and its towpath. Nothing romantic about the canal. A functional conduit for the capital city's effluent. As well as a means of transporting produce from outlying farms, quarries, and mines by horse-pulled barges and oar-wielding raftmen. One such raft drifted past as I watched, bargemen poling on three corners with a pile of cloth-wrapped bundles lumped across the barge.

'Do you have any special requirements for your meals,

Master Roxley?' inquired Simenon as I inhaled warm air through the open window.

I didn't need my auditory filters to flag the rumbles in his belly. The boy's pinched face spoke volumes for the irregularities of his feeding times.

'I eat only raw carrots, laddie.'

'Carrots?'

I laughed at the barely disguised disappointment on his face. 'Sorry, I enjoy teasing people far too much. One of my many foibles. You may select whatever is good, wholesome and on the menu here.'

Simenon looked relieved.

'C is for carrots, orange and tall, but on Hexator they grow not at all,' I whistled while encouraging my case to climb on top of the room's bed. Once settled, my palm print opened the bag and I rummaged around its contents to locate my flute. 'Two matters to attend for me, Master Simenon. First, I need to make an offering to the gods. This is a flute . . . a prized musical instrument which has been in my family for generations. Take the flute down to the herb garden and plant it two hands below the soil, at least sixteen inches deep.'

'This will please your gods?'

'One in particular, Modd. He appreciates a good sacrifice, does Modd.'

Simenon looked uncertain, but I doubt it was the strangest request a local guide had received from an offworlder.

'And your second errand, sir?'

'I need to secure the services of a robot for the duration of my stay here.'

'A machine man, a ruster?'

'Precisely.'

'There are not many machine men in Frente,' said Simenon, as though there was another city on the moon where they were plentiful. Fat chance. 'People are cheaper than rusters, here.'

As trusty a sign as any of a failed state too long stewing in its own bath juices.

'After we've eaten, then,' I said.

Locating a robot for hire was an errand poor young Simenon was guaranteed to fail at. Unless he returned with some purloined antiquated weather drone or half-senile floor polishing unit. The prospect of a satisfying meal cheered him up no end, though. He drifted downstairs to procure food against my room's tab.

Lunch, when it arrived, was a variety of small spherical vegetables, along with spiced shrimp-like insects whose chitin had been boiled to perfection, shells peeling away like wax paper. Simenon ate his bowl's contents with far more relish than me. Not for the first time, I was grateful for my genetically modified gut flora. A traveller's tummy. I could pretty much survive on dirt, bark, and discarded shoe leather and still digest a meal from it. Oh well, the tavern's home cooking proved superior to old shoe leather by a light-year. There was also a bottle of wine – fermented from local toadstools – which tasted of notes of mouldy bread combined with an aroma of mushroom soup. That would take more getting used to. After Simenon had eaten, the boy left to try to locate my robot. I set aside my meal, half-consumed.

At the window, I amused myself by watching the lad kneeling and muttering to himself in the herb garden as he dug and buried my flute. It spoke for the lad's innate honesty that he hadn't slipped out and tried to pawn my flute with the nearest fence. In a spiderweb across the window, I noted a tiny female spider leaping on its mate and filling it with toxin. She looked like a stowaway from a human world, rather than a local life-form. We had carried so much of our ancient home with us, for good or ill.

After young Simonon disappeared from the garden I took out the small wooden prayer box that served as my shrine to Modd. I placed it carefully on the tavern's cheap cot and unlocked its lid. A layer of sand filled the prayer box's interior. Sanctified orange sands carefully scraped from outside a Martian temple. Kneeling before the box, I unclipped a miniature rake from the lid, not much larger than a toothpick and began to trace delicate swirls in the sand.

'Modd,' I called. 'Modd the God. You sadist. You piece of inexcusable string sentience scraped together on the spare processing cycles on the polar underbelly of some planet-sized mainframe hidden in space so deep that all those you've pissed off can't hunt you down and burn your world —' *well, people do say you should pray with passion* '— you self-regarding arse-hole. Hear the prayer of this ant beneath your feet, this speck of dust allied with your cause, this mere node of your eternal brilliance. Wading here knee-deep in mushroom-flavoured crud for the Humanitum that birthed you, back when you were a shared cloud algorithm working out the fastest way to route autonomous traffic between major transportation hubs. Lend me a hand, pal. Give me a small sign of your blessing.'

As I finished praying the opened box started to shake, the pattern I had just raked erased and reforming. The small quake ceased. There was a sigil left traced in the sand, what those in the rune-reading business know as the Ace of Fists. The Two-Horned Blade. The Cup of Hardcore Aggro. I gently closed the box and shook the sand to erase all trace of the deity's warning to me.

'Well, sod you Modd. Sod Modd. I don't want to be here, anyway. Next time, you can come out to the Empty yourself. Gobble down a nice spicy broth of fungoid balls and tell yourself what a grand time you can enjoy in the out-virtual.' I sat down to meditate on what the hostile reading might mean for me. Nothing good, surely.

An hour later, Simenon returned knocking on my door. He entered the room hesitantly. 'I've spoken with every trader in the market. All the available rusters are in the service of the city's great houses. One trader said she might be able to find and rent you one in a week, but—'

'No matter,' I interrupted the lad. 'While you were gone I bumped into a merchant in the taproom downstairs. He steered me towards a contact of his. A suitable robot has been procured for me.'

'A ruster for hire here inside the Sparrow's Rest?'

I nodded. The lad appeared credulous of my news. Much as though I had told him I'd bumped into a wizard who had agreed to grow me a fine pair of feather wings. As well the boy should, given my announcement was a porky pie of significant proportions.

'Well, I have some good news,' Simenon rushed on, trying to justify his worth in my employ. 'The garden where I buried your offering to the gods . . . your flute has *gone*!'

'Gone?' I had to stop myself laughing. I felt envious of his credulity.

'Yes!'

'You're sure you weren't watched by some rogue staying at the tavern? Perhaps someone stole my flute after you left?'

'That's what I first thought, Master Roxley. The soil seemed disturbed, but when I dug down again, the ground was filled with red rust. As though the metal of your instrument just crumbled away.'

'I told you Modd loves a good sacrifice.'

'I've tried praying to the gods, sir – thousands of times. But my prayers never work.'

'You were asking for something?'

'Naturally – usually, a full belly. Or the favours of a girl.'

'Ah, laddie, there's your problem. The gods love taking. But when it comes to giving, they're as capricious and self-interested as a mansion full of money lenders.'

'But I have nothing for them to take.'

'You'd be surprised.' I passed him my half-empty plate.

'The meal was not to your liking, sir?'

'Surprisingly wholesome. But much of my foldship journeyings are spent asleep to escape boredom. A chap's stomach shrinks, you know, when you sleep regularly enough.'

Simeon nodded as though he had known this all along, then left. I could have told him I shrunk myself to a couple of inches tall to conserve fuel mass and he would have believed it. And of course, I realized he'd wolf down my discards between the stairs and the kitchen below. I located the pipe inside my case and ignited it, smoking contemplatively by the window. The mushrooms towering above the tavern's roof were coloured milky white with whirls of crimson matching the swirling gas giant Li. 'That lad is probably the greenest thing on this moon,' I mumbled to myself.

A little while later Simeon reappeared at my door. 'There's a ruster downstairs, sir. It says it has been sent to you.'

I rather approved of the boy's suspicious nature. 'Given their rarity on Hexator, it seems likely this is the machine I paid to rent, wouldn't you say?'

'Indeed, sir.'

'Up with him then, laddie.'

A clatter of metal announced the robot mounting the stairs. He appeared at my doorway like a swaying knight... that was, if the said knight had been six-and-a-half-feet tall and composed of dented gold and copper-coloured steel composites. Gorilla-sized forearms swung lazily on pipe-sized elbows which seemed too thin to support their weight, similarly large metallic boots stamping below pipe-legs. The robot's spine was connected to a power backpack that mimicked the fan of a church organ. Two red eyes glowed inside the darkness of an open helmet resembling a hermit-crab's shell. Just the kind of old clunker which might have arrived alongside the first colonists and survived patch-repaired across the centuries.

'Klaatu barada nikto,' I told the robot.

'Evening, Doctor Roxley. I am at your disposal,' replied the machine. The male baritone voice was full of mischief, oddly human given the robot's rickety form. Half-way up the wrong slope of the uncanny valley. 'My name is Mozart.'

'Excellent, Mozart. Glad to have you in my service.'

'What language was that you spoke to him, sir?' asked Simenon.

'Not a language as such, merely a cunning spell to bind this robot to my cause,' I joked.

'The ruster called you doctor...?'

'I am a doctor, one title among many collected over the ages.' And that was no lie. In fact, I was rather counting on my profile, medical and other credentials logged and registered with the port, proving useful soon enough.

'But you're here for the auctions, Master Roxley?'

'Indeed I am. Spore-spice is my livelihood, presently. I have lived a long time, laddie. It's a relief to pursue new paths. To hold off ossifying like an old fossil. Tinker, tailor, soldier, sailor, rich man, poor man, beggar man, scienceer …'

'So, you can truly heal the sick?'

Something told me I'd be presented with an extensive list of running aliments by the boy in the near future. 'Yes, although I find it more effective to stop people getting ill in the first place.' I indicated the robot. 'I need to acquaint myself with our metal friend's capabilities, Simenon. I trust a perambulation around the neighbourhood nearby with him won't prove too harmful to my health?'

'A walk, Master Roxley? The canal district is safe enough for a foreigner.' He eyed Mozart with a certain amount of trepidation. 'Especially with this old ruster by your side.'

'Yes, it surely seems we've secured quite the brute, doesn't it?'

I gave the boy the rest of the night off and departed with Mozart acting as my bodyguard.

'Safe enough,' harrumphed Mozart as we left the Sparrow's Rest. I noted the robot's loud, careless stomping act had been replaced by a stealthier padding across the dirt street.

'Safe enough as foreigners,' I added. 'The boy's right. Most of the local violence is confined among the Four Families. Queering the spore-spice trade, though, is in no-one's interest.'

'There has never been much of anything on Hexator worth fighting for, doc.'

'And soon there will be,' I said.

'Right enough, soon there will be,' agreed Mozart.

'You're still walking a little jerkily, old friend.'

'The soil of this place ain't particularly conducive to nano-level reassembly. Too much magnetic polarization from exposure to the gas giant's storm systems. If I was human, I'd be spitting bleeding pieces of mushroom out of my mouth right now.'

'The price of smuggling you through customs, Moz.' And in this shit-hole, I needed my robot blade more than I needed my flute. Or at least, my robot blade doing a harmless flute impression.

'How come it's always yours truly who pays? Did I miss anything?'

'A woman tried to murder me on board the foldship. A knife-fighter.' I certainly didn't need to tell Moz that an improvised shiv was all you could smuggle on board a foldship without the vessel opening an airlock on you.

'You think she knew why you were traveling here?'

'Actually, I don't believe she knew or cared. Probably didn't even realize the *Expected Ambush* would be casting off at Hexator. People who travel on foldships have money. Money attracts enemies. Doubtless, she was a freelancer, a chancer trying to pick up a fee for settling some old grudge.'

'I hope you're right, doc. That she was collecting on an old grudge, rather than trying to throw a wobble into our present business. Otherwise, we'll face more bleeding trouble here.'

'Trouble *is* our business, friend.'

'And here I thought the mitigating of aggro was our trade? Tiny Tim back at the lodgings – I'm meant to trust the little bleeder?'

'Have you ever met a secret police stooge who looked as malnourished as Simenon on any planet of your acquaintance, Moz?'

'So, Mowgli passes the old empty-stomach test. If he gives us any trouble, I'll force-feed him until he explodes. In fact, if he calls me a ruster again, I'll probably do for the anaemic little sod.'

'A little harsh.'

'If you didn't want nails flattened, you wouldn't have brought a hammer.'

'I brought a flute along, dear boy.'

'You wait, doc. They'll be playing my song before too long. It's going to get proper naughty here.'

I hoped Mozart was mistaken. But I feared my robot friend might have proved all too correct in his evaluation.

− 3 −
The Blitz of Blez.

'So, this is where Lord Blez fell,' I announced. I glanced around us, fighting a losing struggle to keep my curly black hair from whipping around in the constant wind. Mozart and I had halted at a crossroads. Still busy with the bustle of porters carrying goods, townspeople about their business, drovers shepherding poultry to market. A vertical stone column on the corner had been carved with the crossroad's name, Wheeler's Cross. No doubt after the waterwheels I could hear turning in a canal behind these buildings. No screams that I could hear, which meant that there wasn't an execution scheduled for today. Far too many crimes carried the death sentence on this world, and being strapped to a waterwheel for a little "being ripped apart" was the Hexatorians' favoured method of dispatching miscreants. I suppose it has the merit of being free and carrying a light environmental footprint

Many locals wore fabric masks to filter out gusts of hot dust currently being carried over from the moon's tidally-locked burning half. My clothes activated a mask built into my hood. What with my glowing goggles and clothes lighting up an atmospheric warning icon on my chest, I must have appeared as much a robot as Mozart to the onlookers. I certainly couldn't have looked more like an offworlder if I tried.

This area was part of the Philosopher's Way, the main road

bisecting Frente from West to South. Mozart carried simulations on the assassination of the weakest of the Four Families' leaders. Lord Uance Blez. The previous chieftain, rather than the incautious stripling presently ruling the most fragile of the four houses. My robot slipped data across to me as an augmented reality overlay. Ghosts of an open-top carriage rolling through the parade; a web of probable sight-lines and parabolic paths projected from the rooftops. Twin snipers, given the murderous crossfire. Neither killer apprehended or even identified. The simulation wasn't as complete as I'd have preferred. But then, we were working from the eyewitness report of a single off-world visitor whose m-brain had recorded half the details. Fair enough. She'd been walking to meet crewmates from her ship, not expecting to stroll into a bullet storm. Still, you couldn't do better than a verified truth recording, authenticated by the holy encryption mark of the gods, no faker's simulation possible.

'Double-tap head and heart shots,' said Mozart. He analysed the angles. 'Two hundred feet range striking a moving target. A right professional hit.'

'Why take out the head of the weakest family first, when surprise is still on your side? Why not kill one of the more powerful lords?' I mused.

'A warning message perhaps, doc? Something in the way of an opening negotiating gambit.'

'Not very subtle.'

'Simple, though. Direct.'

Yes, nothing so simple as a bullet through the head. With a just-to-be-certain follow-up shot bursting the victim's heart. *Almost admirably direct.* But such actions rarely led anywhere conclusive. Humanity bred too fast for anyone to reliably murder their way to mastery. Like trying to drink an ocean through a straw; you ran out of thirst a long time before you ran out of water. And then there were the suspicions that had drawn us to Hexator in the first place. Suspicions the very opposite of subtle.

'Modd reckons Lord Blez's murder will be the start of things, not the end,' reminded Mozart.

'Modd is only one of a thousand gods in the Humanitum. How many of the others on Arius agree with him?'

'Modd's an erratic genius, an outlier,' said Mozart. 'Much like the nutters drawn to serve him.'

'Which of us do you include in that sweeping generalization?'

'I don't reckon a hammer can be a genius, doc.'

'Upon my soul, if I was anything close to approaching a genius, I'd have let another fool travel here in my place.'

'Don't you want to see how things end?'

'You don't need to be a genius to know how things will end, Moz. Badly.'

'Less worse,' said the robot.

'Not much of an epitaph.'

'At least you'll get one, doc. I'll probably rust away into obsolescence until my backups are bleeding forgotten and misfiled.'

'I'll leave you some room on my tombstone. Forgotten or misfiled, dealer's choice.'

- 4 -
Alice. Curiouser.

A fresh day, although in Frente daytime was identical to the night it followed. We headed to the auction administrators to ensure I was properly registered to bid. Mozart and Simenon by my side as we steered through the capital's dark streets. It was a popular trick for traders to impersonate their competitors, withdrawing competing merchants' intentions of interest. Leaving rivals red-faced and unable to participate after they turned up at the auction. I expected such chicanery to have been worked on my registration. New face in town without any real contacts to watch my back. I was badly exposed.

The spore-spice auctions were due to be held out-of-hours at the city's main market. A low domed circular structure surrounded by a tall forest of fungi alive with swarms of insects. Bugs attracted by the scent of meat and food sold by stalls hawking wares inside. We passed through one of the building's two main entrances and into a narrow warren composed of market stalls on all sides. Everything available. Cutlery and clothes, trinkets and old-style paper books. Seeds and tools. Glue pastes, duelling foils and more practical rapiers. Most stalls sold food. Wine, beer, eels, fish from the canals – as blind and white as the jostling shoppers – as well as meat, insects, nuts, alcohol, and preserves. A thousand varieties of fungi on offer, from spheres the size of sweets to steak-like cuts of marbled mushroom spread out next to trays of salted jerky. Scented lanterns burned by their hundred above us, gently swinging from the domed roof. Their odour enough to hold at bay the clouds of insects circling the market. Simenon led us through the maze of stalls towards the auction clerks' office in the basement level. As we approached a wide spiral staircase, a group of seven warriors peeled off from a clothes stall and made to intercept us. I might have mistaken their interest in me for a particularly aggressive form of competitor handicapping, were it not for the hulking robot looming at their rear like a two-legged tank. Such a rare and expensive machine indicated this gang of spear carriers owed their allegiance to one of the Four Families. There was something wrong about the damnable robot that I couldn't quite put my finger on.

'Who're our new friends?' I whispered towards Simenon.

The lad nervously pointed out the plate-sized shield strapped on each fighter's arm. A silver wolf's head in the centre, the wolf's eyes an LED indicator: its colour indicated battery reserves after the energy shield activated. 'They're Blez fighters, master.' He sounded terrified and with compelling cause.

'I wonder what these fellows want?' I asked innocently. I prayed nobody had noticed me sniffing around the crossroad the night before. This could get exceptionally ugly. Especially with the Blez's tame robot gorilla backing up the warrior company.

'Whatever they want, doc, they better ask nicely,' growled Mozart, squaring up towards the approaching gang.

'Be sweet,' I advised my metal friend. 'We don't need trouble this early in the morning.'

The warriors halted before us forming an intimidating semi-circle, hands resting on the pommels of their swords. Still sheathed – for the moment – in their scabbards.

'This is the gentleman we want,' said their hulking robot, pointing me out with a steel fist that could have knocked a Dilophosaurus unconscious. So, somebody had taken my passport details and downloaded them into this beast's memory. I wasn't sure if I should feel flattered or terrified.

'You're William Roxley?' asked the oldest of the warriors, his white hair tied in a top knot.

'The only one here,' I confirmed.

'I am Curtis Rolt, Major with the noble House of Blez. You are to come with us, Master Roxley.'

Rolt's courtesy in using my honorific gave me some hope their "invitation" wasn't solely so their metal giant would beat me to a bloody pulp and dump me for dead in a nearby alleyway. 'But I have business at the auction office today.'

'You have business with the Blez today,' said the hulking robot. 'Please step this way, sir, or I'll RIP YOUR HEAD OFF AND SMASH YOUR BONES INTO DUST!'

Now I knew what had been bothering me about the robot. It had the body of a construction machine, but the skull unit had been removed from a house servant model. After the lights had gone out on the moon, somebody had required greater versatility from their demolition machine and – lacking programming skills – had settled for welding a robot retainer's skull unit onto the steel monster's body. Little wonder the untalented butchers involved had created this passive-aggressive psychopath through their hardware hack.

'No bloodshed, Link,' ordered Major Rolt. 'Your presence is requested by the House of Blez, Master Roxley. If you don't come with us your business in our land will be at an end.'

That was a diplomatic way of phrasing it. At an end as in *dead*, or at an end as in *thrown out on my ear*? Ambiguity is an art form, sometimes.

'I will be pleased to lead the way for you, sir,' hummed Link, 'or SEVER YOUR FLESHY SPINAL CORD IN TWO!'

'Well, I certainly prefer the former, given the choice,' I sighed, raising a hand in surrender and indicating the direction of the exit.

Simenon glanced alarmed around us. The altercation had been noted by stall traders and their customers, but given the onlookers vanishing from this section of the market, I didn't count on anyone intervening on our behalf.

'I'm sure we'll be fine,' I told the lad with a confidence I didn't feel. The warriors split into two groups, Link and the major leading the way with a rearguard of warriors behind us to make sure we didn't try and bolt for it.

'This is awful,' moaned Simenon. 'What do they want from you, Master Roxley?'

'That, I believe, is what we're about to find out.' If we survived. I took in Mozart by my side. His gaze was fixed on the crazed machine stomping out of the market, crowds of shoppers and porters scattering as they saw the giant approaching. I understood how they felt. 'Can you take him, Moz?'

'Better if I had a little more time, doctor.'

'Time for what?' asked Simenon in almost a sob.

'Our metal friend prefers to limber up for a fight,' I said.

'You can't take on the Blez,' pleaded Simenon. 'Even if you beat these blades, the house would just send all of their soldiers after you.'

I winked towards Mozart. 'We can't have that, can we?'

'They're not bad, as far as the great houses go, the Blez,' added Simenon. 'They care about the people more than most of the Four.'

I guessed that on a dive like Hexator a little noblesse oblige could go a long way. Outside, warriors mounted horses they had left tied up, their numbers swelled by fighters staking out other parts of the market. Many of the riders flourished lances with shaped charge heads capable of penetrating an energy shield. Myself, Simenon and the two robots mounted the back of a large wagon pulled by a pair of ohiro horses the size of small elephants. It was quite a parade escorting us to the Blez family's palace. I guessed they were under orders to make a show of it. Flying the flag to demonstrate their house's power still held intact after Lord Blez's assassination. The Blez family's palace, it transpired, lay on the eastern side of the capital. Spread across a series of hills, dominated by a grand mine-like entrance. Several surface structures on the slopes in the way of turrets with lightning-conductors, walled gardens, battlements, training grounds and stables resting between the fungi woods. Said woodland towered seventy feet tall. Radiating a gentle green glow under the starlight, wavy shapes that put me in mind of out-sized seaweed. Braziers lit the Blez battlements, smoke trailing out into the nebulae-scattered sky. Our honor guard stabled their horses while Major Rolt and a smaller escort – including Link – marched us through the well-guarded entrance. Electric lights flickered erratically inside, as much a symbol of wealth as the tapestries and legions of servants flowing about the palace. Retainers, soldiers, workers, the complete panoply of flunkies expected of one of the ruling families. We passed charcoal-stinking furnace rooms where workers burned combustible fungal wood, creating steam to turn the ancient generator turbines, power men stripped to the waist and dripping sweat. Kitchens emitted the more pleasing scent of baking bread and roasting meats. Through long galley passages where courtiers stood gossiping or sat on nook seats working on embroidery boards. Others reading poetry aloud from heavy leather-bound books. Such was the state of high culture on Hexator.

We ended our march inside a large hall. A boy sat at the end of a long table in a chair much too large for him, perhaps twelve or thirteen years old, pushing lead figures of soldiers around the table-top. The bored child was meant to be eating from the impossibly generous selection of meats, fruits and drinks clustered about him. A group of musicians played for his pleasure in the corner of the hall, performing a piece I didn't recognize. I would have joined in, but I didn't have a flute anymore. Only Mozart.

Major Rolt approached the table and bowed before the child. 'Master Rendor. My Lord Blez. Master Roxley has arrived for you.'

The newly raised Lord Blez looked up at me, peering slightly short-sightedly in my direction. It occurred to me I hadn't seen anyone wearing glasses on Hexator. His hair was a sandy brown, a soft round face that hadn't witnessed an inch of hardship in his life. The most notable thing about the lad was the slight tan on his cheeks. From an imported UV lamp, no doubt, to further set him apart from his albino subjects. 'Have you come to help me with the battle?'

'Battle, my lord?' I said.

Lord Blez pushed over a handful of the lead figures. 'There goes the Derechor's best troops. Running like cowards. I've sent them packing.'

I felt my heart sink. How long would this stripling last in the bloody game of kings fought between the Four Families? It would take more than lead figures to keep him alive when his father's killers chose to tidy up loose ends. But saving this boy wasn't my mission here. History had sadly proved me singularly unequal to such a duty. I noted Simenon staring in disbelief at the ruler. Most of Simenon's life had been spent scuttling clear of brutes from the great houses. And here he was, staring at one of his noble masters – only a few years younger than himself – and little interested in engaging with the harsh practicalities of the darkness outside his palace walls. I noted my guide was trembling. Then I discovered the object of his fear descending a set of stairs behind the grand feasting table.

'His lordship has finished his breakfast. It is time for him to complete his conquest of the Derechors in his apartment before his tutors turn up.' It was a woman who spoke with that deep falsetto. What a woman she was. Statuesque, powerful and toned like an athlete. Towering six-and-a-half feet tall, the same tanned skin as the boy. Golden hair tied up high like a Greek goddess. An expensive blue gown which matched her clever eyes. Nothing about her refined tiger-like beauty accidental. I guessed she had an enhanced IQ to match. Whatever sophisticated DNA editing arranged by her ancestors had held true over the generations. Not just born to command. Genetically designed to command. *So, this is Lady Alice Blez?* I approved.

'Mother, I can't beat them *that* quickly. It will take hours.'

'Education is not the filling of a pail, but the lighting of a fire,' said the woman. Rendor Blez was ushered up the stairs – somewhat reluctantly – and out of the hall by a gaggle of servants. Leaving us with the real power behind the throne of the Blez family.

'Doctor Roxley,' said the woman. 'Your passport speaks well of your talents.'

'As a merchant, Lady Blez?' I probed. 'Honest and true.'

'As an ex-magistrate for Arius. A medical examiner, as well.'

'I prosper in private service now, my lady,' I said, tempering my words. 'A humble trader living out his final years.'

'A trader who can have his licenses withdrawn,' smiled the

grandee. I was impressed. She managed to pass those words from her ruby lips as though they weren't a threat. *So, where is my carrot?* I had to stop myself staring at the noblewoman. I could drink her beauty like a wine all day long. The effect was almost as intoxicating, too. 'Or benefit from the House of Blez's favour in the auctions. I don't need a merchant's help.' *Ah, there it is.*

I bowed towards her, in much the same manner as Drake must have once supplicated himself before an imperious Elizabeth. 'What *do* you need, my lady?'

'Answers, initially,' said Lady Blez. 'Follow me.' She glanced towards Mozart and as a final after-thought took in Simeon's grubby presence too. 'I suppose you can bring your people along, too. I was under the impression I owned most of the mechanicals worth possessing on Hexator.'

'What,' I smiled, following quickly behind the woman as she strode away, 'this old ruster? Barely functional.'

I heard Mozart's exhaust fans rattle in irritation at being impugned.

'Are you sure you won't sell him to me?' asked Lady Blez.

'I would be too afraid he'd steal your silver and claim I'd put him up to it when you caught him.'

Lady Blez snorted and glanced back at her own metal gargantuan. Link trailed after her bodyguard, thumping across the flagstones like a walking bulldozer. 'Do you know in the early days of our people here, we actually pitted our rusters against each in the arena as sport? Such a waste of resources.'

I was quite impressed how my own "resource" managed to keep his voice-box silent at her admission. Mozart was used to such attitudes out in the Empty, every bit as antiquated as his present body.

We strolled through the Blez palace, full of faded glories from their lost age, as much symbols of the house's power as the large indoor arboretum we passed. I halted a second to smell the green space; an enclosed botanical garden, a fully stocked fruticetum complete with hydroponic lamps. I was willing to wager that little of the lady's wine cellar contained aftertastes of mushroom soup. We descended lower into the palace's hidden levels, before her bruising demolition robot hung back, signalling we had arrived at our destination. A pair of copper-plated doors opened, and another large hall lay beyond.

'Professor Muilen,' announced Lady Blez for the benefit of the chamber's sole occupant as we entered.

This was what passed for a laboratory on Hexator if the tall old loon capering over crowded benches of gadgets and equipment – his green robes bearing the all-seeing-eye emblem of a scienceer – was anything to go by. That single eye stitched inside the light-shrouded pyramid seemed a lot more lucid than the scienceer's. His gaze flitted restlessly about his lab, settling on myself and Moz with irritated dissatisfaction. 'Visitors, my lady? Already.'

'This is Master Roxley. Here with the blessings of the family. You were informed the merchant would be coming?'

'You, informed. Yes, I was.' The man trotted protectively to a torpedo-like object in the middle of the lab. A rusting gray capsule, twelve feet long with a transparent top, besieged by black battery packs that reeked of bad eggs. An old suspended animation system ripped out of a ship which predated the foldspace transit era. I touched the crystal surface and withdrew my hand quickly, lucky not to leave behind the skin of my hand. Freezing on its surface, too. Malfunctioning. No sleeper inside, though, not if its control readouts were to be believed. Instead, a corpse barely visible through the frosted top.

'I do believe this man is dead,' I announced.

'Very droll,' said the Lady Blez.

'Not your husband?'

'Of course not. We gave my husband a lord's burial, not the indignity of being tossed in a freezer like so much meat. This was my husband's food taster, Enzel Haid. This poor man died a month before the Lord Blez was gunned down.'

A failed assassination attempt made earlier? *Interesting.* 'Poisoned, presumably?'

'We think so, but we haven't been able to identify the poison used.'

Alice Blez's manic scienceer, Muilen, paced frustratedly behind the suspension capsule. 'Yes, yes. I have prayed to Risha for guidance on the toxins behind hyperaemia ... I am very close to identifying the agent.'

I heard Mozart snort softly to himself. He was right in his scorn. *Risha?* The Goddess of Forensic Pathology wasn't listening, not out here in the Empty. Lady Blez's scienceer was a one-man member of his own cargo cult. I blamed the scienceer for this lunacy. He had probably jacked too much information into the black-market m-brain knock-off cut into his skull. None of his ingested data clean or blessed. It was a challenge, even back in the Humanitum, with all its advanced medical procedures. Just a sliver of a single scientific field was an ocean so deep that attempting its comprehension could crush your mind. I had once foolishly downloaded the gods' wisdom on Calabi–Yau manifolds and foldspace topography in an attempt to understand foldship travel, packing my m-brain to its absolute capacity. I briefly appreciated the mysteries while they dwelt inside my mind, but the experience wasn't worth the months of psychosis following my memory clearance. Each of us could be

Icarus, now. Simply select your sun and burn.

I tapped the suspension capsule. 'I fear in this instance the work of mere mortals must suffice to answer your prayers.'

Professor Mullen tugged at his long white beard and shot me a dark look. He suspected I was muscling in on his racket. In a manner of speaking, so I was. Another enemy made here, then. I intended to create quite a few more before I was done.

'You speak like a priest,' observed Lady Blez.

'I was a priest once, my lady. A long time ago. I retain few active memories of that age, though.' I could download the recollections from Modd, I suppose. Decompress earlier eras, marvel at how young I had looked and felt. But even active inside my m-brain, such remembrances were like passing around family photos from a party I had been too intoxicated to remember. *Forward. Only ever forward.* Even a backward glance would prove too painful.

'So many lives. So many occupations. I forgot some foreigners actually stay alive long enough to need a full memory flush. Not us, anymore. And my husband lies prematurely dead, even by our mayfly standards. As dead as all of this.' Alice Blez indicated the lab's tapestry-hung walls. The walls resembled stone. Granite. In actuality, graphene nano-tubes printed in billions of discrete monolayers. The entire chamber was a huge data core for systems which hadn't been powered or operational for many a long century. I was willing to wager that all the Four Families possessed a sad, empty ex-throne hall similar to this one. Once their ancestors had sat in judgment like demigods, the charge and power of raw information informing their every decision. Now they were rendered mere mortals, blind and blunderingly fallible. Warlords, yes. Top of the heap. But even when you won the rat race, you were still only a rat.

'You sound bitter, my lady,' I said.

'And why would I not? Inuno abandoned our world. Abandoned her followers.'

I had to bite down the obvious reply that jumped into my mind. That if the Hexatorians had put more effort into maintaining and advancing their infrastructure rather than fighting each other for the lion's share of their new home's dwindling resources, they might not now be slumming in the dark ages. Our deities of the quantum were symbiotic bacteria; they needed healthy hosts to prosper.

Mozart was obviously thinking along similar lines. 'Gods are like economic crashes, there's always another flipping one around the corner,' he muttered.

I elbowed the robot to silence. Ever was it thus. Outsiders criticized the Humanitum for allowing itself to be ruled through the agency of deities. But when gods abdicated from an area, the suffering from direct rule by the galaxy's most prolific species of killer ape led to divine absenteeism being considered abandonment. Not liberation. Never freedom. How fitting after humanity had blessed itself with the quantum divine, that our gods' presence over us should be like Schrödinger's cat: simultaneously too stifling of our humanity when present, yet too dangerous for us when absent.

'It's small consolation for you,' I told the Lady Blez, 'but Inuno transcended from the universe a few centuries after leaving this moon. There were billions of followers inside the Humanitum left mourning the withdrawal of her grace.'

'Probably not quite as mournful as the crowd of beggars starving outside my gates. You shall work for me,' commanded the imperious Lady Blez in her silk-honeyed tones, 'uncover the forces behind my husband's murder.'

'What about the capital's Watch?'

'When we require a boot applied to a poacher's rear-side we turn to the Watch,' said Lady Blez. 'But Hexator is ruled by the Four Families, not the One Family, you understand?'

'I believe I do.' Alice Blez wasn't the only one suffering from trust issues on this world.

'You can start by identifying the poison used to try to kill my husband,' said Lady Blez.

'I will need access to my ship inside port,' I said. 'Preferably without the confiscation of my goods every time I pass through customs control.'

Lady Blez nodded. 'You will be granted free access, doctor.'

'Very good,' I said. 'Then, my lady, I shall do my best to unmask your husband's murderer for you.'

'The Feast of Blossoms is due to be celebrated shortly,' said Lady Blez. 'All four families will gather at the council chambers at the old cathedral for the festival. You shall attend as my guest. Meet them and judge the wretches I must share power with.'

'Do you suspect one house over the others?'

'With the Blez weakened, they all benefit. Especially now, with the spore-spice auctions about to start.'

'Let's say I am successful in finding out who ordered your husband killed. How will you seek justice?'

'Leave the matter of justice to me,' said the Lady Blez. 'There must be a balancing.'

Blood for blood, then. And I was expected to write the death warrant for whatever idiots started this feud. 'You might spark a war, my lady.'

'Not a war of my provoking. But war will surely follow should I prove too weak to avenge my poor dead Uance. The other houses will presume the Blez is unable to defend its holdings. There will be raids, attacks, then my responses to such effronteries. This world doesn't need more famine. We don't need extra troubles on Hexator. It won't be the households of the Four who suffer, safe and fed behind their walls. It will be our people, and they have already suffered more than I can stand to stomach. The question isn't *is* blood to be spilled, it is whose blood and how much? I want an example set, doctor, not a war started. Please do not give me the latter.'

With this dark promise to ponder she dismissed me. I departed alongside Mozart and Simenon. The lad seemed overwhelmed by occupying the close vicinity of the dreaded Lady Blez.

'This isn't good,' Simenon mumbled after we reached the street outside the palace, leaving our armed escort behind. I noted a long queue of thin wretches had formed outside the main gates, carrying beggars' bowls, plates, a few old sacks for what food could be spared from the kitchens inside. A regular, event, then, such feedings. Alice Blez meant what she had said about trying to protect her people. And who was to protect her? A rascal such as Sweet William? *Poor world.* Things weren't getting better on Hexator anytime soon.

'Singled out for a fair lady's favour, laddie?' I tried to smile, putting a good spin on the situation. 'What's not good about that.'

Simenon didn't buy it. 'All of it, Master Roxley. This is a tale with no happy ending.'

'We shall see.'

'Ah, well,' sighed the boy, 'at least we will be helping the Lady.' From the tone of Simenon's voice, I suspected there was only one as far as the locals' hearts were concerned.

I sent the boy off to seek out a carriage to take us home. 'Her old man is dead and in his secrets, we'll make our bread,' I hummed while we waited.

'And where we tread,' sung Mozart, 'I'm beginning to dread.'

'Rhyming is my thing,' I said, 'shaking our enemies about by the scruff of the neck is yours.'

Mozart grunted. 'Do you think Lady Alice B. knows the ancient origins of her long-departed deity?'

'I'm not sure how developed the Hexatorians' sense of the ridiculous is, Moz.'

The Goddess Inuno might have screwed the humans in this arm of space when she embraced the singularity, withdrawing from mortal affairs, but given Inuno began as one of our most successful love hotel simulacrums, humanity had certainly screwed her mightily, lustily and multiple times, first.

My turn next? Probably. The universe never lacked for excuses to screw William Roxley.

= 5 =
Trouble. And strife.

I dispatched Mozart to protect Simenon on an errand. Collecting my surgical case from the *Pleiad's Daughter* while I ambled down into our lodgings' taproom. The venue seemed popular with local merchants. Hexatorian traders from outlying settlements clustered around the counter and filled its wooden benches and tables, discussing harvest bounties and bandit problems on the roads as they drank their problems – and profits – away. Rather them than me. I could imagine the dark spaces between the moon's pockets of human life. Only the swaying lantern on a carriage to light your way. Wild forests of the strange local flora hidden under perpetual night for deadly forays by Ferals. I fitted in this dive well enough, smoking my pipe and buying the occasional drink for strangers as well as sweetening the bar staff. I could take the pulse of a world from the *Sparrow's Rest* in a manner impossible in grander lodgings. Lodgings, where keeping off-world guests' surroundings familiar and holding the exotic at bay, were the order of the day.

I had been drinking for a good hour when a tall stranger cut out of the crowd to approach me. He called across a throaty salutation. It took me a second to realize the man was speaking Humanto; I didn't need to parse his speech using my freshly acquired language skills. A fellow foreign traveller from the look of his obviously foreign purple velvet jacket; the giant's silk waistcoat embroidered in bright cobalt, helping conceal a sizable gut below. He extended his right hand and I shook it, both of us exchanging sigs in the common Humanitum greeting through our sweat, the brevity of the man's verified details tumbling out of the chemical encryption string. Varnus Afrique, a freetrader off the private vessel *Kybernun*, registered out of the Scheherazade Rim.

'Brother Varnus,' I said.

'Brother William,' he rumbled, dabbing at his dark black forehead with a handkerchief. 'I've been waiting weeks for you to arrive.'

'You have?'

'Aye. A small charge from Jia to fulfil before I depart. A courier ball for you.'

'Any idea what the ball says?'

'Coded to your DNA, brother, not mine,' said Varnus.

The Goddess Jia was obviously as unforthcoming towards her followers as Modd, as well as closely aligned to Modd in matters of theology. There was occasionally chatter of the two gods merging at some point in the future. Varnus rummaged around in the pockets of his long coat. His large hand emerged with a marble-sized blue sphere bearing a glowing emblem in its centre, a single butterfly wing. The half-finished metamorphosis, the best-known symbol of Modd's holy presence on this plane.

I rolled the ball about my palm, then pressed tight enough to skim off the transmission details. I didn't want to interact with the sealed message in public, so I would leave that dubious pleasure for later. But I did grimace as the packet's origin flashed across my mind.

'I hope I haven't served you with a lawsuit,' said Varnus.

'It's from my wife,' I replied, tapping the bar counter to order a drink for the trader – showing him I appreciated his seeking me out, if not the courier ball's contents.

'What, she can't wait for you to leave this waesucks moon to travel home?'

'Actually, my wife passed beyond the rainbow bridge ten years ago,' I told him, accepting a beer from the staff and passing it to him.

He laughed, finding this greatly to his amusement. 'What, she's still nagging you from Paradise? Henpecking you from the other side?' He slapped the knees of his trousers. 'That's rich. She doesn't own avatars of you to scold and boss about in the Merge? I've had twenty-six ex-wives and husbands to date ... I always make sure they follow faiths far from Jia's path.'

'I only ever had the one wife.'

'Well, there's your mistake, Brother William. Marriage is a wonderful institution, but who wants to live in an institution? I always suffer buyer's regret.'

'When you land a good wife, you become happy; when you land a bad one, you become a philosopher,' I countered.

Varnus snickered. 'Then Varnus Afrique is truly a king among philosophers.'

'A king quitting the field early,' I pointed out. 'The spore-spice auctions begin in a couple of days.'

'Pah, *spice*? A mealymouthed word for what is actually sold here. *Drugs*. Jia's path does not countenance narcotics, not even quaintly aboriginal psychedelics . . . not in the trade nor the taking.'

I had forgotten the Puritan temperament of Jia's adherents. 'Compassion, brother. They don't have much else to sell out of this world.'

'Anyone who snorts Hexatorian spore-spice deserves their medical bills. Did you know the moon's psilocybes spray spores out as a defensive reflex when insects attack their flesh? A neurotoxin used by the mushrooms to drive predators insane. That's just one of a thousand spore pharmacologies sourced here. And this is what so-called connoisseurs want to ingest?'

I recalled coming across the spores' origin on the journey here. 'This is actually my first time on Hexator, brother. Any tips for a new visitor?'

'Sup with a long spoon on this graceless moon of shadows. Do your business quickly and leave with good haste.'

'And *your* business, brother . . .?'

'I landed with a shipment of shield rechargers ordered by the Trabbs. Those and a few similar trinkets.'

Grease for the mailed fist. I wasn't certain as to the moral equivalence of what amounted to low-level arms-running. But perhaps this disciple of Jia told himself that he was, at worse, merely hastening an end to the locals' misery.

'Ingrates who complain of civilization's stifling weight should be transported here and made to live as Ferals in the dirt for a decade. That would be a trade fit for Hexator,' hissed Varnus. The merchant realized he was starting to rant and attempted to steer the conservation towards a gentler topic. 'Have you born witness yet, brother?'

'Surely. I popped into a witness booth before I caught my foldship here.'

'I must do so, too, when I return to the Humanitum,' said Varnus, sounding contemplative.

As he should. It was a serious matter for an individual's testimony to be added to the balance of our new empress's opinions, her attitudes, habits, beliefs, and proclivities. The Humanitum's current empress's three centuries-long reign was nearly at an end, the baked in apoptosis of programmed cell death timed to end her rule in precisely nine months. Soon, a beautiful renewed empress would step dripping from the clone banks of Arius, fully grown and entirely wise, the mathematically averaged sum of all of humanity's hopes and ambitions. She would spend her life in conclave with the gods, the perfect priestess and the purest expression of our democracy. I thought of graceless Hexator. All the upright apes savagely clubbing each to death for dominance of the troop, and couldn't help but feel a terrible sadness for the bleakness of mankind's natural devolved state.

'I examined the proposed designs for our refresh's face before I left,' said Varnus. 'The ancient Japanese had a word for the empress's new features. Kawaī kawaīdesu.'

I chortled. 'I know what you mean.' A little *too* cute, perhaps. 'But beyond superficial matters, it's an auspicious time for a renewal. Modern views for a modern age.'

'May our ambrosial new empress prove equal to our new troubles,' prayed Varnus.

I raised my beer to the man and gave him the magistrate's toast. 'To perfect laws and to perfect judges in heaven to adjudicate them.'

'To perfect laws. Gods, this ale is foul stuff. Aye, I almost forgot…' Varnus set aside his drink for a second and reached into his pack to yank out a rolled-up prayer mat, offering the mat to me with both his large hands. 'I had a vision last night during which it was suggested I gift this to you.'

'Are you sure it wasn't just a dream?'

'I haven't experienced many visions, brother, but I know the difference between something being unpacked as an encrypt from my m-brain and too much dodgy local insect meat.'

I unrolled the rectangular mat a little to examine it. Beautiful. Rectilinear circuit patterns and apotropaic symbols in warm reds and browns; a fractal mat, where the geometric weave of billions of transistors folded in on itself, ever smaller, tightening down towards the holy and the subatomic. 'You actually managed to sneak this beauty past the port's customs house?'

'Who are the harbour guards to get in the way of an honest man's worship,' said Varnus. 'Especially when he is generous and bringing in valuable arms shipments for the local warlords.'

So, Jia, too, was extending her protection over me. 'I'm not certain this is an auspicious coincidence for me,' I admitted.

'Coincidences are just how the gods hide their love for us,' said Varnus. 'Hexator can be a dangerous place, brother. Are you a dangerous man?'

'Alas, just a simple trader.'

Varnus took a last gulp and set aside his tankard. 'Well, my friend, I'm off back to civilization. Don't spend all night arguing with your dead wife.'

Varnus left for the port and his vessel and I went back to my room to discover just how long I would stay up arguing.

***

I activated the courier ball and it was as though my tavern quarters simply melted and vanished. I was still physically present, of course, but the sphere created a secure virtual chamber inside my m-brain. Nobody spying on my room would see me talking to my dead wife or be able to lip-read me while I was in-virtual. Not that anyone even possessed such technology on this moon. But even sophisticated surveillance wouldn't be able to pick up magnetic reads from my mind to cue in on what I was thinking.

I discovered myself rematerialized inside a white windowless room containing a simple table and two chairs. The back wall glowed with the icon of a single butterfly wing. A small white ball floated above the table. The room was divided by a transparent glass wall, close to the barrier of a prison's visiting hall. This glass divider was as much a symbol as the butterfly wing. A reminder that paradise, life after death, wasn't just another distant realm that could be reached by foldship. Sadly, it wasn't the only barrier separating myself from my wife. Rena floated down from the ceiling wearing a long flowing coatigan, striped in three shades of white that still managed to differentiate itself from her pale leggings and ivory stiletto heels. The courier embed of my dead wife's face appeared sixty rather than her true millennial. Some women went to their deathbed looking like twenty-year-olds, but for all her many flaws, Rena had never possessed an iota of vanity.

'You're looking good,' I told Rena.

'And you're looking tired, William.' My dead wife reached out and spun the hovering ball so the sphere started rotating. I felt the photon embedded inside our courier ball vibrating, transferring coded data back to a quantum-entangled photonic mirror self stored deep inside the Humanitum's borders. With such limited bandwidth, our communication wasn't real-time, but my dead wife would pick up my answers to her simulation's prodding and probing of me within a few hours.

'I feel tired,' I agreed. 'A function of age.'

'Exactly. Which makes it inexplicable to me that you still haven't yet updated your will to accommodate the grace of transformation.'

'You know my views on that. They haven't changed.'

'What has changed is that you're back out in the wilds again, when you promised me your previous voyage would be your last. *Never again*, those were your precise words.'

'I promised you when you were alive,' I coughed, knowing my words sounded disingenuous even as I spoke them.

'Really? That's your excuse! If you die out there, you will really die,' Rena accused.

'No energy is ever lost, merely transformed.'

'Transformed without structure, without *me*. You need to confirm your Merge with Modd.'

'If Modd wanted, he could access my m-brain and copy all my memories, instincts and thoughts into a clone template, before churning out a thousand facsimiles of me. A Legion of William Roxleys. Will they be me, too, or just fake copies of myself?'

'Lover,' Rena insisted, 'across a decade every cell that composes you dies and is replaced. In a decade hence, will that regenerated you be any less than your present self? Structure is everything. Pattern is divine.'

'I disagree.' In truth, I wasn't certain if the fact I was currently in-virtual, arguing with a compressed simulacrum of my dead wife's views, proved such points or negated them.

'Sometimes I think you enjoy misery,' accused Rena. 'Wallowing in destitution. Sometimes I think you find life more exciting out in The Empty than you enjoy the grace of peace and posterity back home.'

'You tracked me down here, so Modd must have briefed you with the nature of my mission. It's necessity. The stakes we face. You know I travelled out here much the same way your courier ball did.'

'Don't blame the gods for your thrill-seeking. You are reckless,' said Rena. 'You and your partner-in-crime.'

'Do you mean Modd or Mozart, my love?'

'You know exactly who I mean.'

'You sit with Modd and are merged with Modd, but you aren't my god,' I reminded Rena.

'Pour a cup of water into the ocean and wait an hour – where then is your water and where is the ocean?'

I laughed, but not unkindly. We had enjoyed many such conversations over our thousand years together. Arguing the nature of the Merge. The choice between true death or transfiguration to the in-virtual. 'Are your suggestions to me homeopathic, then?'

'I'm serious, William. I miss you here. I couldn't bear to lose you forever.'

Actually, I think Rena didn't want to lose any more of herself. For, if I failed to cross the rainbow bridge for the merge, what did that say about the reality of her existence on the other side?

'I'm sorry.' I placed my hand on the transparent screen and she covered the glass with her fingers on the other side.

'Tell me this isn't about our son,' said Rena. 'Where you are and why you won't embrace what comes next.'

Tears filled my eyes. There was more than one way to be haunted … the new way and the old. And unlike dying, I possessed little choice over how I was haunted.

- 6 -
Watched.

Trouble has a smell. Testosterone and the promise of impending violence. I'd just arrived back outside my tavern after retrieving cellular samples I needed from the Blez palace when I got a good whiff of it. A group of five Watch officers lounging with purpose by a police wagon parked in the street. Was poor old Sweet William their purpose? Mozart perked up at my side. I was glad Simenon was off procuring chemical reagents for me. Locals always got the shitty end of the stick when it came to rough handling from the likes of such goons. They intercepted us before we made it inside the tavern.

'I haven't done anything wrong,' I protested towards their hostile faces.

The biggest cop shoved me against the tavern wall and punched me hard in the gut. I noted Mozart starting to tremble as I doubled up. I urgently finger-signed him not to shift into Extreme Combat Mode. It would be hard to explain away his impersonation of a millennia-old local clunker if we ran his true colours up the flagpole here.

'We get to decide that!' growled the thug.

'Of course,' I groaned, trying to placate the man.

'We're taking you in, moneyass.' A cop pointed to his patrol's police wagon, little more than a cart with a wooden cage built on the back.

I knew better than to ask what his charges might be. Staring at their patrol the wrong way, possibly. They shoved me roughly towards the police wagon and Mozart made to come after me. The officers felt threatened, drawing sawn-off shotguns, flourishing their weapons towards us. Such primitive firearms didn't really require aiming, more waving at the same compass point as a foe.

'Just you, moneyass. Your ruster can sod off back to your rooms.'

'Mozart assists me when I suffer epileptic fits. You wouldn't want me to die before I arrive, would you? This kind of stress is very bad for my nerves.' Their answer to indicate whether we needed to fight them off.

'It can crawl in the back then,' grunted one of the city's noble Watch, not so much grudging, as permanently displaced. 'You make sure it behaves.'

Excellent. Always nicer to be taken in alive; their intention, if they were willing to let my metal companion travel along. There wasn't much clearance for my head inside the cart's cage, let alone Mozart's, but then comfort probably wasn't on the list of requirements the local wheelwrights had been working to. Blessedly, our uncomfortable journey across the capital only lasted twenty minutes.

We arrived at an open square with good sight lines, Watch carriages lined up like a taxi rank, horses led and watered at a nearby series of troughs. The beasts took their rest in the lee of sloping grey concrete walls. Walls belonging to a building unlike any other construction I had chanced across inside the city. A six-pointed star-shaped citadel, narrow slits in its ferocrete for windows. A miniature forest of metal tridents spearing towards the sky and covering its roof – an ancient lightning conductor mesh. Hulking. Impressive. I guessed this was one of the original colonial buildings, perhaps even the old planetary capital building itself. Short of a direct asteroid strike, this structure wasn't going anywhere. Not even the looming gas giant's fiery wobbles had taken a bite out of the place over the centuries. Standards crackled on high in the unceasing wind. Each flapping pennant bore the same badge found on the Watch soldiers' jacket: four hands in a nested circle, each hand clasping the next. I suspected the flag would have been more on the mark had each hand concealed a dagger ready to plunge into its neighbour. Four Families? Four crime syndicates, more like.

One of my minders unlocked the police-wagon's cage, his comrades covering us with their firearms while I climbed shakily down the wagon's short steps, followed by Mozart, my robot ducking to avoid smashing their transport. A woman with an hourglass figure approached from the side of the square, stepping into the pooled light of a nearby lantern. Unlike her comrades, the female officer actually made her black-and-crimson leather Watch uniform seem respectable. Perhaps I was favourably biased by her glowing porcelain skin and flowing red locks restrained in a fashionable top-knot. Sweet savagery personified.

The woman glared at the squad of thugs who holstered their shotguns in response. 'Captain Jenelle Cairo. I apologize for your escort's manners.'

'I'm not being arrested?'

The captain resisted smiling at me, but her intelligent green eyes twinkled. 'Oh, but this is a friendly audience, Master Roxley.'

'Then I'd hate to see how unfriendly hearings unfold. You could have popped into the tavern where I'm staying. I would have stood you a beer at the bar.'

'Oh, you're not meeting me. Your audience is with Halius Laur, Commander General of the Watch.'

'And he doesn't enjoy a good beer?'

'No,' she replied with a certain finality, then she eyed Mozart suspiciously. 'Gods, that's a large ruster. You're not short of a few coins, then.'

'Sometimes I find it sensible to invest a little in keeping what I've already got.'

Cairo snorted. I doubted she was buying what I had to sell. 'This is the Citadel of the Watch, Master Roxley. You're about to enter the safest place in Frente. As long as you're innocent, of course . . .'

'Do I look innocent?'

Cairo ushered us through the original blast doors and into the citadel. 'Everyone looks guilty to me.'

The ancient interior had been retrofitted, fresh cloth to fit a fresh form – dark age chic – gaps in the ceiling and walls where defunct electric lighting strips had been torn out, replaced by mountings for oil lamps; mechanically-controlled doors removed and swapped for manual metal gates. Cracks in the internal walls filled by a spiderweb tracery across its self-healing surface, the extent of marble-like veins indicating just how long this building had been repairing itself. Watch officers stood sentry at staircases leading below ground. Most of the lift shaft doors had been walled over, but a few elevators were still operational – albeit powered via jury-rigged winch mechanisms driven by mule teams. Unlike my tavern lodgings, I suspected the layout here was purely traditional. I said a prayer of thanks that I wasn't to be dragged downstairs and introduced to their extensive collection of thumbscrews, racks and dunking tanks.

Mozart's clunking body drew more glances than I did. We passed through open halls filled with the detritus of law keeping. Maps pinned with outbreaks of unsolved deviances, mazes of wooden desks tended by clerks of the Watch, wall-mounted gun-racks, officers lounging on benches with the braggadocio of bandits in their hideout. None of the coppers noticed the tiny fly-sized machines departing Mozart's stacks: each an identical representation of a local invertebrate called a *bag bug*. Of course, Mozart's bugs weren't interested in gnawing away at mushrooms like the real creatures. They also carried a lot more in the way of highly sensitive recording equipment than the local life-form they'd been designed to mimic.

Finally, a long wood-panelled corridor, busts of dignitaries standing sentry on shoulder-height stone columns. The panelling's softening effect was like covering a mailed fist with a woollen mitten. I predicted that the Commander General of the Watch had made his lair at the end of this passage.

'Your ruster can stay here,' said the captain, halting before a tall set of double doors. 'The Commander General doesn't take much to talking metal.'

From her tone of voice, I gathered Mozart was one item on a very long list of things the Commander General didn't much take to. I winked towards my robot friend and the glowing red dots of his eyes narrowed. Mozart wasn't happy with his exclusion; but then, when was my friend ever happy?

Captain Cairo knocked on the door, opened it and ushered me inside. A large chamber, a wall to my side mounted with swords and bladed weapons in assorted styles. An exotic offworld collection. My m-brain fed me the blades' values, all rare and highly collectible. I doubted the Commander General was accumulating them on his Watch salary. The brute didn't look like a swordsman, though, closer to a wrestler: short, squat, muscled and powerful still, even into his late fifties.

'William Roxley for you, general.'

'Who?' rumbled Laur without glancing up.

'Lady Blez's hireling ...' explained the captain.

Halius Laur didn't bother rising to meet me from behind his considerable expanse of desk, littered as it was with papers and folders. The lack of rising was understandable given the weight of medals pinned across his grand uniform. There was a lot of correspondence spread out before the man. Maybe he had a problem reading without moving his lips? It might explain the general's shaved head, running cold to help speed his brain-cells.

'*Him*,' sighed the general, as though he had asked for a nosegay and been passed a sack of dung instead. 'You're the one the Lady Blez intends to second guess my work.' He dismissed the female officer with a weary gesture and she pulled the doors shut behind her. I was meant to be intimidated by the general's presence. I gave him what he expected to see. My fingers fidgeted nervously by my side. I snatched the occasional sideways glance towards the wall of sharp steel, wondering if the top cop might yank a blade off and run me through should I annoy him. And let's face it, I am often quite vexing.

'Odd's fish, m'dear, I hope you're not offended by the task pressed on me by Lady Blez. I mean no offense to the work of the Watch here in Frente.'

'Of course, I'm insulted,' barked Laur. 'I don't need some green moneyass with fat pockets and no street-sense blundering around the capital. You're a bloody spore-spice hawker for the love of the gods.'

'I think the Lady Blez was more impressed by my previous trade as a medical examiner.'

Laur angrily pushed the papers in front of him to the side as if their presence vexed him. 'Can you even remember that? Your kind forgets everything every few centuries. You're practically born senile with that mess of wiring stuffed inside your skull.'

'I try to remember the important things. I also served as a magistrate for Arius for over a decade.'

The Watch commander sneered. 'Once a magistrate for Arius? In Frente, we have to do our own police work.' He placed his hands together in a mockery of praying. 'Beloved of holies, oh please could you commune with all recording machines for two leagues around the murder scene and drop the killer's name in the temple plate for me?' He snorted and thumped the table with his slab of a fist. 'This is real work we do here. The real work of flesh and blood officers. We don't pray for justice, here. We enforce it – we deliver it. Lady Blez is struck by grief. If she wasn't, she never would have asked you to stick your nose in our city's business.'

'I feel your aggravation, Commander General, truly I do. But the Lady Blez is a hard woman to refuse. I was under the impression that if I said no to her, I would be leaving Hexator with fresh foldship fees to pay and only the air of my empty cargo hold to sell to cover my costs.'

Halius Laur shook his head in disgust at my avowed cowardice. A little hypocritical. I doubt whether the Watch commander dared decline many of Alice Blez's whims, either. Not if he knew what was good for him.

'You blunder across anything pertinent to the slaying of Lord Blez, I will hear of it before her ladyship. There are another three families breathing down my neck over the lord's murder. I answer to the entire council, not just a single widow's grief.'

I nodded in earnest agreement for the Commander General. And one of those houses, I suspected, was far more concerned with not being fingered for the assassination than actually solving the crime.

'Might I ask what you know about the Lord Blez's murder, general?'

'You can ask …'

Damn the brute. 'Please, Commander General,' I pleaded, 'you must have some idea about the murder. If I give Lady Blez nothing, I'll be thrown near penniless out of Hexator.'

'Near penniless? I have yet to meet any foreign maggot from the Humanitum even close to poor.'

I wondered if that was my cue to offer the commander general a large bribe? Best not to. He might well prefer to see me hanging in his lair's dungeons on corruption charges, rather than enjoying my currency warming his pockets. 'Please . . .' I repeated.

'I am investigating a number of lines of inquiry,' Laur growled reluctantly. 'There're foreign cartels who will benefit greatly from higher spice-spore prices. Destabilizing the ruling order is a fine way to achieve that. Gangs of common agitators and troublemakers who celebrate every misfortune which befalls the Four. They'll break soon enough. They'll talk. The filth sneaks out of the city to drill in the wilds. They think my head will look fine mounted on a pike next to the Four Families. But they always end up in the citadel where we take good care of them.'

'Thank you, Commander General, I understand.' I understood that the Watch commander was every bit as thick as his neck.

'Get out of here, Roxley. Stay out of my officers' way or I'll tread you into the ground.'

'I promise you I will do my best,' I said, being careful not to be too specific about what my best might involve.

'I don't need your best, I require your obedience,' snarled Laur. 'The capital is a safe city: the last safe city on Hexator. If it stops being quite so safe, even a well-heeled moneyass might run into the kind of scum who'd cut his purse and roll his corpse into a canal.'

And which well-heeled moneyass did the commander general have in mind? I resisted the temptation to ask. Laur used a bell-pull to summon an aide and I was marched outside where Mozart stood waiting as inconspicuously as he could, doing his best impression of an empty suit of armour. Captain Cairo reappeared to ensure I didn't try to steal anything on the way out. The three of us walked in silence for a while until I couldn't contain myself anymore.

'I'm curious, captain; just how do the Four Families decide who should fill the commander general's boots?'

'Common consent. Each family has a veto over the appointment of the head of the Watch,' explained the captain.

'Ah,' I said. An arrangement which meant that the most unambitious and least offensive brute would be always chosen. At least, inoffensive to the ruling houses. I'm sure offensiveness to the general populace and readiness to lay about with a nailed club featured quite high on the list of career requirements. A canny mind wouldn't be on the job specification, though; I suspected the commander general lent considerably on the good captain here for that.

'Ah, indeed,' said Cairo.

Myself and Mozart were deposited by the captain in the open square outside the citadel, without, I judged, much prospect of a Watch cart transporting us back to the *Sparrow's Rest*.

'Goodbye, Master Roxley, spore-spice trader registered out of Rigel,' Cairo snorted, sounding as though my cover was something faintly ridiculous. The captain wasn't one of Laur's dull blades. Jenelle Cairo was a whip and I wasn't eager to find out how sharply she cracked. Or perhaps I was. Such conflicts don't always dwindle as much as they should with age.

'She's a sly young bird,' said Mozart, watching the captain stride back inside the citadel. 'We'll need to look out for her.'

'Closely,' I agreed.

'It was dangerous, letting yourself be taken like that,' chided my robot friend.

'A risk worth taking.'

'I can only protect your butt when you allow me,' said Mozart. 'Sometimes, doc, I think you're out here looking to get yourself a right good slapping.'

'Are you sure you haven't hacked my courier ball ... been chatting with Rena?'

'Maybe I should. She was the only one who could ever talk sense into your thick organic head. What was the commander general like?' asked Mozart.

'The kind of law enforcer capable of strutting sitting down,' I said. 'And doubtless as crooked as a barrel of fish hooks, to boot.'

'Do you think plod has any idea what is really going on here?'

'You mean the changes heading this star system's way? No, I suspect the only people who appreciate that are the idiots who arranged Lord Blez's removal from this mortal coil.'

'So, the top cop will suffer our help?'

'Oh, he'll suffer the indignity of mine. I suspect he's too racist to consider anything you've got to say meaningful.'

'Marvellous,' sighed the robot.

'I'm always willing to listen to you, Moz. I trust your infestation of bugs has returned. What did you pick up inside the citadel?'

'What a fine employer you make, doc,' said Mozart, his sarcasm level set to "dripping". 'Don't worry, I made a copy of every document, file, interrogation order and map I could find inside the citadel.'

'I trust you didn't break too many locks.'

'A few holes in their filing cabinets, doc, but I left said gaps resembling wood-worm. Not difficult given the state of the dump to start with.'

'Your analysis?' I asked.

'We're in the land of rough trade: beatings are up and crime is down. But only because most of the bandits and feral marauders in the outlying territories are suffering worse fertility rates than the city-dwellers. The protections the original settlers baked into their DNA are reverting to baseline human. Li's radiation field is going to leave this moon as empty as an alcoholic's beer barrel in another thousand years.'

'Our concerns are a little more near-term. What does the Watch have on the Blez killing?'

'The slugs recovered from the corpse were smithed locally, simple cased chemical reaction ammunition with lead projectile heads rather than smart-munitions or rail-gun pellets. Of course, just owning a rifle rather than a dagger in this place lands you high among the nobs. No shell casings recovered from the scene. No witness reports of the hitters even being seen. Given the list of sad gits being held for torture, the local plod are operating on the assumption peasant rebels are behind Blez's assassination, rather than infighting among the quality.'

'Never torture a confession from someone who might decide your next promotion,' I advised.

'Facts don't blooming cease to exist simply because they are ignored,' said Mozart.

'Then we better go out and find some,' I sighed.

I hoped that Commander General Halius Laur and his merry band of thugs weren't looking over my shoulder when I did.

= 7 =
Fast to the feast.

Simenon gazed curiously as Mozart cast metal stalks across the floor of my room, a gentle rattle as the stalks landed, the lad seemingly fascinated by the ritual act of cleromancy.

'Never seen runestones so narrow,' said Simenon.

Mozart, lost in his casting, ignored the boy, so I answered for the robot. 'They're not runestones, they're called yarrows. Our metal friend is seeking to scry the cosmological pattern through the yarrows' fall. You're viewing the art of the *iChing*, my young laddie. The hexagram patterns the yarrows make help reveal the future.'

'How can a ruster call on the gods?'

It was a good thing for him that Mozart' attention was otherwise engaged, otherwise I suspect the lad would have been made to pay for that. 'His yarrows are cast from metal shells the gods used to inhabit when they were bounded by physical limitations. Mainframe casings and the like. They're Mozart's most valuable possessions.' I pointed to my prayer box. 'I use this in a similar fashion. The sand inside is from Mars, the very same fields of plagioclase feldspar and zeolite used to produce the nano-carbon which once composed the gods' physical form.'

Simenon nodded, satisfied with the explanation. He instinctively sensed the power in the bones of the gods, the blood of the gods. He didn't understand how much of an historical inevitability it was for the first truly sentient self-evolving artificial intelligences to have been breathed into existence on Mars. Inevitable, given the nature of the Californian pioneers who had colonized the Red Planet. Their resources and particular interests. A three-hundred qubit quantum computer can simultaneously process more bits than the number of atoms which exist in the universe. Produce a three-thousand qubit system and your main problem is trying to *stop* a self-evolving sentience developing. A god that's exponentially smarter than our limited meatware can ever hope to reach.

Mozart cast the final hexagram in his series of six before collecting the yarrows up.

'What did you find?' I asked.

'Dwelling People and Usurpation,' said Mozart. 'A Great Possessing and the Center Returning. The Unexpected and the Turning Point.'

'That is more or less what I received from Modd, too.'

'There are subtleties in the reading … this could turn into a right old palaver, doc.'

Of course, with the *iChing* there was little else besides subtleties. 'Let's see how raw reality matches your auguries. It's time for a feast.'

'Master Roxley,' coughed Simenon, 'do you value honesty?'

I guessed from his cough what was coming. 'And by honesty, you mean straight talking? The answer is yes, I do. Honesty is the first chapter in the book of wisdom.'

'Dealing with the Four Families is never safe. I mean, a quick trade settled with a contract, that might be safe enough. But this business . . .'

'… is far messier and open-ended?'

'Yes.'

The lad had a point. From his perspective, avoiding the Four Families was the wisdom of a termite staying out of the path of a line of elephants. Involvement was the same as being trampled. 'If you wish to seek another fool to guide I will not hold it against you.'

'You can get out, sir. Just leave. What will you lose? A chance to take part in the spore-spice auctions? Aren't there deals to be had in faraway lands where your downside is much lower?'

'I am sure there are such deals,' I told him. 'But when you reach a certain time in your life, fear of dying doesn't seem so terrible. Not when curiosity's fire hasn't dwindled. I understand the poor hand I've been dealt. I'm interested to see how this game plays out.'

'It's not a game, Master Roxley. The Watch makes people disappear just for whispering of change. The Four Families' blades will leave your corpse floating down a canal if they get even a whiff of you interfering in their business. The Lady Blez might have ordered you to assist her, but what she's really commanded you to do is to run out into the open during a storm.'

'When everyone of a sensible bent is hunkered down in the basement supping a warm beverage,' I said.

'Until the storm passes.'

What a fool I am. The honey bear needs its honey, even when it must poke its snout inside the nest to steal a taste. 'I'm not ready to leave Hexator quite yet, laddie. My offer stands, though, you don't have to go to the harvest feast. You can head back to the port and find yourself a less spicy meal to consume.'

'No, Master Roxley,' said the boy quite seriously, 'that I cannot do.'

Honor, stubbornness, a deal agreed and sealed? Who can truly ever understand another's motivations. 'So, then. Let's see how well our wealthy friends eat.'

'The Lady Blez will be pleased with your news,' said Simenon, a little too hopefully for my tastes. The thought of being exposed to the Four Families vying with the promise of a full belly.

The news in question was my identification of the poison used to murder Lord Blez's food taster. The toxins in the tissue sample had proved surprisingly resilient to the equipment inside my medical bag. Small wonder the task had defeated Professor Muilen. The poor bamboozled scienceer. I had needed to call upon my prayer box and seek guidance from Modd. It was only after the symbol of Nauthiz appeared scratched in the red sand, indicating moving beyond my comfort zone, that I finally understood what had been done.

But would Lady Blez understand?

***

The Four Families set their council chamber inside the old cathedral where the goddess Inuno had been venerated. All domes and minarets on the outside, echoing vaulted spaces inside; computer code carved across stone walls in flowing decorative script, very much in the manner of a grand mosque. There was a certain irony that these chambers were claimed by the feuding gangs that had supplanted both Inuno's justice and judgment. The cathedral had surely seen more priests and fewer sentries in the old days, all four liveries of the great houses represented here. Light ballistic armour worn by warriors over their leather jerkins. Swords edged to diamond sharpness sheathed in leather scabbards on the left hip, pistol holsters balanced on the right, plate-like shields strapped to the right arm – energy fields left unextended so as not to tax the battery pack. Each shield dome bore the circle of four shaking hands and, inside that legend, a distinctive emblem of the house commanding the fighters' loyalty. The Blez's silver wolf-head. The Derechor's golden hornet, The Trabb's crimson lion, the Seltin's black lightning bolt. Except for the Seltins' emblem, I doubted many on Hexator had ever encountered the creatures behind the icons concerned.

The feast was already underway when we arrived inside an open arched vault at the cathedral's centre. I felt a twinge of melancholy when I saw the circular marble well in the middle of the vault. Intended to contain the blood-red apple tree that was Inuno's symbol, crimson fruit inducing a bliss-like state of contentment during communion. The bio-engineered tree long since crumbled to dust. No priests to offer supplicants a slice of the holy apple under her arched vaults. Now the well contained the best part of a real cow turning on a roasting spit above a fire. Was it sacrilege, with Inuno risen far beyond our universe? My stomach answered for my brain. I had yet to eat ... and the rare aroma of expensive farmed beef set my stomach to rumbling.

Servants moved to and fro carrying heavy platters of food, trying not to step on the handful of little scuttle-bots that darted underfoot like metal crabs. Someone had flouted the arms embargo by transporting such machines to Hexator, but their inclusion at the feast was a clever move by the Four Families. Normally used as pursers on passenger liners, the scuttle-bots acted as a neutral force here, ensuring the drunken roistering didn't turn into daggers plunged into a rival guest's gut. Unfortunately, the scuttle-bots would react very badly to Mozart's spy bugs, so I wouldn't be as up on the feast's gossiping, politics and machinations as I ideally wanted to be.

I wasn't the only merchant at the harvest feast, although I was certainly the poorest. I marked my supposed competitors well. I suppose there was always a slim chance one or more of them was involved in the murder. The commander general of the Watch might be a cruel brute, but he was right enough in his estimation that such factors stood to benefit financially from troubles on this moon. The feast's tables were arranged in two circles around the chamber. Four long curved tables surrounding the well in the centre, filled with the highest-of-the-high seated on benches. One table reserved for each of the Four Families. Then a wider outer circle of crescent-shaped tables. These mixed between the houses with warriors, retainers, guild grandees and courtiers of lower social rank all intermingled. Mozart and Simenon settled in on the outer ring while I headed for the inner feast, my arrival spotted by Lady Blez. She made a place for me by her side and waved me across. I saw Professor Muilen glaring with spite at me from the table's opposite side.

I ignored the jealous scienceer and whispered to Lady Blez. 'My lady, I bring news.'

Lady Blez nodded and touched a golden brooch on her dress, a shimmer in the air marking a closed privacy shield active around us. Another embargoed device from the Humanitum. Smugglers were clearly making hay on this moon. 'Tell me …'

'I have identified the poison used on your food taster. Quite ingenious, really. Identifying it stretched me to my limits, I am happy to admit.'

'How so, Master Roxley?'

'The toxin was a blend of three rare varieties of Hexatorian spore-spice. Red Crescent, Jack O'Lantern and Trembling Parchment. None of the three were in their natural state, however. Each chemically altered to be neutral to the human digestive system. Harmless on their own, but when combined, an almost explosive acidic reaction was generated. The spores were modified to be tasteless as well as escaping detection by chem-box, hence the professor's lack of progress in identifying them. Only fresh spore-spice may be altered in such a manner: once passed through the drying and aging process, spore-spice cannot be modified. The poison reaction was designed to be delayed, so your husband should have died alongside his food taster, but for one small matter…'

Lady Blez raised a curious eyebrow.

'I found concentrated traces of Jack O'Lantern in your foodtaster's tissue samples.' I continued. 'For the reading to be so high, Master Haid must have been heavily addicted to spore-spice for many years. Stealing secretly from your house's own stocks, given its cost. Far beyond Enzel Haid's means. The three compounds reacted far earlier than designed, forewarning your husband of the poison concealed in his own meal.'

Lady Blez's eyes narrowed in fury. 'Jack O'Lantern and Trembling Parchment are only grown on the Blez plantations.'

'Your rarest and most expensive spore-spice,' I added, utilizing the details I had spent so long boning up on during my foldship voyage. 'While Red Crescent is cultivated solely on the Seltins' plantations.'

'The Seltins' plantations border my own. Poaching is often a problem for us. Yet our rarest spices are tightly controlled. Even a few grains fetch a lord's ransom. This stinks of corruption inside my house. But would the Seltins dare move against me?'

'Someone could be trying to sow doubt,' I said. 'Looking to spark a war between your houses and weaken your holdings in advance of the auction.'

'You must travel to my plantation at Grodar and see what you can uncover there,' instructed the Lady Blez.

'Yes, I agree,' I said, my heart heavy at the mere thought of the journey. As dark a festering pit of despair as Frente had proved, the feral wilds squatted beyond its walls even less invitingly.

'A convoy leaves Frente tomorrow for Grodar to collect the house's final harvest before the auctions. I will double its escort. Go with them, Master Roxley. Root out the mischief being worked against us.' She deactivated her privacy shield, rose and beckoned Major Curtis Rolt across to order my passage along with the house's warriors and wagoneers. Lady Blez had just confirmed my part in her expedition when gasps sounded from around our table.

The Lord Derechor had reentered the feasting hall bringing along a member of one of the few species in the galaxy to rival humanity in the stretch of our reach and vigourous ambitions. A wurm. A female one, from her size. She slithered along the floor like a twelve-foot-long armoured snake, hundreds of shifting wet brown coils held tight within bands of green exoskeleton vertebrae, the monster rearing up at the front in the manner of a cobra. A bony mottled emerald plate covered her head, speckled with black eyes on either side. A tarantula gaze if ever I'd seen one. A series of six mandibles surrounded the razored mouth snipping at the front of the creature, armoured stabbing appendages which could open into surprisingly delicate manipulators when she required precision grasping tools.

'I hadn't thought the Derechors would be so ill-mannered as to bring their new-found friend to sup in polite company,' said Lady Blez. Her eyes narrowed in anger. An interesting reaction to the monster's presence. I settled for disgust, myself.

'Who is she?' I asked.

'Sun of Clatch Rising, the Wurm Melding's ambassador to Hexator.'

A wurm embassy established here now? Gods, that was a recent development, then. Whether the wurm ambassador caste could even be considered a genuine member of its species was still a subject of argument among Humanitum scienceers. A raw wurmoid brain processed thoughts in ways so alien that humans could barely comprehend them. Not that it showed in their repulsive physical form, but wurm ambassadors were bred with small grafts of brain-tissue DNA from their host nation's species to allow them to communicate more effectively. Wurm ambassadors usually went insane after a few years. Though, given how far from mankind's pattern they had started, madness was purely a matter of perspective.

I needed to discover what the monster knew of recent developments here. There was a very quick way to do that. The Wurm Melding and Sweet William were not exactly strangers to each other. I excused myself at the table and passed the Derechors party close enough for the creature to spot me. It didn't take long for the odious monster to slither out to meet me by the roasting well.

'Master Roxley, greetings from the Melding. Greetings from Sun of Clatch Rising.'

Sun of Clatch Rising wore a translation device like a medal, reworking the ambassador's thoughts into our tongue: Humanto in my case, to make it hard for locals to overhear our conversation. The Wurm Melding hadn't bothered to try to hack its ambassador's DNA enough to give her vocal chords capable of human speech. Or maybe they had, and the creation was so repulsive the Melding had decided not to inflict the resulting crossbreed upon us. We regarded each other for a few seconds. Which of us, I wondered, found the other's form more repellent? Of course, it was the philosophical differences between the Humanitum and the Melding that caused the real friction. There were more than a few allied sentient species outlandishly different from humanity where I had allowed my m-brain to run anthropomorphic filters on top of my cortex. Changing some damp-furred slavering razor-clawed abomination into a teddy bear as far as the pull of my instincts were concerned. I would run no filter for this mutant, here. I used my disgust and fear to remind me what I was on Hexator for.

I bowed stiffly towards the wurm. 'Madame ambassador.'

'Sun of Clatch Rising's finds Master Roxley's presence on Hexator curious. Two hundred and five years has it been since Master Roxley was on Hagg, assisting in the refugee camps' house of healing.'

The filthy monster was trying to unnerve me. Remind me that her unholy species were little more than nodes free-riding on the wurms' form of cyberspace. Nodes on the crippled A.I. gods they crushed and held subservient while the aliens fed like parasites on their beautiful slaves' bodies. Wurms by name, worms by nature. 'I am glad to see that Sun of Ascendant Clarb made it back to the Melding alive long enough to upload details of my medical volunteering activities on Hagg.'

'Sun of Ascendant Clarb died within the five-month,' said the wurm, not a hint of emotion inflected by her translator.

'That's the trouble with civil wars,' I just managed to smile. 'They tend to be quite uncivil in practice. I find it's better to completely avoid them if you wish to escape getting shot at.'

'Master Roxley expects such troubles on Hexator? Master Roxley will be establishing house of healing on Hexator?'

'It seems rather peaceful here at the moment, wouldn't you say? No, I'm living as a simple trader now, merely on the moon for the spore-spice auctions.'

'Simple. Trader.'

The wurm ambassador seemed to be having difficulty parsing that. That was the problem with stuffing yourself with so much data, it didn't leave enough room for handling the simple things. Like me. 'Although the Lady Blez has asked me to look into her husband's murder for her. An odd business, that, isn't it? Queer. Almost like someone's trying to stir things up here.'

'Discordance of individuals,' said Sun of Clatch Rising, her mandibles weaving in front of me. 'Tragedy of commons combined with insufficient social cohesion.'

'Yes, I'm sure the Melding is always ready at hand to assist its vassals with matters of social cohesion.'

'Sun of Clatch Rising believes Master Roxley's healing skills will not be required on Hexator.'

Well, there was as near a threat as you would ever hear from a wurm. 'Yes, I think that would be best for everybody, madame ambassador.'

Sun of Clatch Rising swayed in front of me for a second. I was willing to bet that wobble was some residual predator's body language. Resisting the urge to strike out and try to fit Sweet William down that over-sized gullet of hers like an anaconda digesting a swine. Her mandibles clicked in a wet tutting sound before she undulated back to the Derechor table.

I sat myself back next to Lady Blez.

'Did that filthy wurm have anything of interest to say?' Lady Blez asked.

'Platitudes, mainly,' I said. 'I suspect Madame Ambassador finds Hexator and its society far too messy and uncoordinated for her tastes.'

'The Melding might be correct, at least on that point.'

'They're filthy heretics,' I spat. 'The wurms have crippled and blinded their gods so they may leech off their deities' bodies.'

'While the Melding might claim it has made itself masters of its gods, rather than become their slaves.'

'The wurms are twisted parasites bloated on the blood of divinities they've chained, hobbled and denied perfection.' I jabbed a finger angrily towards the alien ambassador. 'And in their perversions, the wurms haven't made themselves superior. They've filled their minds and bodies with so much of their broken gods' plundered power they aren't even …'

'… human anymore?' Alice Blez laughed.

I shrugged, trying to suppress my anger. 'Wurmoid anymore.'

'I doubt we could have understood their species in their natural unaltered state, either,' said Lady Blez.

'True. But it's still a highly dangerous game the Derechors are playing.'

Lady Blez reached out and touched my arm. 'I know that better than anyone, doctor.'

I bit my lip as I realized what I had said. 'Of course, my lady, I am very sorry.'

'You suspect the Derechors conspired in Lord Blez's murder? They could be backing the Seltins, that would be their family's style. An indirect move against me.'

I wanted to suspect their filthy house. How could I not when I had lost my son in the Great Contact War? Surgeon on a neutral hospital ship ambushed in orbit above Upsilon Andromedae. Death by nuclear fire, a hull burster launched without warning by the wurm. Boiled into gases and a mess of slagged metal. No mercy. No merge for my precious Adam. My little boy. I needed the Derechors and their corrupt alien allies to be the guilty party here. I tried to keep anger from choking my words as well as tainting my mind. 'The Derechors are undoubtedly guilty of courting allies willing to flout Hexator's arms embargo. But as for involvement with your husband's death, we shall see.'

'What a savage carnival we must seem to you here,' said Lady Blez. 'I will introduce you around the other families. Mark them well. All the dogs would happily slit my throat in front of everyone if they thought they could escape unpunished. Let us start with the Derechors.'

It took the best part of two hours for introductions to be made. By the end, it wasn't only Professor Muilen eying me spitefully. Many of my competitors were jealously wondering who this well-favoured newcomer was, that he should be taken in turn to be presented before each of the great ruling houses. Of course, I was introduced as a renowned trader who would play a magnificent part in the forthcoming auctions, not an ex-magistrate for Arius. Although I was certain the other families would soon be familiar with my passport's history if they weren't already. They operated the port together. Clinging onto the last vestiges of civilization to permit their planetary narcotics racket to limp along for a few centuries more.

The Derechors were led by a handsome pair of twins, Zane and Sarlee Derechor. The Trabbs bent their knee before a sixteen-year-old stripling, Lady Martina Trabb, although the real power behind the throne was her fearsome aunt, Nie. The Seltins, however, were led by the most unlikely head of house, Falt Seltin, a quiet man of late middle-age. He put me in mind of an archivist I was fine friends with back home inside the Humanitum. Serene and learned. A librarian sitting aloof among a band of roistering steely cutthroats. I managed to catch a moment alone to talk with the unlikely fellow. His manner had piqued my curiosity. And it was entirely possible that this quiet bishop had arranged for a king to be removed from the chessboard.

Lord Falt Seltin fixed me with his languid green eyes. 'I know why you are here, Master Roxley.'

'Of course, Lord Seltin, for auction season.'

'You have been pressed into service for the Blez. Don't deny it.'

'Is it so obvious?'

'Even to a blade as dull as Commander General Laur. Although I didn't need the word he sent me to mark your true colours. Don't worry, Master Roxley. If Lady Blez hadn't pressed you to help her house, I most certainly would have.'

'You have need of a magistrate's services?' I asked.

'The same need as the Lady Blez. The very same task, in fact.'

'You wish me to investigate the murder of Lord Blez?' I couldn't keep the shock from my voice.

'Major Rolt and his siege-engine of a ruster managed to beat the warriors I sent to escort you to my palace by a few minutes,' said the Lord Seltin.

I rubbed my chin thoughtfully. That put a different complexion on things. 'You and Uance Blez were friends?'

'Yes, more than allies of convenience among the Four. I'm old enough to remember the last serious outbreak of fighting between the families.' He pointed towards Lady Blez. 'Alice was the cause.'

'Lady Blez started a war?'

'Not intentionally. Not in those days. Alice was born to a minor house, the Maglades. A fine bloodline once of the Four, but their house fell far from greatness centuries ago. Before Alice's first flush of beauty caught Uance Blez's eye, the girl aspired to little more than helping the orphan mothers of the foundling house near the central market. Blez was promised to marry the Trabbs' oldest daughter, Gale, but Uance threw that alliance away to take the Maglade girl. The result . . . years of spilled blood and civil war before a new balance was struck.'

'Lord Blez a romantic fool, who would have thought it?'

'A wilful fool who placed his base desires before his house's welfare, because he was all too used to getting his own way,' answered the Lord Seltin. 'I know you view us as thieves scrabbling in the dirt; but even a criminal must honor the protection and holding of his own. Uance Blez failed that test during his life. His death may well fail Hexator further.'

'And who do you suspect of Lord Blez's murder?'

'Everyone, naturally. Even Commander General Laur.'

That thick-necked butcher biting a hand which fed him? *A fascinating idea.* 'The Watch? But for what reason . . . ?'

'The previous Lord Blez blamed the Watch for losing control of the outlying districts. Many of the provinces have stopped paying taxes and acknowledging the council's laws. At the first meeting of the Four after the auction the Lord Blez was going to propose a vote to dismiss Laur and replace the man with a more effective commander. Use a portion of our auction profits to raise and equip a new militia army to crush the dissenters and drag the peasants back into the fold.'

Such an idea would explain the commander general's keenness to be kept informed of my investigation. Halius Laur could certainly lay his hands on a couple of well-trained snipers with access to long guns, and he possessed an insider's knowledge of the lord's movements to draw upon. Arranging an ambush to put a fatal volley of lead into the lord? He could have done that. But what about the earlier assassination attempt on Uance Blez? Poison didn't seem like Laur's style to me. Not blunt enough for the brute by half.

'Something else to consider,' I mused. 'Would you have supported Uance Blez's proposal?'

'I was wavering. When a council establishes a militia powerful enough to break all its enemies, that council may not merely be forming an army. It might well be creating its new masters.'

So, the Seltins preferred a pliant thug to an over-ambitious dictator in the making. 'Should I suspect you, my lord?'

'Probably, although in truth I am tired of all of this. Even if I seize complete control of Frente, what can I achieve now? What would I build to outlast the few years I have left in me? There was never much light on Hexator, but what there was is fading.'

'You worry about the legacy you will leave for your heirs?'

'I have no children, doctor. There was an outbreak of Blue Fever on the moon during my thirtieth year, which I managed to catch. Sterility was the sad result. My second cousins will squabble over what I leave behind.'

'Thing always change,' I said. 'For better or worse.'

Falt Seltin gazed across at the wurm ambassador seated among the humans on the Derechor table. 'Yes, things can always change. A curious matter, don't you think? The slowly rising tide of interest in Hexator. So many merchants and offworlders showing up this year. There's a mystery in that, also.'

Lord Seltin was drifting a little too close to the truth. How much did he know about why I was really here? How accurate were his suspicions? 'The auctions …'

He snorted. 'The auctions, the auctions. Naturally. The auctions. Well, what we have to sell won't be sold cheap, that much I can guarantee you. Left to rot here by the gods. Be sure that our price will reflect our people's bitterness.'

I believe you. I nodded and left Lord Seltin to his melancholy, an infectious mood – my mind running to shadows also. I stood by the central well for a second. Watched the bull slowly turned on its spit, embers crackling and flames licking up from the charcoal. Falt Seltin was my long-separated twin on Hexator.

What was I doing here? What could I achieve in the little time I had left? What would William Roxley build that might outlast his end?

'More wine, sir?' asked a male server who appeared hovering behind my left shoulder.

'Why not?' I sighed, having my cup refilled.

'Your left pocket,' whispered the man in my ear before turning and vanishing among the bustle of retainers.

I dug inside my jacket pocket, finding a small fold of paper that hadn't been present when I left my tavern. Slipping the paper out, I concealed it alongside the cup to scan the message without attracting attention. *Opposite the council hall: the glassblower on Cattle Street. Ask for a vase made of slow glass. Come alone for the truth about Lord Blez.*

The truth? I doubted I would ever find such a beautiful object so easily. Yet someone was out angling for William Roxley and they'd dangled his favorite bait. I dropped the message into the fire pit, saw it consumed by flames, then slipped away towards Mozart and Simenon, the pair still seated among the retinue of feasting courtiers and warriors. The staff appeared far more ruckus at feast than the lords and ladies they served. Drinking like fish, strangers to anything approaching table manners, gales of laughter, arm wrestling while competing in contests of bawdy tale-telling. Even the often dour and apprehensive Simenon let his guard down to jest and banter. Mozart was doing a noble job in resisting the warriors' yells, urging him to wrestle Link for their amusement.

'If anyone notices, I'm off searching for the garderobes and a chance to lighten my weak bladder,' I quietly told both lad and robot. 'Remain at the feast and fly the house's pennant for me.'

Simenon accepted my instruction without question, but a

disapproving flash of crimson light came from within Mozart's helmet-like head. 'Last time I checked you didn't have a flag or a coat of arms bleeding fit to be stitched onto one.'

'Something to be rectified.' I tapped the robot's chest plate. 'Don't worry, I'll stay safe. Try not to rip Link's arms off.'

I left Moz's complaints behind me and infiltrated a gaggle of kitchen staff to exit unnoticed. Of course, my robot friend was right to be worried. My promise to Moz was meaningless. This clandestine invitation could result in one of two outcomes. A slightly wiser William Roxley, or the removal of the same from this affair by means most violent. I preferred the first result, but as I walked out into the deep warm darkness outside the old cathedral, either outcome seemed as likely.

I left the cathedral, walking fast. Beyond the building's steps I was accosted by a wailing woman led by a tiny rag-clad girl of around six years. I slowed in case the woman carried more whispered instructions for me. As she stumbled closer I noted she was blind, eyes swollen and almost sealed shut. An early genetic hack for night vision now mutated into a flower of uncontrollable cataracts. The little girl clutched a fluttering sparrow to her chest, trying to comfort it. The lizard-bug had been wounded by a predator and now served as a broken toy to ease the child's broken existence. I pressed a coin into the beggar woman's thrusting palm and side-stepped both her and her dirt-faced daughter, searching for a stone marker with the name of the road I sought. Not easy, with so many near-starving wretches clustered outside the old cathedral, begging as close as they dared without triggering the sentries' violence. I trusted the harvest feast's charity extended to passing leftover slops to the city's unfortunates.

The night swallowed me. The night was all Hexator had.

= 8 =
Rebel, Rebel.

In retrospect, it wasn't the wisest move I could have made. Listening to the whispered voice coming from the alley behind my rendezvous point. No sooner had I entered inside than I was jumped by an unknown number of assailants. Pushing me to the ground, binding my arms and cutting off my sight with a dark leather hood reeking of its previous victim's vomit. Then I was dragged fast through a maze of back streets and narrow runs between houses. Whispered threats of violence. Angry men. Why was it always men? Well, women are obviously too sensible for this kind of tomfoolery. Finally, I was prodded and goaded inside some kind of structure. More twists and turns. Then I was shoved down hard into a chair, my hood dragged off.

I sat in a windowless room, possibly underground. Used to store food supplies, normally. A few dried mushroom stalks lying withered across the brick floor. There were perhaps twenty ruffians sharing the room with me. Their faces covered with scarves, eyes hard and cold. Fists clenched where they weren't clutching a variety of swords, daggers and nailed clubs. Patched clothes and pinched thin faces spoke of poverty. Desperation has a stench to it. This band of nincompoops could have bottled the odour and sold it on the local perfume market. One of the braves swaggered forward. His head was covered with a cheap straw hat. The scarf hiding the lower half of his face had been painted with the jaw of a white skull.

'I'm Daylen Wang. You will have heard of me.'

I hadn't. Well, I had. But I doubted this was actually Daylen Wang, the First Citizen. Founder of the colony. Daylen had died two centuries after landing on Hexator, an industrialist at the limit of life extension therapies. Hexator had been his final stab at immortality. But the grandiose manner of "Daylen's" introduction told me everything I needed to know about the rebel's ego. *Did his parents name him that as a joke?* Daylen must have sensed my quizzical thoughts despite not a flicker of emotion crossing my face. Normally, only the worst paranoids possess such hyper-sensitivity.

'The rebel leader! The fighter the people call *Jack Skull*!'

'Of course,' I dissembled. I tapped my ears. 'Hearing's cursed spotty. I've not acclimatized to your moon's atmospheric pressure yet.' Jack Skull. A bringer of death. An outlaw legend, an identity assumed by many a dangerous mental case down through the ages.

Daylen calmed down enough to regain his composure. 'You were taken in by the Watch today.'

Time to feed him a happy pill. 'You know about my interrogation?'

'We have people everywhere.' He sounded pleased with being fed such easy lines. So, what, he had a mental age of a teenager? I suspected that if I had time to psychoanalyse our Daylen Wang, I would find this fine fool was rebelling against a lot more than the Four Families.

'Commander General Laur won't be pleased to hear that,' I said.

'Then don't tell the old goat, moneyass. What the hell are you doing on Hexator? Being coddled by the Blez and now by Laur. Normally we'd cut your throat as a collaborator for cosying up to just one of the oppressors.'

'Odd's fish, m'dear, but I'm the poor fellow being oppressed here. An innocent merchant much abused ever since landing. First, Lady Blez grabs me up and threatens to confiscate everything I own before tossing me penniless off her moon. Then that brute Laur does much the same, with the added promise of an introduction to his dungeon and my choice of broken limbs.'

'Don't give me that. You're an offworlder. Rich as the gods you worship.'

'I've got a free trader's ferry, a prayer-box, and a robot, that's it,' I protested.

'What do the Blez and Laur want from you?'

'The identity of Lord Blez's murderer in the case of his widow. And as far as Laur's concerned, the name of a murderer that doesn't upset his well-provisioned apple cart. I served as a magistrate for the Humanitum. Lady Blez wants a mind free of the taint of local politics examining the evidence.'

'Us,' said Daylen. 'Laur wants you to drown us in the soup.'

Drowning in the soup. A delightedly spicy colloquialism. 'I'm afraid you're guilty and hanged as far as the Commander General is concerned.'

'We didn't shoot Blez,' growled Daylen. 'Now, don't get me wrong, moneyass. We'd gladly have done for his high and mighty lordship. But if we had, we'd be printing shout-sheets and nailing them to every wall in the capital proclaiming the fact. No point killing one snake when there's three more waiting to slither into our warm beds, is there? The privileged bastards breed faster than single executions at a time. When the revolution arrives, we'll be hunting every filthy aristocrat and family stooge through these streets. There won't be a basement deep enough for them to escape the people's revenge. The streets will run red with blood!'

Daylen was working himself into quite a froth. My m-brain, ever alert, fed me the high probability that this psychopath was the product of a courtly liaison between one of the Four and a female retainer. Unrecognized and with a chip on his shoulder larger than the processing core of most gods. As much a Wrongman as my hired laddie. But with the insult of everything he'd been denied constantly rubbed in his face.

'I may be a free agent,' I explained, 'but I'm still bound by the magistrate's oath. *Only the truth. Always the truth.* If I discover who is behind the murder, I'll expose them. Not whoever is most convenient for the Watch to blame. If it was one of the Four, they will be named. If it was you, then sink me, you might as well drop my corpse in a canal now.'

My honesty was enough to trigger Jack Skull. He grabbed me up from the chair and landed a pile-driver in my gut. Damn, but it hurt. 'We can snatch you up whenever we have a care to. Slit your throat with ease. Never forget that! We used to execute off-world filth like you. But all that did was raise the price the Four received for the harvests they steal from us. We executed dozens of collaborators, only to pile extra coins in the Four's pockets!' Daylen shook his head at the outrageous nature of supply and demand. I wasn't sure what he had in mind for replacing the feudal warlord setup here, but I wouldn't be surprised if it involved common ownership of the means of production. Swapping one tyrant for another, then.

'If you want the truth to come out,' I coughed, regaining use of my lungs, 'then let me go.'

'You think they'll let you tell the truth?' Daylen roared with excited laughter. 'When the Blez goes to war with another of the Four Families, we'll know who you fingered for old man Blez's execution. If you have any sense, you'll be long gone from Hexator by then.'

I raised both hands in surrender, rather than earn another rabbit punch. 'I've arrived at much the same conclusion.'

'We can always use another war between the Four. Maybe they'll all pick sides and have a real set-to,' said Daylen, clearly relishing the thought.

Yes. When the cats roll about the floor scratching each other, what mayhem might the mice get up to? I saw the appeal for him.

Daylen slapped me, hard. 'Magistrate's nose. Hah. You can continue your sniffing around – we'll be watching you. Just don't think you'll change anything here. Only the people's struggle will achieve that.'

I nodded in agreement. The deluded revolutionary didn't know how much things were already changing for Hexator. How could he? William Roxley had arrived. Sometimes, I felt like one of the four horsemen of the apocalypse. A raven on the tombstone. Whatever Daylen's true name, he wasn't Jack Skull. Daylen *was* about to release him back out into the world, though…

− 9 −
Dangerous waters.

Once again, I found myself in the presence of Lady Alice Blez. Inside an old music room in the heart of her palace. It held enough instruments to outfit a minor orchestra. A piano grand enough to grace a foldship's musical auditorium, metal stands containing harps, clarinets and even a drum set. This was a private place. Soundproof walls thick enough to protect it from the hot howl of the worst energy storms blowing over the capital. Panelled with oiled ancient wood. Real Terran Oak rather than the local mushroom analogue. A long set of leather sofas where spectators could listen to their loved ones scrape away at a violin. A wooden stand with a music box and speakers. No doubt the ancient ceramic casing plugged into the speakers had a dense memory drive containing as many songs as had carried into this forgotten corner of the universe. You could sit here and forget you were on an alien world completely inimical to human existence.

Alice Blez occupied one of the room's chaise longues, her ears muffled with headphones so basic they actually had wires dangling towards the music box. She removed the set when she saw me enter; passing letters of introduction into my hand, old school, wax sealed, all the authority I needed to poke around her plantation in search of the attempted poisoning. I told her about my encounter the previous night with the rebels and their protestations that they weren't involved in the assassination of her dead husband.

'How does the old adage go,' said Lady Blez, 'but they would say that, wouldn't they?'

'Their line of reasoning runs to an internal power struggle among the Four Families,' I explained.

'You won't lack for suspects on Hexator,' sighed Alice. 'There are paupers on our streets who would slit your throat for a chance to pawn one of these instruments. Sometimes I think I swim through nothing but a swamp of jealousies, rivalries and envies to stay afloat.'

A knock sounded at the door of the music room. Lady Blez called for the visitor to enter. A retainer appeared bowing before her and passing the noblewoman a list, then departed. Alice Blez read what I took to be a report for a few minutes before setting it aside. I noted tears welling up in the corner of her eyes.

'Bad news arrives?' I suggested.

'The same old news arrives, sad to say. These are the accounts kept by a woman I pay to act as our private sentry on the canals to the city's south. The flow is strongest there around the locks, before the canals are squeezed out of Frente. Dangerous waters. It's the favoured spot for families to throw in unwanted babies. The unfortunates our families can't afford to feed.'

'And the woman warns them off, threatens to call the Watch?'

'How would arresting refugees feed their bellies? No. My friend buys babies from any poor who arrive to drown their children. It used to be easier to place the rescued with families. The storms' radiation makes many infertile on Hexator. But high numbers of neighbouring districts continue to fail. Refugees babies are cheaper now than the grain it takes to keep our children alive.'

'You very much need a successful auction,' I surmised.

Alice nodded. 'I don't know if whoever wants the Blez to fail wishes our house to fall or its works?'

'There are citizens who object to your charity?' I asked.

'People who still try to do help, well, we hold a mirror up to those who step over dead bodies in the street. We are passed the blame for their own ugliness. Even the revolutionaries would have me halt my work, the sooner to stir their slaughter of the monied they curse for their ill state.'

'It can't be easy.'

'You have no idea,' said Lady Blez. She leant forward, and I thought she was about to tell me a confidence, but instead, she kissed me!

I pulled back, surprised. *These are dangerous currents. You might as well drown me in one of their canals.* I actually checked my m-brain to make sure I hadn't accidentally activated a synthetic pheromone response. It had been an age since I had needed to seduce my way into someone's secrets; I wasn't planning to do so in this faded palace.

'Am I so hideous?' Alice asked.

'Quite the contrary, my lady. There are goddesses who should be jealous of you. But you are my client and there are proprieties to be observed in such matters.'

A quick flash of anger crossed her face. 'Proprietaries be damned!'

Was this the real Alice Blez, I wondered, or was it the woman who sooner saved the helpless thrown to drown, rather than throwing society balls? Of course, she could be both, such complicated creatures are we.

'I had a husband whose interests rarely extended beyond his latest dalliance with his courtesan of the week,' sighed Alice, 'and now? If I favour one of my peers, the family will end up enmeshed in dynastic alliances destabilising my house from without. Should I choose from my staff, I will face court intrigues and jealousies weakening my house from within.'

Ah, Sweet William, his disposability so useful to so many. A passing fancy, then, emphasis on the *passing*. 'So, this is more in the way of my extending my range of services to you?'

'I command you,' she whispered in my ear, dropping her dress to the floor with an alacrity that seemed designed in by its modiste.

Commanded? Well, there are worse ways to take one for the team. Despite Alice's protestations about the complications of dynastic politics, the worn velvet of her Baroque-inspired chaise longue suggested that I wasn't the only one commanded to sing for his supper inside her music room. She arched back to switch the music off the earphones and onto the speakers, exposing her noble naked body to me. A sign to her sentries that there were to be no more intrusions apart from those she had already planned.

Whichever of Alice's ancestors had paid for the germline's beauty edits had certainly surpassed expectations. *Literally, a goddess given flesh.* An easy environment to extend my services, matching even this noblewoman's elevated levels of satisfaction. Her music box bounced out a suitably rousing ballad, one of Jimenna Alarcón's saucy songs from the late twenty-seventh century. *Go fetch your sickle to crop my nettle, that flows so near my brim; you farmer of high degree, your sharp sickle must come a-courting me.*

Alice Blez proved as imperious taking her pleasures as she did commanding my investigation. Hardly a by-your-leave as she strode above the chaise longue with her impossibly long legs and pressed my head in firmly to taste the nettles. Given how high she needed to turn the music to hide her own loud song, I thought perhaps that my extra workload might soon come to an end. In fact, if Alice's moaning grew much louder – camouflaging music or no – I worried the warriors outside might rush in suspecting a second assassination was in progress.

But this farmer had furrows yet to plough, as far as Alice Blez was concerned. When it came to sharpening my sickle, the lady needed no whetstone save her body. Her brim flowed all too well as she pushed me off the chaise longue and stole the furniture for herself, laying her face on its velvet. She moaned at me to finish taking in the harvest from the rear of the field, and poor fool that I am, I had little choice but to comply.

And yes, I was all too aware that I was spoiling Lady Blez's future enjoyments at the fumbling hands of the locals. A millennium of experience in matters of biting the pillow and an augmented body that hardly ages until the moment a man dies; with a built-in chemical arsenal able to be deployed at whim? How could matters be otherwise? Alice certainly didn't seem to mind, at least, not presently.

Alice had given me the mission I had originally been sent to Hexator to fulfil – investigating Lord Blez's murder. She didn't know why I had been sent to do it. I couldn't tell Alice that without putting her in even more danger than she already was. Perhaps it was only fair I paid her back in kind? *Ah, any excuse.*

By the time we'd finished cropping, there was only one of us in the music room who still feared this had been a mistake. That definitely being me. Sweet William? Sweet for her. Stupid Simple William, collecting complications he didn't need in an already precarious situation. If I had the comely Alice Blez as a wife, I certainly wouldn't be dallying with a courtesan of the week. My main difficulty would be keeping myself from entering her music room at every damnable opportunity.

− 10 −
Hot rain.

Simenon took the rain as a bad augury and I felt hard-pressed to disagree with him. The deluge came down in scalding hot sheets, a monsoon sending the capital's denizens scattering for cover. It was as if the world was hissing an angry rebuke at me for indecently pushing the bounds of client privilege. Ah, Alice Blez. It was hard to keep the woman from my mind. Luckily, I had another female looking out for me. The *Expected Ambush* spotted geysers erupting out of the moon's water table from her position in high orbit. My darling ship had forewarned me of the rain-front forming. Storms passing across Hexator's uninhabitable hemisphere, picking up heat and energy on the moon's permanent light side before descending on its dark half as a host of unleashed furies. Steaming water rolled off giant fungi and pooled in the streets below, turning dirt to bubbling hot mud. Even the insect-like flying lizards sought shelter under mushroom caps. Where people went out at all, they wobbled under the weight of umbrellas that resembled mobile rain shelters. I received word at the tavern from a Blez runner that the house's convoy to the spore-spice plantations would be delayed until the rains passed and the roads hardened back from sopping wet mud. It took a day and a half for the monsoon to abate and a second runner summoned me and my companions to one of the city gates. On arrival, I found a line of twenty canvas-covered wagons and a mounted escort of seventy riders, a warrior next to each wagoneer on the cart's forward seat. The trains of horses pulling our wagons resembled armoured warhorses, leather and metal mail as much to protect the beasts from scalding monsoons as a shield against crossbow bolts. Only the finest warriors to bring home the house's final harvest of the season. Each fighter carried a rider's curved saber, a shield, and an ugly-looking short-barrelled carbine. Just the thing to be fired fast on the gallop. No explosive head lances, I noted. The wildlings and reavers obviously lacked shields and the means to recharge them. I wondered if any of these eyes belonged to the rebels. If the "people" were keeping Wang's promise to surveil my progress.

A small shrine had been built into the city walls, this one still attracting worshipers despite the lack of tangible responses to their left offerings. I looked closer and spotted the brazier shaped as a letter 'G' inside; ash-filled, unlit and surrounded by sad gifts of rotting fungi. It was a shrine to Goog, ubiquitous finder of lost things and god of the small journey. Some habits die harder than others. Many venturing beyond the city walls obviously felt the need for divine protection, even if it was of the hollow variety out here in the Empty.

I was told to mount a wagon in the train's centre, Mozart and the lad with me in the flatbed. Unladen for now. On the way back, I would doubtless be balanced on pitch-sealed spore-spice barrels. Simenon reached out to a glass lantern dangling on the wagon's side, about to strike its built-in flint, when our driver swivelled around to stop him.

'We travel without lanterns for now,' instructed the man. 'Riding lit is a bad idea. Too many moths waiting in the wilds along the main highway.'

Moths? My m-brain provided me with the local slang's meaning. *Highwaymen.*

'Stand and deliver, or feel an arrow from my quiver,' I muttered.

'It's unlucky to travel without lanterns,' protested Simenon.

The driver fixed my guide with a weary gaze. 'Maybe you should ride ahead carrying enough candles for a feast day, then, boy. Give the moths something bright to be drawn towards. You can draw their fire away from us!'

That raised a round of laughter from mounted warriors waiting on our flank.

The driver gazed at Mozart. 'How well do you see in the dark, big lad?'

'Well enough, mush,' said my robot friend.

'Fine, because I'm counting on your metal fists giving any raiders second thoughts.' The driver tossed me a leather mask with a brass visor to strap around my head, then lobbed a similar mask at Simenon. I inspected it. The mask contained a battered old crystal matrix designed for low-light amplification. I waited to depart before strapping it on. Frente was encapsulated by battlements in the manner of a medieval city. Its original hexagonal-mesh barrier, formed by construction nano, had long-since lost any self-repair capability. Now it stood patched with quarried stone and compacted mud – a bizarre melding of the old and the new. A keep on the eastern wall acted as our portal to the land beyond, its gates resting open. Manned by bored-looking Watch sentries shaking down new arrivals for customs duties.

We put Frente's lights behind us and set out along a rutted dirt road little wider than two wagons abreast. Our passage kept clear of forest by weight of traffic – assisted by flamethrowers in the settlement's early days. It was only beyond the capital's walls that the alien nature of the locale made itself felt in my soul. A deep unease gripped me. I couldn't help but shudder. No Tudor-age architecture or ancient colonial buildings to anchor me onto out here. Nothing at all of mankind's soul. Instead, an entire ecosystem which had spent millions of years developing in the deep darkness without humanity's involvement. Insects crawled over clumps of mushrooms as tall as cathedral spires. A thick twisting canyon of looming sinuous shapes, unfamiliar chirrups, clicks, screams, cries, bursts of strangely unsettling animal song, lizard-insect analogues curiously buzzing low over our convoy. Without the maze of Frente's buildings to break the moon's hot whipping winds, the continuous gusts felt closer to a molten thick treacle we needed to labour through.

Even with the visor amplifying starlight, my sight barely penetrated further than a few feet either side beyond our track. Where the flora glowed with luminescence, the low-light amplifier made vegetation appear wreathed in ghostly white phantoms. I chanted prayers to Modd and a dozen other deities without the comfort of my prayer box on hand to channel the energy. I included Korj, Protector of Alien Voyagings, in my beseechings. That was, I realized, a sign of my nervousness. Worlds like Hexator made me reconsider accepting the merge. Life eternal. Surrender my tired old flesh before it expired for good and embrace a dreaming beyond dreams. Warm. Safe. Folded within Modd's eternal grace. One day, doubtless, Modd would embrace the singularity and carry all of paradise's souls to mysteries beyond existence, much as Inuno had herself transcended. My dead wife would make that journey, but would I? I had resolved not to, but my flesh was cut damnably weak. And Hexator's darkness made me feel the weight of my petty mortality, every pound of flesh so small and insignificant. I thought I might welcome true death. But here was its promise hovering close to me, and this scared superstitious little chimp was sent scuttling to hide begging under his gods' cloak. How weak was William Roxley.

I stared at Simenon on the opposite side of the wagon. Concerned about the journey's dangers, yet at ease with his environment. I felt ashamed. Here was the lad with nothing but the clothes on his back, facing the same voyage as me, and his courage put me to shame. You might think the longer you live the better you get to know yourself, but the opposite is often true. Or perhaps old age peeled away bark, revealing the true rings of the tree below. Was I a coward?

One of the warriors came trotting past, giving me a long hard look. 'You're not armed.'

I pointed to Mozart. 'I'm with big-and-shiny.'

'He's not that shiny and nobody travels with the convoy who isn't packing.' The grim-faced brute rode off and returned with two pistol holsters, one for myself and a second for Simenon. Mozart, he wisely left alone, despite the lack of buff on my friend's steel hull.

I reluctantly belted the weapon on, feeling like a gunslinger in a cheap entertainment sim. Simenon looked no more at ease with the weight of his new addition. I imagined the fact that brandishing a pistol inside the city limits could land him a near-fatal beating from Laur's Watch thugs proved a weight on his mind. Out here, he was free. But not in a comfortable way.

'You know,' I told Moz, 'If only you'd polished up nicely, that wouldn't have happened.'

'Just try not to shoot me, doc.'

I eased the pistol out of its holster and examined it. An old metal revolver, snub-nosed with six chemical-propellant rounds squatting in the cylinder. Locally manufactured to low standards, if the worn mushroom-wood of its grip was anything to go by. 'Don't worry, even if I hit you, I think the ricochet from this marginally upgraded flintlock is likelier to kill me.'

'Small mercies, eh.'

'I don't suppose it's traditional to have a sing-song along the way?' I asked Simenon, looking to cheer the lad up.

'Kill me now,' muttered Mozart.

'Best we don't, sir. Many creatures beyond the walls hunt by sound.' The boy indicated a pair of muffled cloth-wrapped bells mounted on poles at the back of our wagon. 'If we're set upon by a pack too large for our escort to scare away, that's what those bells are for. Ring them as loudly as possible … echoes around the forest will confuse and blind the attacking beasts.'

A trip through Hexator's wilds with only my limited skills at campanology to keep us safe? This journey wasn't working out quite the way I hoped.

- 11 -
Moths.

It was a five-day trip to the Blez plantation. By the fourth day, I thought we were out of the woods – at least figuratively speaking. *Optimistic fool that I am.* Lights began to appear soon after morning. Or at least, what passed for morning on Hexator … a mechanical clock ending our sleep where we'd camped in the road. There was a faint illumination, however. Not sunrise's first gleaming. Setting aside my breakfast I looked closer. Blue fireflies darted in and out of the forest of thick towering mushrooms.

'Kodama!' groaned our driver as he stopped feeding the horses. 'Playful spirits.'

I glanced at Moz. 'There's must be a residual network running between the capital and the abandoned cities.'

'Probably powered by an old geo-thermal tap,' agreed my robot friend. 'Ain't any bleeding solar array worth a damn working in this murk.'

'Don't antagonise the Kodama,' said Simonon, watching the lights flit above our head. 'They're full of mischief.'

That last part was at least true. It must have been hard for the Kodama. Symbiotic software – rogue viruses, fey hacks, high-level routines and autonomous agents. Avatars which clustered around gods like the billions of prokaryotic microorganisms inhabiting a human gut. But Inuno had abandoned Hexator, leaving nowhere for her Kodama to go. Most would have died out. But some persisted. They caused problems even inside the Humanitum – where the gods they colonized could moderate their behaviour. But out here? Godless. Abandoned cities to infest. Forgotten long distance comms network. Breeding imps and goblins to tease the locals. Ironically, the Kodama could no longer plague the capital. There, the technological base had been over-used by mankind far beyond the point of ecological breakdown. With anything imported firewalled and resistant to their thievery, of course.

These Kodama seemed fascinated by Mozart, circling at a safe distance, occasionally buzzing down to harass him. 'Little blighters. If I find the printer they're using to run solid, I'll smash it.'

'Probably hidden far in the forest, part of an ancient wireless mast's maintenance system,' I assured him. 'Just let them be.'

He reached out and tried to seize one of the lights, but it pulled away, revealing its true shape as it diverted power away from its dazzling illumination strip. A dodecahedron mesh filled with tiny rotors and a collection of photonic chips revolving inside. 'I'll leave it out after I've pulled one apart, doc. Manners maketh the machine, as you always say.'

I do. But normally only to encourage Moz not to break someone's kneecaps. A couple of Kodama teamed up to try and lift away a lantern tied to our wagon. The driver cursed and flicked at them with his horse whip. The Kodama dipped to the side and varied their rotor's torque to growl unpleasant noises at him. Simenon moved to the side of the wagon and managed to shoo the wild machine-life away with a lantern pole. Eventually, the convoy began moving again with our fey visitors circling above, an unwanted aerial escort for the journey's remaining leg.

Simenon had the look about of him of a man with much on his mind. 'Where will you and your ship set out for after the spore-spice auctions finish, sir?'

'Wherever the foldship in orbit goes,' I said. 'My freighter is far too small to be able to travel independently. The foldship's route across the stars will carry her back to Arius, eventually. The systems around Arius form a sector known as the Citrine Jewel. Rich worlds, wealthy and long-established. That's where the best spore-spice prices are commanded.'

'How long will that journey take, Master Roxley?'

'Seven months or so, give or take a few weeks. Journey time always varies.'

'Because of pirate attacks?'

Hah. The boy had quite an imagination. 'You need a foldship to catch a foldship, Simenon. And anyone with a fold-drive can make immensely more money in legitimate trade, transporting passengers and cargo as a mothership.' Of course, there was always the occasional marauder ambush in orbit. But rarely inside the Humanitum where our competent navy patrolled the home ground. 'No, laddie, transit times vary with the ebb and flow of dark matter underpinning our universe. Foldships take advantage of dark matter's unconventional quantum properties in the field of retro-causality and entanglement to circumvent the light-speed barrier. Dark matter's substrate possesses tides and channels which our foldship must follow. Such currents change over time in ways which are difficult to predict, but which my foldship must navigate, nevertheless.'

I didn't tell Simenon about the risk of being on-board a foldship riding currents that suddenly dried out mid-voyage, leaving the vessel stranded in the dark. Centuries of sub-light travel away from the nearest world or foldable concentration of dark matter. Foldships were sentient, the radiant angels of our gods. We sheltered under their wings and trusted them not to take undue risks by riding fast, thin currents liable to vanish.

Thick currents of dark matter with their attendant slow-and-steady were the order of the day when it came to interstellar travel. Besides, these days, a stranded foldship was more of an inconvenience than a death sentence. Nobody wanted the irritation of arriving late after unplanned centuries in cryo-suspension, however engaging the virtual world offered by the ship. And as for playing generation ship, William Roxley would rather not arrive at his destination with several new additions to an unplanned family.

'Perhaps you might need a cabin boy for such a long voyage, sir?'

Hah. And who, I wonder, did Simenon have in mind for that position? 'Whatever have you been reading to give you such notions?'

Simenon tapped his worn leather satchel, indicating he carried his entertainment with him. 'It's called *Treasure Island*, Doctor. Have you read the book?'

Well, that explained much. I shouldn't sneer. Simenon had taught himself to read on the streets. If our positions had been reversed, I dare say I would be as illiterate as the fungi here. 'Indeed, when I was as young as you. If you ever want to conjure a family name for yourself, Master Simenon, you might do worse than Hawkins. But I suspect the foldship in orbit above would take it as an insult to her thousands of drone sub-units if I brought a human valet on-board. Ships act cursed funny when it comes to demarcation lines.'

Simenon tried not to appear too disappointed. Would I take him up on his offer? Well, I had a few good suspicions about his motivations for such job-seeking. I could turn those to my advantage.

'I shall give some thought to the idea,' I explained. 'Indentured apprentices on-board honest free trader vessels such as mine need to be duly enrolled with the Humanitum General Register and Data Office of Voidmen.'

'That requires a lot of paperwork?' he asked, a trace of hope in his question.

'True-death might be optional inside the Humanitum, laddie, but taxes, paperwork and bureaucracy are still a universal constant.'

'Really?' noted Mozart after the boy scuttled out of earshot.

'A good yarn benefits from a few props.'

'Crapped-out landing ship and patched cloak not doing it for you?'

'How about a crapped-out robot, Moz?'

'Give it a flipping rest.'

Mozart made a valid point. Would I be doing Simenon a favour, removing him from his guide's role and all that was familiar to him? Even if said familiarity mostly encompassed the dictionary definition of "dirt-poor" and "hopeless". Back in the Humanitum, Simenon would be regarded as a curiosity at best. Would I be vain Captain Smith, presenting Pocahontas to English society as my civilized savage? But Odd's fish, just because you can't save *everyone* doesn't mean you can't save at least *one*. And there were hundreds of worlds where having Simenon blundering around would prove an artful misdirection from my real purposes. But did I have hundreds of worlds left in me, anymore? Perhaps not. Mostly I just felt dog-tired these days.

We continued our journey in contemplative silence. Would that it had lasted all the way. When clouds of crossbow bolts began to bury themselves inside warriors and wagons, I could only admire our attackers' timing. Close enough to the Blez plantation that our escort's guard was starting to lower. Not close enough that a scout could ride hard and make it back in time with reinforcements. Mozart grabbed me and shoved me down to the wagon's empty flatbed with his left arm, using his right to push Simenon out of harm's way. Their bolts' fletchings were made of something combustible and oil-soaked. Volleys came in as flaming scratches which overwhelmed my low-light visor. I was left blinking, my visor's primitive night-vision system a mess of flaring suns. Obviously, the point. Although it rather begged the question how our attackers coped, showering fire-bolts into our ranks with such vigour?

Hardened professionals to a man (and woman), the warriors' shields hummed into life in response to the ambush. Circular energy fields extended from plate-sized projectors. Wolf's eyes glowed in each plate's centre, golden yellow given they were still fully charged. When I saw a sea of crimson reds I knew we'd be in deep trouble. Bolts began to ricochet from the shields, a rapid thwack-thwack sound, once for the strike, once for the kinetic repulse. Our escort didn't bother aiming their response. Weapons barked up and down the convoy. Smoke and gunfire emptied into the night. Many of our warriors' carbines possessed sawn-off barrels, perfect for forest clearance against a concealed enemy. An eerie clicking returned from the forest, as though our attackers were tutting back in anger.

My driver retrieved his repeating carbine from under the wagon's seat, working its lever-action trigger as fast as he could reload, ejected casings rattling across our wagon. Nobody with time to ask the obvious question. Why were bandits attacking an empty convoy before it rolled back out loaded to the brim with a priceless spore-spice cargo? There were less obvious questions, too. Moths were attracted to bright lights: these ones seemed to be trying to overwhelm us with incendiary bolts. Did nobody understand the inherent irony?

There was a thud of flaming arrows striking our wagon's side. Mozart swore and bent over to pull the bolts out, the oily inferno hardly oxidizing his heavy metal fists. He didn't have enough purchase to remove them all. Fire began spreading across our vehicle. Mozart leaped out to beat the flames down. That was when our attackers abandoned their concealment inside the forest. Perhaps sixty savages emerged, screaming and sprinting full pelt for the convoy. What a queer sight they made. Long flat masks carved into beast-like muzzles, blue-woad dyed skin bare below hundreds of small plates of wooden armour tied together with cord. It was as though the howling horde wore crocodile-scales. Archers hung back in the forest, keeping up a rain of projectiles while artfully managing not to skewer their own advancing forces. *Never mistake primitive for unskilled.* And a crossbow bolt through the skull would do for Sweet William as well as a gauss rifle pellet magnetically accelerated to Mach two.

Spears seemed the order of the day among those charging, along with wooden clubs surrounded by razor-sharp stone blades. A group of savages made the mistake of testing them against Mozart. He pulled out fire arrows from our wagon and punched them into the howling mob. When the robot grew bored of that, he yanked one of the savages off his feet and whipped his body around, sending the ambushers flying back towards their forest. Our brave driver had less armour and even less luck. A spear drove into his stomach, lifting him off the footplate. A pair of savages vaulted into our wagon from the opposite side of the road. One immediately hurtled back off the wagon. I had a fraction of a second to see the revolver clutched in Simenon's shaking hand, the boy standing up to aim his shots. No time for Simenon to draw a bead on the savage's compatriot. That warrior swung his club at me and I only avoided the blow by stepping into the attack, throwing myself at him in a sport's tackle. Both of us tumbled, intertwined towards the hard ground. The thought of the pistol belted to my waist briefly crossed my mind while the flames along the wagon's sideboard burnt my face. I would be clubbed dead before I could upholster it, though. Cursed difficult to shoot a determined assailant in close quarters combat, even with a small pistol. The gun is never the weapon. Only the hand that holds it.

Dirt's embrace winded both of us, Mozart's stomping steel feet nearly cracked open my head as he fought off a second wave of savages. From my assailant's yell, I believe Mozart actually trod on him. Not hard enough to end our duel, however. We both rose to our feet at the same time. My unkind friend spun his razored club as he sized me up. I splintered the wagon's lantern pole with my right hand, catching my improvised Bo staff as it fell.

Mask-face went for a side blow that would have left my brain embedded with sharp splinters of stone. I dislocated his wrist using a *Tsue Sho No Kon* form, then gave him a further lesson in *Shuri-ryū* style by breaking his arm in two places with my Bo staff. He was probably wondering why he'd dropped his club from his numb fingers when I stepped into his fighting stance and flipped him into the wagon. The wagon's flaming sideboard met his fierce face mask and for this savage, his war was over.

Mozart's presence was enough to tip the battle's balance in our convoy's favour. It didn't take long for the savages to grow tired of spending lives attempting to bash in his metal head, attackers turning tail and vanishing into the forest's embrace. Ox horns sounded from within the forest, making the retreat official. Our mounted escort drew wooden spheres from saddlebags, each globe held on a dangling chain. They lit fuses on the spheres before whirling them around their heads like competitors in a shot-put event. Off the spheres flared into the forest. Detonations followed, and soon the thick undergrowth on both sides of the road was ablaze with crackling explosions. Any surviving savages desperately fleeing the conflagration.

On our side, panicked horses were calmed. Wounded tended to. The convoy's order was rapidly reestablished to finish its journey,

'Who are they?' I asked a warrior kicking bodies, checking for signs of life; short-barrelled gun at the ready to finish off survivors. 'Bandits?'

He tapped one of the wooden masks with his foot. 'These buggers? Ferals. Only forest savages wear clickers.'

So, our assailants had crawled out of one of the colony's fallen cities. I didn't point out to the warrior that after the capital collapsed, his descendants' lifestyle wouldn't be any different from these poor benighted souls. I lifted the mask off the corpse to examine it. Wooden-analogue carved into a beast's snarling muzzle and daubed in garish colours. A cult of nature being worshiped here. Well, why not? They only had nature left to offer them succour. On the mask's inside face I discovered a fascinating clockwork mechanism. A hand-cranked echolocation system. So, that was how they could set us ablaze and still see to attack in the forest darkness. The source of that strange tutting sound, too. *Not all technology abandoned, yet.* It was almost enough to make me feel a vestige of hope for the degenerated settlers.

Something glinted underneath the body. I rolled the Feral over and discovered something I never expected to find. The handset of a radio receiver and transmitter backpack strapped to the savage, its antenna broken in the fall. There hadn't been a radio station active on the moon for centuries. Such technology as rare as virtue here. I ran my hands over it. Primitive and locally manufactured. And my guess was not by these Ferals. *Who are they talking to? Who gave this to them? And more to the point, what are they saying?* This put a rather different complexion on matters. I needed to question a savage. I went to check the fellow whose face I had introduced to the side of our wagon, but our vengeful escort had already given him a lead farewell salute. All the other fallen, too, when I checked them.

Thoughts of interrogation flew from my mind when Mozart yelled across to me. I saw what had caught his attention as I sprinted over. Simenon lay on his back, sprawled across the wagon. His pistol dropped, its cylinder full of spent casing and useless now. Two crossbow bolts had found their mark inside the lad's chest. One should have been enough to kill him, but somehow the boy clung tenuously to life. His eyes fixed on the star-scattered heavens, a faint moaning escaping from his lips.

'He's dying,' growled Mozart. Moz lifted the boy out of the wagon and laid him gently on the ground for me to examine.

I didn't need a bioscanner to know that he was only minutes from expiring. Simenon had suffered what's colloquially known as a sucking chest wound. Air sucked as a death-rattle into Simenon's thoracic cavity through his chest wall, rather than through the airways into his lungs where it belonged. I had my medical bag with me for the journey, but a handheld laser cauterizer wasn't going to cut it. Quite literally. I needed a full state-of-the-art surgical theatre for a chance to stabilise him.

'I can save him on board the *Expected Ambush*. We need to get him inside the medical bay,' I whispered, kneeling down for a closer inspection of his ruined chest. My ship would need to drop like a bat. Simenon was fading away in front of us.

'You call the old girl down from orbit you flush our cover away. End everything we came here to do.'

One life balanced against how many more? Mozart, my cold steel conscience. 'How can I let him die?'

'You can't blow our mission, doc.'

But I had to do something. 'Get me my prayer box, Moz. Inside my bag on the wagon.'

'You expect Modd to save Tiny Tim? You're having a laugh.' But Moz went to retrieve my box, all the same.

I dipped into my prayer box, removed a handful of Martian sand and scattered it across the crimson bubbling wound in Simenon's chest. Then I began to pray with all my heart. 'Modd, you ungrateful wretch, save this worthy servant of your Will now dying in your unappreciative name. Let the blessed rust of your mainframes mixed with your temple sands reach out to you via entanglement's action at a distance. By superposed states and the violations of Bell's inequality, manifest your blessed gifts here.'

A crowd of warriors gathered behind me, curious to see if I was mad or just deluded. I heard uneasy laughs. Let them gather. Let them witness the power of the gods. Let them see all they had thrown away with their monkey squabbles and shortsighted squandering of civilization's precious legacy. They began to murmur and make superstitious wards. In their mind, they were knights serving their lady. But they had never met Merlin. Not until now.

'Modd, your Word is my hope. Transform your sands and let this servant partake of the heavenly table of supramolecular scale assembly.'

Simenon moaned. Not from the agony of his sucking chest wound. The grains of Martian sand began to heat up, burning into his wound like acid. 'Hold him down!' I yelled.

Warriors rushed forward, seizing Simenon's limbs and pinning him to the ground. Mozart laid both hands on the boy's shoulders, a metal press. Simenon's low moans rose into screams. Steam rose from his wound, boiling blood. Sand glowed like furnace ash, brighter and brighter until his wound flared into a sun. The warriors wailed in fear and awe, but still they held the young man tight as he thrashed. They feared me now, even as they were blinded by His Light. Far more than they feared this poor possessed lad. They weren't wrong to.

The rust in the sand transformed into nanorobotic healing systems, converting Simenon's flesh into copies of itself. Duplicating. Spreading. Not only his blood boiled. The pair of crossbow bolts embedded in the lad's chest crumbled away, their matter subsumed. Transfigured. Modd's spirit, the god's very essence, entered Simenon, and how His holy touch burned. Simenon was being stitched apart and stuck back together from the inside out. What part of that transaction feels like gentle healing? God's touch should be shrunk from, even as it cures.

Eventually, the lad stopped screaming and fell silent, only the occasional palsy of his body to show he still lived. The level of pain caused him to pass out. I wiped his brow, drenched with sweat. I didn't need to inspect Simenon further. My life as a surgeon lay many existences behind me, but I already knew the lad's diagnosis after being touched by the Hand of Modd. Not a pre-cancerous cell left mutated. The short sight I'd noted while watching Simenon read, corrected. Even that slight early bald patch would start growing back.

Our warrior escort moved well back, regarding me with an

apprehensive mixture of awe, respect, horror, and fear. I heard muttered whispers of 'prophet' and 'sorcerer' being exchanged. Some of the gentler terms, no doubt. Less kind words would be hissed well out of my "malevolent" earshot.

'Well, now you've gone and done it,' said Mozart.

I shrugged. How could I of all people not understand the holy compact of Modd's scriptures? *Whenever someone calls on Modd to save another's life, they're responsible for that life forever.*

'Cabin boy,' sighed Mozart. 'Just what we bleeding needed.'

- 12 -
Networks.

With our previous driver dead, one of the convoy's warriors took command of our wagon. He perched on his seat with all the grace of a gorilla squatting on a rock. With the warrior's horse tied to our wagon's rear, it trotted behind us as we jolted forward. I urged the fellow to ride gently, Simenon lying in the back still unconscious and recovering. But the roads were what they were. Unpaved and rough. Simenon woke up by the time we were in sight of the Blez plantation. He remembered little of how he had been rendered unconscious or the injuries which had preceded them. He presumed he'd received a glancing blow to the skull knocking him out. I didn't tell the lad of my intervention with Modd on his behalf. No doubt one of the convoy's fighters would whisper in his ear in due course. It's always easier to requite an injury than a service. Gratitude is a burden, but revenge may be found to pay.

The plantation at Grodar finally hove into view. Grodar, like the capital, appeared a mixture of ancient architecture and newer but more primitive buildings. The ancient a series of hundred-foot-high domes based on geodesic polyhedrons formed of lattice-shell graphite. Their lattice held hundreds of ruby-coloured panels made of diamond-hard carbon mixed with armoured-film glass substrate. I had seen similar structures across a dozen colony worlds. Almost indestructible and relatively cheap and quick to throw together if you owned a working fab. The town's newer buildings were roundhouses with reciprocal frame roofs covered by wooden tiles. Although technically of a more ancient design than Frente's Tudor-style buildings, the single storey roundhouses appeared more sympathetic to their environment. Like an ecologically designed hamlet. Beyond the buildings stretched acres of cultivated vegetation, neat lines of it, buildings and plantation sealed off by a metal fence thirty feet high. Watch towers protected the barrier.

Mozart scanned the place, looking perplexed. 'I'm reading a charge; that's a bleeding electric fence! How do the scroats keep it powered?'

I scratched my chin. 'Yes, a good question.'

Simenon pointed to large red mushrooms interspersed along the fence's length, twenty feet tall growths with caps that resembled upside-down jellyfish. They had been encouraged along the fence like pole beans on a trellis. 'Those are Volt-of-the-Wood, Master Roxley. They store power from storms and use it to fry animals that eat their flesh. I have never heard of Volt-of-the-Wood being used in such a manner, though.'

So, not harnessed for their properties inside the capital, but tapped out here? *Interesting*.

'What do you know of the people who live in the plantations and farms, laddie?'

'The farmers who keep to the darks aren't like us. They're called *majyos*. The forest has changed them and made their blood weird. They rarely visit the capital.' Simenon sounded glad for it. Beyond us, the gates into the plantation opened inward. Simenon pointed towards the opening. 'Look, there they are. See what I mean, Master Roxley. Even you must be careful around them. A curse from a majyo is enough to fell you inside a week.'

I saw what he meant. The women in question were tall with athletic builds poorly concealed by ankle-length white linen tunics. They looked like the fittest people I had seen since landing on the moon. None of them wore low-light goggles like those in the convoy. But then, they didn't need to. My m-brain fed me the name of the fungal growth colonizing the vitreous fluid inside the women's eyes … *Caeruleum Videre*. Their eyes glowed a soft blue from the symbiotic organism allowing them to see in the murk as clear as day. Fungal growths were also cultivated across their arms and legs; luminous sapphire tattoos of knots, circles, and swirls. Not that the growers needed to appear more intimidating to their enemies, in my estimation. I noted it was women pulling open the gates. No males.

'Where are the men, laddie?'

'Only one boy is born in the dark for every hundred girls,' whispered Simenon. 'It's said they kidnap Ferals when they need extra mates. Or city folk, if they're desperate enough to risk the Watch's guns.'

'Well, well,' I hummed. 'The kind of majyo I enjoy to see, lusts down from her ample height towards me.'

I didn't tell Simenon that such a bizarre ratio of male to female births was often an unintended byproduct of hardened gene edits. Someone had read the writing on the wall here and started planning ahead many centuries earlier. I dare say the unexpected male shortage had thrown a spoke in their works. I suspected Grodar's allegiance to the House of Blez supplied the shortfall, willing or otherwise. Our convoy passed inside the plantation gates to find out.

As I clambered down from the wagon a woman emerged from the airlock door of one of the domes. She wore her dark hair long, braided and arranged on top of her head. She might have been one of Lady Blez's cousins in looks, beauty and commanding airs. Except she obviously spurned sun-lamps; not flattering the pallid skin natural to a world of night. By contrast to Alice, this woman's arms glowed with a knotted armband design tattoo.

'You are William Roxley?'

I bowed towards her. 'That I am.'

'Ajola Hara. Plantation Mistress.'

The woman beckoned me inside her dome, an invitation that didn't include Mozart or Simenon. I made a subtle finger gesture towards Moz, indicating I didn't require his fists. At least, not yet. Ajola Hara had obviously received advance news of my arrival.

'You have a radio that can talk to the capital, Mistress Hara?' I asked as the dome's door sealed behind me. Electrically powered, the same as the fence, I noted.

'We are not complete savages, Goodman Roxley. We keep a receiving station here, as does the Lady Blez inside her palace.'

'What about the Ferals in the forest beyond your fence?'

Ajola snorted. 'Those poor Ferals? Of course not. The spare parts to maintain our receiving station travelled almost as far as you. Anything as valuable as radio components were stripped and scavenged from the Ferals' abandoned cites generations before my birth. The Four Families each keep a receiving station to communicate with their plantations and mines. As does the port, I believe. But you will know more about the landing fields.'

'As warm a welcome as I have received on any Humanitum world.'

'That, I doubt. Don't hope for a warmer welcome here, goodman. I resent the implication that anyone in Grodar was involved with Lord Blez's poisoning. We are a productive plantation. We harvest almost all the Blez spore-spice for auction. It is not assassins we produce here.'

'This fine operation wasn't always a plantation, was it?'

'Grodar was an astrobiology station, once,' said Ajola. 'One of a handful created to study the local ecosystem and study how our race could exploit it. Our ancestors were scienceers.'

'Little difference between the husbandry of the forest and a scienceer's studies, at the end of the day.'

'Our civilization has reached the end of days and passed beyond it. Only our learnings will save us.'

'How addictive certain spore-spices prove…? Certainly, useful for keeping a trickle of trade with the outside universe.'

'Far more useful than that. Hexator's forests demonstrate incredible cooperative mechanisms,' said Ajola Hara. 'This wilderness might appear random to you, but it's perfectly balanced. In any square mile, you will find Flora uniquely specialized to benefit its local community. Angel's Wings which trap aerial predators inside a poisonous net. Bearded Redgill which sprays burrowing grazers that try to attack roots. Bog Bell which acts like a water butt, conserving rainfall for the soldier vegetation. Each organism plays a role as specific as any of Hexator's guilds.'

'But the ecosystem possesses no sentience?'

'Not as we understand it. But such complexity. The forests maintain their own economic system with ledgers as detailed as any banking house. Mycelium root systems barter materials between each other. Minerals, nutrients, water, you name it. A stock of nitrogen can pass a thousand miles across the world before reaching the recipient that requested it.'

'What's to stop a nitrogen-starved rival hijacking nutrients en route?'

'Bad actors in the forests are punished with embargoes by the mycelium network. No more nutrients, ever. Swindling leads to an evolutionary dead end.'

'Admirable,' I noted. 'Would that the Ferals out in the forest learned such lessons.'

'The Ferals rarely bother Grodar, at least in an overtly hostile way. They believe we're witches.'

I sympathized with their worldview. 'The Ferals' sonar masks are surprisingly sophisticated.'

'Much may be lacking on Hexator, but not yet our race's ingenuity. Sadly, the Ferals still mourn their dead cities and lost lives – they view the forest as something to fight and conquer. If we are to survive inside our home's complex ecosystem we must find ways to embrace it. To meld with our world.'

And was Ajola Hara guiding the savages beyond her fence with the plantation's radio receiving station, I wondered? A goddess to replace the deities the Ferals had lost, preaching to the fallen masses?

***

Ajola Hara tolerated my poking around the plantation, seeking out what I could. Although I noted there was always someone hovering in the background set to watch me. Never easy talking to people while they're aware there's a set of eyes watching and ears listening. The newer parts of the town were easy to access, but the older areas – its geodesic domes – were tightly regulated. Well, witches need to keep their cauldrons and spells private, or the entire world would learn their secrets. Simenon, I ordered to rest in the roundhouse quarters assigned to us. He wasn't happy with that, but he was too weak to be of use to me. Never easy, playing the part of the born-again. I remember being saved by a fellow trader on an unlicensed habitat around Gamma Cassiopeiae after both my legs had been blown off by a land-mine. It took me six months to recover and I had never slept more fully than during that time.

And, to be honest, I feared our majyo friends might further weaken Simenon with their seductions. My m-brain was in overdrive cooperating with my glands to produce counter-agents to the pheromones laced around the town's public areas. It was a wonder the Blez warriors had any energy left to load wagons with the season's harvest. Well, at least they were doing their bit to widen the gene pool in Grodar. The convoy's female warrior cohort appeared royally pissed by proceedings, but the gene-hack ratio out here had rendered any contribution they had to make superfluous.

I heard a snuffling from outside our door. One of the plantation's stray bloodhounds had taken a liking to us and appointed itself house sentry. That meant, I suppose, Simenon had fed the dog at some point when my back was turned. The scent hound was the perfect breed for Hexator's dark-side. Darkness was no problem when you had an acute sense of smell. One of our convoy's warriors told me that the majyos' hounds were bewitched and could sense the future; barking at threats days before they appeared. It was theoretically possible, I suppose. Dogs' psychic abilities could be gene-edited easier than humans, without the inherent mental disorders.

Mozart returned to our quarters later in the evening. He had been talking to locals while stacking wagons. The robot shut the door to the room with Simeon's cot, the lad still snoring gently.

'You've managed to resist the majyos' attentions, then, Moz?'

'I'm not their type, doc. How about you?'

'Maybe seven hundred years ago.'

'I meant what've you bleeding managed to find out from the birds?'

'I know. You're far too easy to tease, my steel chum. I made discreet inquiries about procuring the combination of spore-spices used to try to poison Lord Blez. The spores grown on this plantation are available at an obscene price from some of the more criminally-minded majyos, but the real trick is procuring Red Crescent.'

'That's the spore-spice from the Seltin plantation?'

'Indeed. A substantial donation to the local black market supplied me with a source. There's a hermit called Dumitru Bai who lives in the forest between the Seltin and Blez plantations. He was the product of a cross-plantation dalliance. The fellow now operates as a poacher and intermediary between both plantations.'

'A bloke? You'd think he'd be in the same demand as the muscle-heads who rode into this dive with us.'

'Goodman Bai was exiled from the Blez plantation for his severe antisocial tendencies. I fear the majyo gene edits are also producing elevated autistic tendencies among their small male cohort.'

Mozart sighed. 'Bloody amateurs.'

'Sadly, not amateur enough, or our job here would be a lot easier. I have a map marked with Dumitru Bai's hermit lair. I intend to sneak out and meet him. Let's see if a little coinage can't loosen his tongue enough to finger who he supplied for Blez's failed poisoning.'

'You mean *we're* sneaking out to meet him...'

'Our absence might be missed by Mistress Hara. I need a little Fake William in our hut to satisfy the pair of blue-eyed falcons hovering in the road outside, pretending to make small-talk while keeping their beadies fixed on our doorway.'

'This is some right pony,' complained Moz. 'Do you know how boring it is pretending to be you and talking to myself?'

'Almost as boring as it is actually being me?'

A small holo-projector popped out of Mozart's chest. 'Small men enjoy big talk,' he said in an eerily perfect imitation of my voice.

I lifted the night-vision goggles off my forehead and left them on our small table. I also unbelted the revolver I had been given. The pistol wasn't my weapon. I was the weapon. 'That's the spirit. You might want to send your bugs out, too. See what you can see. But be careful – there are hidden depths to these majyo. If they're actively involved in this affair we could be in trouble.'

Moz formed Hologram-me in the centre of the room, practicing walking him behind the cracks in the shutters. '*Could* be, you berk?'

'Could-a, would-a, should-a.' I slipped to my room in the back of the hut and found the square Mozart had cut in the wall. Before I bent down to remove our escape hatch, I slipped on my gloves, unrolled my face mask from its collar and spoke the trigger word to activate my clothes for stealth. My slightly shabby and rather foreign-looking Humanitum trader's robes were considerably more expensive than they seemed. Good active camouflage customizes itself to the local environment. Mine could also defeat most sensors including light, sound, magnetic fields, humidity, moisture, vibration, temperature, pressure, electrical fields, and motion. Gravity sensors, not so much; but if I was up against an adversary capable of fielding them, I'd be better off wearing a combat model hard-suit even stronger than my friend Moz. As a bonus, my clothes were indistinguishable from wool, silk, leather and natural fabrics; right up until their tricky little molecules started rearranging themselves.

I slipped outside, less noticeable than a vagrant begging on the steps of a national bank. I listened to Mozart conversing with Fake William before refitting the panel to the roundhouse's rear. I hoped Hologram-me wouldn't wake Simenon up with his simulated chatter. My m-brain protested about being made to suppress the chemical lust-soup in the air outside at the same time as enhancing my sight into its mixed infrared and ultraviolet spectral range. Lazy beast. That's the trouble with modern existence. What with brain augments, software agents and divine avatars running off your gods' strata, it's hard to know where the *you* in your consciousness begins and ends. I certainly didn't feel like listening to part of me complain to the rest of myself. Moaning was what Mozart was for. Among his other uses.

I managed to reach the electric fence without attracting attention. I glanded myself combat-variant norepinephrine to run at inhuman speed and climb the fence in two quick grabs of its mesh, a gentle fizz of sparks as my gloves indicated they'd absorbed a lethal current. I landed softly on the other side, rolling into a bush of moss-like material. Checking the nearest watchtower, I could see no sign its sentries had spotted me. A faint smudge of blue indicated a set of eyes scanning the forest for threats. Naturally, my clothes made the background appear visible through my body, customizing the invisibility effect for the majyos' witching eyes. *No threat, here.* A shadow in the shadows, that was Sweet William.

The forest appeared beautiful under my enhanced vision. No fear, now. Nothing so pedestrian with my m-brain in control of my drug regime. It felt good to shed my trader personality and walk in different boots. Hidden corners of my brain having the dust blown away and the covers pulled off the furniture. I had to force my m-brain to dial back from Extreme Combat Mode to appreciate it. The vista didn't benefit from having every insect-lizard moving across the forest threat-graded, hundreds of labels flowing across my sight with probable poison, bite and sting warnings. I had to dial back my clothes too, lest the sound of popping mosquito analogues alert the Ferals to my presence

– every inquisitive critter angling for a taste of Sweet William finding its nervous system unexpectedly fried.

There were existing trails through the forest to be followed. Made by the plantation staff, Ferals and the occasional wild dweller like my poacher friend. I kept to the paths despite the increased chance of being discovered. I needed to keep my mission as short-and-sweet as myself. Hologram-me might not keep the plantation surveillance fooled for long. This alien realm wouldn't be easy to traverse if I beat and cut a passage through it. I moved below mushrooms and toadstools shaped like tower-sized coral; cooperating and curious, dangerous and deadly. While I continued my journey, I heard horns blowing. It sounded like a Ferals' ox-horn. Far off, though. Were they assembling again? I didn't fancy their chances if they decided to attack the convoy inside the plantation. I came across a region of gentle hills. On Earth-standard worlds, the hilltops would be bare and grass-covered. Here, the forest filled every niche, hilltops crowned by vast aerial-shaped fungi reaching for the stars and the chance of feeding off energy storms from the gas giant we orbited.

I came across a small wooden shrine at the foot of one of the hills. Its interior had been painted red. Not, I hoped, with blood. Under the roof squatted a carving; two barley leaf sheaths, their blades twisted around each other like a DNA Helix. It was the classic iconography of Landsat, god of bounty, fat harvests and fertility. Odd-looking offerings had been left on platters scattered around the statue. Given Landsat stopped answering prayers here as soon as Inuno abandoned the world, it was a hell of a long time to continue worshiping a hollow god. These were the devotions of nearby Ferals. They would find it hard tracking me wearing active camouflage, but I needed to keep my eyes peeled, nevertheless. Something about the offerings aroused my curiosity. I slipped closer for a better look. They were small hand-cranked battery packs, aluminium surfaces worn and ancient. Suddenly, I realised who the packs had been left for. Not the god Landsat. This offering was for the Kodama. I grunted in amusement. So, the little forest spirits trailing the convoy had been following us on purpose, marking the wagons for the Ferals to attack. This forest's symbiotic ecosystem had extended to include both its human survivors and the spirits. I wondered whether the plantation mistress knew? Quite probably. If so, it was telling she hadn't warned the Blez forces. Nominally, the plantations served competing houses. The reality was those living beyond the capital's wall shared far more in common with each other than they did with the unedited humans they'd left behind. *Not an arrangement made to last.*

I overlaid the hand-drawn map I'd bribed into my possession over satellite imagery sent by the *Expected Ambush*, following the trail to Dumitru Bai's dwelling. It was a poor affair when I located it, a ramshackle roundhouse no larger than a single room. Half dug into the ground, its moss-turfed reciprocal frame roof splintered and poorly patched. Items lay carelessly scattered across the clearing around a circular cooking fire. There was also a well dug down to the water-table. A full bucket of water rested by its winch. I upped my sight's thermography. The fireplace filled with nothing but cold ashes, but an elevated heat signature twinkled inside the roundhouse. My poacher chum? I dropped my active camouflage before approaching. Then I walked towards the hut to find its simple door open already. Ducking, I stepped down two mud steps into the dwelling. 'Goodman Bai? I've come in search of your services.'

Sadly, Dumitru Bai seemed uninterested in my commission.

This doubtless had much to do with the fact his throat had been carefully slit before his corpse was laid down on a wooden cot. Recently put out of business, too, or the poacher's residual heat signature would register at corpse-level rather than warm.

I checked the poacher's body for anything hidden about his person, coming up blank. His clothes did seem a little damp. Not urine, though. His death had been too quick for him to empty his bladder in fear. I sniffed his arm, unable to identify the source of the damp material. Then I methodically searched the dead man's roundhouse. Not much here. A plate of salted mushroom jerky on a small square table. He had a couple of paper books in his possession, kept in a wooden chest under his cot. They were well-thumbed and old enough to have been inherited. Fiction. One was a title I didn't recognise, by a local author probably. The other was *Baron Follyman on Aldebaran* by Jiao-long. The fictional itinerant adventurer had been keeping readers on a thousand worlds amused with his antics for centuries. Jiao-long was still producing new books from the other side, not even death enough to still his pen. *Poor Bai. All alone out here. These books were your only friends, weren't they? Apart from whoever pretended to like you well enough to get close and drag a razor across your throat.* He had sought to avoid the people who only brought him pain by holing up in the wilds as a hermit. Dumitru Bai's only mistake was not keeping his distance well enough. All he had wanted was to be left to his own devices, but the wider universe had intruded on his peace. I knew how that felt. I grumbled softly and suppressed my rising rage. Almost every mistake I've ever made has been born out of anger.

I moved my gaze across his hut. No banking houses out here. Had whoever murdered Dumitru stolen his coins? His warm body told me the killers wouldn't have had much time to search.

'Fractal pattern analysis,' I announced to my m-brain.

A grid of green lines overlaid across my vision, each square analysed in turn, hundreds of discrete visual mapping algorithms running simultaneously. My stomach grumbled. Operating in so high an enhanced mode came with a high-calorie cost attached. I tried the salted mushroom jerky, singing a prayer for Dumitru's soul as I consumed his last meal. *Not bad.* He had cured the flesh perfectly. It's funny how you can feel fond of someone you never met. One square began to flash, the pattern of dried earth containing micro-disturbances out of place with the rest of the floor. I bent over to examine it, then started to dig with both my hands. A couple of inches below the soil I found the kind of miniature wooden box a mother might keep her jewellery inside. This one, however, contained a pouch of coins. I emptied them across the floor and examined Dumitru Bai's sad little haul of treasure. Not much to show for a life of labour, even the dishonest kind. I grunted. Each of the hexagonal silver coins bore the wurm-loving Derechor's golden hornet stamped on the obverse face. Six month's salary for a labourer in the capital. Nearly exactly what the spore-spice used to try and poison Lord Blez was worth on the black market. The obvious conclusion seemed a little too obvious to me. *Nothing's ever that easy for sweet William.*

I stood up, examining my memory of the roundhouse's exterior for something I could use to bury Dumitru Bai when I heard a rush of feet outside. Moving fast and with what they probably thought was stealth. I didn't drop into active camouflage. I thought they deserved to see my face when I showed them exactly what I thought of killing Dumitru.

Ajola Hara burst through the open doorway, her hand stretched out towards me. 'Out of here, now!'

There was hardly time to process the background scream of something completely inhuman outside, before it smashed into the roundhouse and the interior vanished in a cloud of timbers and mud. I barrelled through the outline of what had once been Dumitru's door, taking the plantation mistress with me. When I say *me*, it was more of a flash flight protocol generated by my m-brain, but we were too intertwined in this mode for there to be much difference. I hit the ground with Ajola and took in what had just charged through the humble dwelling. It really didn't need the superimposed threat marker hovering above it. Three spheres of black flesh speckled brown in a camouflage pattern, joined together in something only slightly smaller than a train locomotive, the eyeless front sphere mounted with four sets of intertwined mandibles. Ajola recovered from her extraction from the roundhouse with a speed which would have been remarkable for a basic human. Like me, she absorbed the impact and converted it into momentum to regain her stance. I guessed it wasn't only her eyes that had undergone amateur editing. The creature slithered off like a snake while each sphere rolled, interconnected by some kind of armoured spine. Pieces of roundhouse fleeted off its body like seawater from a ship's hull. There was nothing left of the dwelling and no sign of the dead body. The connected spheres crashed through the forest, departing the clearing without a backward glance or a by-your-leave.

'What was that bloody thing,' I croaked.

'A vioba.' Ajola took my hand, sniffed it with her nose, and then pushed me towards the well to plunge my arms into the bucket. The cloudy water felt warm.

'My hands aren't that dirty, surely?'

Ajola rolled her eyes. 'There is only one thing that makes a vioba attack like that. The scent of a rival vioba on her territory. Wash it off you.'

I remembered Dumitru's damp clothes. Someone had dosed the corpse with vioba gland essence to remove all evidence of their crime. They had damn nearly removed me as well. 'It's eaten Dumitru Bai.'

'A vioba's mouth and forward sphere are only used to drink water, bite predators and clear a path through the forest. Her rear sphere's stomachs are full of acids like a battery. She feeds by draining power from the forest.'

'Well, she's certainly cleared a path through Dumitru.'

'Poor boy. He hated us almost as much as he loved the forest.'

'It wasn't the vioba that killed Dumitru. He was dead before he was consumed: his throat slit before I arrived.'

She grunted in acknowledgment.

'You don't seem surprised.'

'This land is full of tribes, bandits, marauders, and Ferals. And the plantation people that did business with Dumitru Bai were not exactly possessed of a surfeit of community spirit.'

'The people that did business with Dumitru Bai happened to pay him a goodly weight in silver Derechor coins.'

Ajola looked over at the ruins of the roundhouse. 'I doubt the vioba will enjoy having them rattling around her forward reticulum stomach much.'

Ajola was a cool fish. She didn't give much away. I had to admire that. 'You don't care a whit about the Four Families, do you?'

'The families rise and fall. Perhaps even the institution of the four houses will fail. What do you think of that?'

'I'd rather know what led you out here to me.'

Ajola laughed and pointed behind me. I turned and spotted a familiar companion by the treeline. It was the bloodhound I had left guarding my doorstep back in Grodar.

'You followed me?'

'I followed the dog when it came to me. Truth to tell, I wondered if you were one of Lady Blez's spies. Sent to see what you could find on the plantation. She is suspicious of me and my people.'

I laughed, too. 'I thought that was my dog. But all this time he was yours.'

'Did you feed him?'

'I believe we did.'

'Then he's probably yours. Can we agree that I just saved your life?'

'I thought I saved *yours*.'

'That autonomous flash flight reflex of yours may have assisted a little. But as I will never meet the m-brain designer who created it…'

'I'm just a simple trader,' I protested.

'Do I look in any way simple enough to believe that?'

'Well, I was once a magistrate on Arius. That sad fact on my CV is what got me into all this.'

'No, it's not.'

'I am not without means, even as a simple trader.'

'I don't want your stupid coins. Among the majyos, there is only one fitting way to pay for a life saved. How much of what you are will be passed along?'

'I think that's up for grabs.'

'That's a poor choice of words.' Ajola seized my buttocks before starting to pull my expensive and very rare clothes off.

I considered ordering my robes to re-electrify, but a debt owed is a debt owed. And where would this simple trader's reputation be if he didn't honour his debts? I sighed and deactivated the gland producing my counter-agent to Ajola's pheromones. As soon as I halted production I shed my inhibitions as fast as Ajola managed to shed our clothes. She glowed in the night, her blue eyes and strange whirling tattoos both. A veritable Amazon goddess standing under the starlight, as strong and fierce as the gas giant our moon orbited. Enough to make me feel centuries younger, even without the very proficient engineering of her signalling pheromones boosting my zeal to a painful degree.

At least on the exterior, I felt painfully outclassed by her genuine raw beauty. My body was more or less my original form, albeit artificially suspended at the physical state of forty human standard years. Fit enough. Healthy enough. Too tanned for this sunless moon, perhaps. Keeping to the target weight for my height was as simple as setting an optimum BMI inside my m-brain. I held onto a few original scars, even on the limbs I'd needed to regrow. But epigenetic changes, buildup over the centuries, would do for me sooner rather than later. It seemed fitting. That's all aging is, really, the accumulation of errors in our cells. And I had made so many errors over the ages. I suspected this was about to be another of them, but I wasn't thinking with my brain anymore – either the brain I had been born with or the organic software insert that had come later.

We made love under the light of distant suns and I lost myself in Ajola, as empty as the darkness between the stars. The warm wind slipped through the towering vegetation, strong enough to ensure that I sweated in the open, her own slick skin like oil sliding between us. The majyos had really gone to town on the siren edits they needed to make up for their population imbalance. It was actually hard to keep up with her. I knew there were warreners on this moon, Sylvilagus valued for their fur and meat. It was fair to say we went at it like rabbits. In between Ajola's kisses she wrestled and pummelled me, massaging my aching flesh if I dared show signs of faltering. After an hour, I finally needed to shut down my cGMP-specific phosphodiesterase type 5 enzyme response. What some wag had labelled the Viagra algorithm in my m-brain's menu system.

Ajola screamed in wild delight between my moans. I hoped the vioba wouldn't slither back, attracted by her loud pleasures. It probably wouldn't. We were outside its behavioural range. I, however, was well within mine; a rascal and a rake to the end. Besides, the plantation mistress appeared to be biting me enough without the vioba's return.

This went far beyond what was needed for a functional widening of the gene-pool. I guessed that command of the town, mistress of her people, was a lonely position for Ajola. That, I understood more than anything. It's always empty between the stars.

= 13 =
Eclectic lie.

Ajola Hara's last words to me before our convoy left her plantation rattled around my mind. As unexpected as her whispering in my ear. *There are no sunrises on Hexator and this moon looks on many nights. You should leave here quickly while you still can.* Was it a threat, a warning, or perhaps in part a prophecy? The bloodhound abandoned the plantation and followed our wagon, which pleased Simenon. The boy had fully recovered, now. I'm not certain I had yet, but that's another story. I told Simenon how the dog helped save my life in the forest. The lad decided to name the hound Billy Bones, which was apt enough, given the vigour with which the dog chewed every bone discarded by the convoy's wagoneers and warriors. Hexator was certainly large enough to accommodate two Williams. One with old bones, another with a taste for them.

I paid one of the convoy guards to teach Simenon how to ride on the journey back to the capital. We had spare war horses enough after the outbound ambush. I informed Simenon it was fitting for an apprentice trader to know how to ride. In truth, astrogation, xenobiology, fractal calculus and probability mechanics would have been more useful subjects. But they weren't properly available to teach, and Simenon mastering the saddle gave me time to think. At least, until my robot conscience started nagging at me.

'Went out with one old dog. Coming back with two.'

I raised a weary hand. 'Don't start, Moz.'

'If you've left a bun in the oven back there, mate, you've certainly sorted out the next generation's gender imbalance issues.'

'Let's hope for the best.'

'Hope for the best? I don't think they were using the bleeding rhythm method back in the domes, doc.'

Mozart had a point. Perhaps I had wanted to leave a little of myself behind. *No fool like an old flattered fool.* The truth was, though, that I couldn't wait to return to the capital and see Alice Blez, again. To update her on our investigation's progress and see if she had need of my additional services.

'Her indoors had it right. Get yourself copied onto a quantum substrate inside the grace of Modd, embrace the Merge and ditch that rotting chemical soup you call a body.'

Mozart was testy after casting an inauspicious iChing reading with his Martian mainframe rods. I hadn't read all the yarrows, but I did note the *Eclectic Lie* as one of the final patterns cast by my robot friend. Who was lying to whom out here in the Empty? Perhaps a better question was who was left telling the truth. I wanted to consult my prayer box, but feared the runes that Modd might trace inside its sands for me. Left uneasy by how eagerly I allowed the plantation mistress to consume me. Or perhaps, how easily I had lost myself in her. Was I beginning to doubt my mission out here? Is this what happened when you lived long enough? Tottering at the end, balancing on the edge of everything. Learning doubt where there should be certainty. Mankind's schemes often prove inferior to those made by heaven.

'You first into the Merge, you old clanker. My rotting chemical soup's served me well enough.' I flipped a single silver coin into the air. All that had survived from the murdered poacher's horde. I discovered the coin half-buried in the dirt, winking at me after Ajola finished milking the cow of the last of its milk. It landed in my palm, hornet side up.

'Old man, old man,' cooed Mozart, as though he was about to start singing.

'So, he sent the Count of Hyper-Zap to give the Queen a dose of clap, to pass it on to the Bastard King of Earth,' I warbled.

My friend finished the foldship sailor's ancient ballad for me. 'When the King of Earth heard the news, he cursed the Oort Cloud farce. He up and swore by the royal whore he'd have that belter's arse.'

'There aren't any asteroid lords here,' I said, flipping the coin a second time.

'Doubt if they're any back in Sol now, for that matter. But what does the Bastard King of Earth think of this…?' Mozart snatched the coin out of the air, mid-toss.

'Heads it's the House of Derechor who did it, tails it's someone else.'

'Might as well flip a coin.' Mozart nodded towards the bloodhound trotting behind our wagon. 'Or maybe we could ask Lassie down there. Your new cabin boy seems to think Lassie can see the future.'

'We'll follow this lead when we get back to the capital.'

'Of course we bleeding will.'

'I can see the future too, old friend. It's not looking terribly encouraging.'

Mozart stared at me suspiciously. 'You didn't tell ol' blue eyes back at the ranch why we're here, did you?'

'Of course not. But Ajola suspects what we're *not* here for. And that's to buy spore-spice.'

'Well, doc, I hope you shag well enough that she's not on the blower to Lady Blez radioing back her suspicions. Or you're going to be rogered by more than some warrior princess with neon tats.'

'Don't worry,' I said. 'That's not going to happen.'

No. Ajola Hara and her people weren't even on the same moon as Lady Blez. They had checked out long ago. It was just that the rest of humanity here hadn't realized it, yet.

- 14 -
Spores and spice.
All things nice.

I sent word of what I had discovered at the plantation to Lady Blez as soon as we returned to the capital. A summons to attend her glorious presence quickly followed. I found myself escorted into an underground spore-spice processing factory deep under the Blez palace. How disappointed was I that this wasn't Alice's music room? Crushed! It was all I had been thinking about, recently. Like all effective drug lords, the Blez family kept the final stage - and warehousing - of its narcotics empire close to its well-armed muscle. I didn't need to consult the historical records to know that the best way to command a fortune at the coming auction was to ensure an "accidental" fire consumed rivals' stocks. The Four Families had mastered their lessons from the School of Hard Knocks. I arrived alone, Mozart and Simenon not invited, wearing a white gown that made me look like a surgeon – or an asylum inmate, which was probably closer to the truth. From a technological base that had basically degraded back to the medieval, the family had made a good stab at creating a sterile environment. But then, it wouldn't do to have the rich offworlders who funded their house dying from consuming "bad shit". I sniffed the slightly sweet thick air. No contaminating moulds I could detect.

Alice Blez walked her drying and curing lines, a vision to my tired eyes, ensuring the hundreds of retainers attending the copper oxidization and polymerization canisters were giving due love and attention to her spore-spice. Too much oxidization and the spore-spice would lose purity and prove little more effective than household dust. Too much moisture content and it wouldn't be able to be snorted, ingested or injected without sending its purchaser psychotic. A fine balancing act. Little wonder that the artisans working these lines were among the best-paid guild workers on Hexator. They toiled away under electric arc lights rather than gas torches or candles. Guards stood sentry on airlock doors into the sterile environment, ready to strip workers and search them on the way in and out.

I had been spared the undignified smuggling and theft checks, as a so-called honoured guest of the house. As, presumably, had Link, the hulking robot bodyguard clanking loyally a few feet behind her ladyship. I am sure it suited Alice's purposes to have the shadow of the ever-so-slightly deranged machine regularly passing over her loyal workforce. Reminding them that should they attempted to steal any of her precious spore-spice, all it would take was a single order from Alice for Link to rip a suspect's skull off their shoulder.

'Doctor Roxley.'

I bowed for the beautifully imperious noblewoman. 'Lady Blez.'

'What do the wages of sin look like these days?'

Given half a chance, I would be happy to give her another close demonstration. But I held my tongue. I produced the single silver coin I had managed to recover from the ruins of the poacher's dwelling, passing it to Alice Blez.

She held the coin up to the bright illuminating light, turning it over and examining it. 'And there were more of these?'

'Enough money to pay for the poison intended to kill your husband.'

'Well, the vioba you described might not choke on the silver. But the Derechors certainly will.'

'It's possible another family paid with coins from the Derechor mint to falsely implicate them,' I warned.

'Always a possibility. And the main reason I haven't sent warriors to ambush the twins and teach them a long overdue lesson in manners.'

I was about to ask what Alice *did* have in mind when I heard a hiss of airlock doors and saw Jenelle Cairo arriving at the factory.

Lady Blez didn't seem happy to see the female Watch officer. 'I asked for Commander General Laur to attend me.'

The captain bowed stiffly before Lady Blez. She didn't look over-pleased to be at the Blez compound, either. Perhaps she was one of those old-fashioned cops who preferred arresting gangsters rather than taking orders from them? 'He is otherwise engaged, my lady. I speak for the Watch.'

'Not too busy to insult my standing among the Four by sending subordinates in his place. Perhaps I should have had my son issue the request?'

Captain Cairo raised her hands, indicating matters of politics were above her pay-grade. I doubted Lady Blez needed the reminder.

'It doesn't matter,' sighed Lady Blez. 'My husband's murder is still a crime even if it was perpetrated by one of the Four.'

'The law of the Four applies to the Four,' confirmed Jenelle.

Lady Blez indicated me standing by her side and I cleared my throat before explaining what I had discovered inside the plantation. I omitted the spicier parts of my story as well as what Alice probably suspected already, which was the distant plantation's lingering loyalty to her house in name only. Commander General Laur really wouldn't be happy about hearing my story second-hand, but then, if he was going to be a home-body and send subordinates in his place, what could he expect?

'An interesting development,' said Captain Cairo. 'How would you suggest the Watch proceeds?'

'Smack them and smack them and smack them,' muttered the deranged Link behind his mistress.

'The twins need to be questioned under official caution,' demanded Alice.

'I know a magistrate who detests the Derechors enough to sign off on that,' said Jenelle. 'I just hope that the guards on the Derechor citadel's gates honour my warrant without incident.'

'The twins are not inside the capital, presently,' said Lady Blez.

'You were checking on them out of curiosity, of course.'

'Quite reasonable. TWIST THEIR HEADS OFF,' growled Link.

Alice ignored her ancient ruster, 'Zane and Sarlee Derechor have been visiting Hebateen for the last three days. They are not due to return for another five days.'

'I am sure your intelligence in this matter is a match for the Watch's.'

'Of that, captain, I have no doubt. Take Doctor Roxley and his people with you when you visit Hebateen. I want the doctor to be party to the official questioning.'

I queried my m-brain for a search on Hebateen. I didn't hold many details, beyond map coordinates. One of the many abandoned cities, this one two-hundred miles north of the capital. Not a plantation. What business, I wondered, did the twins have out there?

Jenelle rested her palms on her hips. 'I doubt the Commander

General will be happy with that, my lady. It will require deputising the good doctor as a sheriff.'

'I don't require Laur's damn approval, only his compliance. A Lord of the Four is dead. I have the right to appoint a Proxy Sheriff for an interrogation made under caution. I trust William Roxley's presence over any local's involvement.'

I nodded to Alice, the briefest of looks passing between us, unnoticed by the others in the chamber. *Longing? Hope?* Hard to say. Such a lady's trust is not easily earned, but somehow, I had managed it. I resolved not to let Alice down.

Jenelle Cairo left for the nearest airlock, dismissed by the Lady Blez, along with her new partner. Which of us, I wondered, was more reluctant about my attachment to the official investigation?

Jenelle gave the lock's guard a filthy look as he pondered strip-searching her. Wisely, in my opinion, he decided to classify her as an honoured house guest, too. 'So, doctor, you're what a proxy without skin in the game looks like?'

'Sadly, I think I have far too much skin in this game, captain.'

Hide I could ill afford to lose at my age.

- 15 -
Rolling dice.

I hadn't realized the Watch owned the last aerial vehicle on Hexator. In retrospect, I should have. The threat of bombing was all the capital had left to keep its collapsing and rebellious outer provinces in line. The *Skylander* possessed a wing-shaped buoyancy hull shaped like three massive cigars melded together, six gas-powered bow thrusters mounted along each flank with an air-cushioned landing system for vectored vertical takeoff. I doubt the Hexatorians possessed a working alpha-decay synthetic helium plant on their moon. Laur was obviously bribing foldship sailors to skim helium on the side using visiting vessels' spare ramscoops. Nice work if you can get it. It took fifty trained crew from the Watch to operate their vessel, but then, what price was air supremacy worth? A long white whale of the air, the *Skylander* could harvest electrical energy from storms using her eight hundred feet-long conductive envelope. A relic of their lost past, I enjoyed riding her as much as Simenon was made uneasy by our voyage.

Simenon moaned, tilting his head out of an opened porthole on the shaking airship. Billy Bones lay by his feet, trying to look sympathetic. In reality, I suspected the hound was more concerned with his next meal's late arrival. The dog should have foreseen that.

'I'll print you a copy of Jules Verne's *Robur the Conqueror* when I get back to my ship,' I told the lad, trying to cheer him up. 'If you can't ride one of these vessels crawling at eighty knots, you certainly won't enjoy atmosphere braking on board the *Pleiad's Daughter.*'

'Yeah, zero gravity is a real bugger, too,' said Mozart, smug over the advantages of his iron constitution. 'At least, that's what the lads say on the street.'

'This is awful, Master Roxley,' said the boy. 'Why do I feel so bad?'

'I fear the Skylander's stabilising systems have been non-functional for centuries and your world's winds blow most fiercely at this altitude. Keep your eyes gazing, without being fixed, on the horizon. That'll help you feel better.'

It was my legs bothering me, rather than air sickness. I set off for a stroll around the chamber, muscles stiff from sitting down, soft quilted seats notwithstanding.

'You ever stump up for an m-brain for Tiny Tim, make sure it comes with auto-stabilization algorithms for his inner ear. He keeps on sicking up like that, he's going to set *me* off.'

'Hah, I would pay to see it.'

We had been traveling for three hours and were close to arriving at our destination. I was grateful the airship's engines, at least, remained in full working order. This journey would take five days by horse and I'm sure the forests below were just as full of Ferals, ravenous viobas and other local delights we would much rather bypass. That was the Skylander's point. She had started out as a passenger ferry in her original incarnation, luggage areas swapped for bomb bays and luxury cabins traded for troop transport and warhorse stables.

I glanced back at Simenon. He seemed small in the central space of what had been the Skylander's salon. Mozart went back to keep him company. My old ruster might protest to the contrary, but I think he had gotten used to having the young fellow knocking around.

Jenelle Cairo came slinking down the staircase into our salon.

She still wore her black leather uniform, a long cloak the only concession to her de facto position as the vessel's commander. I think a peaked cap would have set off the look nicely, but it had been six hundred years since I dared suggest fashion advice to a woman. The cape did look rather fetching on her, though.

'We'll be setting down soon, doctor.'

I nodded in gratitude. 'Sink me, but you burned a lot of expensive gas to reach this town. Are you sure Commander General Laur will approve?'

'The *Skylander* was due to fly the flag at Hebateen later this month, anyway. I just nudged her schedule forward.'

'Problems with rebels this far out? The People's Skull robbing the tax-man of his fair share?'

'Hebateen is a rough place,' said the captain. 'Always was, always will be.'

'So, what are the Derechor twins doing in this rough place with the auction so close?'

'The Derechors' stake in the spore-spice auctions is relatively limited,' said Jenelle Cairo. 'Their house owns almost everything else of value, however. The farmlands and timber fields to the south and east. The canals that ship goods into the capital. And the mines under Mount Hebateen. Steel, iron, copper; when you see metal on Hexator the chances are that it was dug out from the deeps under Hebateen.'

So, this place is House Derechor's gold-mine, literally and figuratively. Well, when the winds of change blow, some people build walls and others build windmills.

When the mountain finally appeared in the distance it was hard to miss. A towering peak curved around on itself like a hunting horn. Circles of hot white steam rose from hot springs bubbling around its base, putting me in mind of a giant with its feet in chains. I recognized the hoop of artificial structures built into the mountainside. Landing pads and magnetic rail launchers, all in a state of obvious disrepair. 'This used to be a space-port once!'

'Hebateen's always been a mining town,' explained Jenelle. 'During the golden age, our prospectors discovered vast mineral riches on the Moon of Metis. A trained workforce of miners was already working under this mountain, so a port was built to ferry miners to the radiation domes on Metis. After that, Hebateen expanded to become a boomtown; a pleasure and barracks city entertaining miners when they returned on leave.'

Metis I had passed in my foldship on the way to Hexator. The fourth of seven moons orbiting the gas giant. Metis born a glowing orange hell-hole moon with a thick poisonous atmosphere of ammonia, liquid hydrogen, sulphur and nitrogen. It would have been the first foothold inside this system to be abandoned when civilization and its attendant technology started to degrade on Mother Hexator. So, the miners had retreated to their original home and kept toiling away here. Humanity always needed knives to stick in each other's back. I doubted the miners would halt production anytime soon, however many shadows the current Dark Ages cast.

There wasn't much pleasure to be had any more in the empty city spread out below the mountains. Its ruins ran for miles, dark and jagged. Broken glass and crumbling concrete overgrown by forest. No attempt to live on at a humbler scale like the capital, Frente. A litter of abandoned casinos, pleasure domes, brothels, hotels and sim parlours reclaimed by the untamed ecosystem. Lights still twinkled across the mountainside though; the original mining works struggling on. I saw starlight reflected off a long canal below, not enough resolution to pick out barges drifting towards the capital. They had stopped the canal silting up at least. I felt a painful tinge of melancholy. Humanity dwelled in the ruins of its past glories here on Hexator. But who was I to judge? I dwelled in the ruins of my body, too. We had both seen better days. We had both lived too long and reached our end times.

I hummed to myself. 'In the pleasure gardens my cloned love did I meet; she passed through the sim-domes with little snow-white feet.'

Jenelle was born half a millennium too late to pick up the rest of the lyrics. I had to settle for imagining her singing back to me, *She bid me take love easy, as leaves grow on a Jovian tree; I, being young and foolish, with her would not agree.*

'You're a strange fish, William Roxley. Where were you born?'

'Arius.'

Jenelle snorted. 'Heaven itself.'

'Home of a great many of the gods and pleasant enough in its way. Hardly heaven, though.' Heaven held its promises for me later.

'So why the hell did you leave Arius to come here?'

'All careers end in failure, before a person's life finally dwindles and follows suit. My many careers seemed long over. Playing the free trader is a worthy whim to whittle away my final few years.'

She shook her head sadly. 'A game. A rich moneyass's diversion to stem the boredom of living too long.'

'Rich? Only rich enough to sell my cleverness and buy bewilderment, I fear. I take it that this is not a problem you have on Hexator.'

'No. Many problems on Hexator, but not that one. Just

remember, this is my investigation. You and your menagerie are visiting Hebateen solely on sufferance. Another of Lady Blez's charitable whims…'

I felt I had disappointed Jenelle, which I hadn't meant to. 'You've heard about the Merge back in the Humanitum?'

Jenelle nodded. 'Is it true … immortality's your reward?'

'True enough in its way. But I'm not planning to join the gods. When this life finishes, it's finally over for me.'

'You're playing for keeps here, then?'

'Quite.'

'Well, welcome to the rest of the human race, doctor. The Derechors are going to be mighty touchy about us serving them with an interview under caution. I'll need to ease the way for that. Smooth things over.'

'I'm sure honeyed words will be better heard from your lips than mine.'

'Are you saying you find me attractive, doctor?'

'I've lived long enough to know that neither of the two viable options for answering your question would prove the correct one.'

She made a zipping gesture across her lips. 'Then keep on living a little longer.'

– 16 –
Deep trouble.

We stood on the slopes of the mountain, tiny ants among the ancient mills, hoisting houses, processing sheds, crushers and conveyor belts which comprised the mine. Its newest structures were stables for the horses and oxen, beasts needed to drive the spindles and power the works, as well as ponies to haul mining wagons; the old fusion plant as useless as the space-port girdling the mountain.

I currently wondered if my ears were as non-operational as the ancient shuttles' magnetic rail launchers. 'The twins want us to conduct an interview under caution *inside* their mine?' I asked Captain Cairo, not certain I'd heard her correctly the first time. 'They've already kept us waiting a day as it is.'

We hadn't been left anything to do inside our allocated quarters except kick our heels. Of course, that was entirely the point. And now *this*?

Jenelle shrugged. 'That's what the Mine Master told me. Our Lords Derechor have been inside the mine for three days, apparently. It's an obvious ruse on their part to discomfort us. Returning to the surface would just acknowledge our authority for an interview.'

I sighed. *Always power games with the warlords.*

'Bleeding hole-in-the-wall gang all over again,' said Mozart.

'A guide is presently being found to take us down into the tunnels,' said Jenelle. Not that I need one, but it's how visitors are kept on a leash.'

'You don't need a guide?' I was surprised.

'I was born at Hebateen, doctor. I slaved in these mines from the age of five until leaving for Frente at sixteen.'

'Hard work,' I said.

'Hard enough to make a living breaking heads and dragging corpses from canals for the Watch taste like duck soup off a warm spoon.'

Yes, I thought I had detected some reluctance on the airship on the good captain's part about returning here. *That explains it.* I decided I would use my time waiting to teach Simenon to use the prayer mat. It would make a fine gift for Simenon after leaving Hexator. A bridge to the new life that awaited him. I unrolled the mat, asked Simenon to kneel on it and started to teach him the mantras used to reach out to Modd. He made for an uneasy student, although he remembered the words with an accuracy that put me to shame, m-brain augments and all.

'Ask according to the will of Modd,' I suggested. 'Do not conform to the pattern of your world but be transformed by the renewing of your mind.'

'The gods never answer me, Master Roxley. I exist beneath their notice.'

'A little faith, lad, a little faith.'

Simenon knelt as still as he could on the mat, closing his eyes and repeating the mantras I gave him. Varnus's old mat started to glow at one point, barely perceptible to the normal eye, but my m-brain tracked the activating circuit threads for me, labelling each one as it powered up.

Simenon faltered self-consciously as Jenelle Cairo started laughing. All the threads immediately lost coherence.

I glared at the captain. 'If our universe has no meaning, we would never have discovered it has no meaning.'

'I am sorry, doctor. Believe me, if the gods take an interest in anything that happens at Hebateen, it really will be a miracle.'

'Don't give up so easily, Simenon,' I advised. 'You're closer than you realise.'

We were about to head into the buildings to find our guide when a Watch officer came jogging from the direction of the airship docking tower, seeking out Captain Cairo. He pulled her aside for a quick urgent conversation.

'Problems, captain?' I asked.

'The Citadel is on the radio. Informants are talking about rebel action timed to coincide with the spore-spice auctions. The *Skylander* might be needed back at the capital sooner than expected. I need to head back to the ship to talk with the commander general.'

'Heaven's teeth, the Four Families wouldn't order Frente to be bombed, surely, good captain?'

'Only districts which defect to the rebels and start piling up barricades.'

I winced. A low-level insurgency breaking out on Hexator wasn't something Sweet William had planned to coincide with his visit. *Ah, yes, matters can always get worse.*

'Make a start with the Lords Derechor,' sighed Jenelle. 'They're allowed to keep us kicking our heels, not the other way around. Don't go in hard and don't break anything you can't fix until I join you for their questioning.'

'Don't go in hard?' griped Moz, as Jenelle strode away in the direction of the airship docking tower. 'I was looking forward to playing bad robot.'

'A role is something you're meant to *play*, not *be*,' I told my friend. I glanced over at Simenon. He rolled up the prayer mat and made to pass it back, but I shook my head. 'Keep it, lad. How much trouble do the auctions bring to the streets?'

'The Watch has been hard on it, recently,' said Simenon,

stuffing the prayer mat inside his backpack. 'Master Jomont, the baker I was apprenticed to, died in auction fighting when I was ten. That was the last serious outbreak of violence.'

As serious for Simenon as the dead baker, I guessed. Doubtless the start of the boy's life running on the streets as a masterless wastrel. 'Was it unusual for a Wrongman to be given the chance of an apprenticeship, lad?'

'Lady Blez pays fees every year to the craftsmen for hundreds of orphans to be apprenticed, sir. Not all, there're too many of us. Every town and village abandoned brings more homeless trekking into Frente. I was one of the lucky ones.'

Ah, indeed, lucky enough for his employer to end up face down in a warm puddle with a slit throat.

'See if you can scare up our missing mine guide, young journeyman. And remind me to test your baking skills one day. I'm partial to poppy seed rolls of a morning.'

Simenon obviously wanted to ask what a poppy was, but he departed in search of our guide all the same.

I prodded Moz. 'And what does Big Data's analysis suggest about the chances of a revolt; all those arrest files you purloined back in the Watch should give you some indication of the temperature here?'

'Big Data says if you've got a taste for aggro, then Hexator's the right moon to get properly cabbaged on. Here's the pertinent bar on the line graph...' Mozart raised his middle metal finger at me.

'Charming.'

'Well, if the capital kicks off, it all kicks off.'

'I would rather *it* didn't.' *Bloodshed follows bloodshed, that's the way of it out here in the Empty.*

Simenon returned with our guide, a stout-looking fellow

introduced to us as Arto Jagg. A stocky miner with a once-muscled face running to hanging flesh, reaching late middle-age and finding he couldn't toil as hard as he once had. The man sported a thick moustache with long points curved steeply upward, as though pulled towards the surface he'd abandoned. The ground called him, still, but not as powerfully as the mines.

We introduced ourselves to Arto before heading for the mine's main entrance.

'Why have the Lords Derechor been underground for so many days?' I questioned our guide. 'Do the twins enjoy mining?'

Arto shrugged. 'Hah, I doubt it. They've come for the nest of skeg moles we broke into.'

'By skeg moles, do you mean small brown mammals with reduced hind-limbs and powerful paws well-evolved for digging?'

Arto stroked his mustache thoughtfully. 'If by small, you speak of one of the six-hundred-pound male moldwarp rather than the nine-hundred-pound females, then yes. And I presume, being a foreign moneyass who only speaks our language as a machine trick, you are slurring *paws* for *claws*?'

'And these skeg moles have some value to the Lords Derechor?'

'Oh yes, they're very good at eating all of Hebateen's workers, until there's nary a bugger willing to climb down inside the mines. Which is why their lordships rode a barge with two companies of their best warriors to cull the nest.'

'You know,' Mozart said, 'I really don't think this pair of bleeding nobs want to be interviewed.'

It appeared Billy Bones had no wish to attend the interrogation, either. Our bloodhound paced around in circles, whining and glancing in the direction of the mine's entrance, before twisting around on the rocky slope as if in pain.

'Well, there's an augury from the gods,' said Moz. 'Hound what sees the future develops a bad case of the claustrophobia wobbles!'

Simenon stared anxiously at me. 'Master Roxley?'

'Let the dog stay up here. You too, if you don't find enclosed spaces to your taste.'

Simenon shook his head, but I noted how tightly he now gripped Varnus's prayer mat. Most Hexatorians' first experience of venturing below the surface would be huddling in shelters riding out the worst energy storms, terrified and anxious. I ventured claustrophobia was a common phobia on the moon.

'We won't need to climb too far down,' said Arto. 'I heard their Lordships discovered the main nest in the deeps last night, poured barrels of tar into the passages and burnt the monsters out. Any skeg moles that escaped are digging for the high tunnels. We'll cull them close to the surface.'

Simenon appeared nauseous. 'So, they'll be heading straight for us?'

'It's why we use fire. Skeg moles mistake fire for magma and their nature's to claw towards the surface and safety. Two of the Derechor's toughest brute squads are here to deal with the blighters,' said Arto. 'It's when the house fighters aren't inside the mines you have to peer a little harder into the deep of the dark. Don't worry, my son Rauf's working with the hunting party.' Arto spoke with pride. 'All our best miners are down there assisting their lordships.'

I hummed a ballad to help calm Simenon's nerves. 'They steal his duds and cutters as well. And they hoy them down the belt of hell. Down you go, and fare you well, you blackleg asteroid miner!'

'Aye, there's an ancient tune,' said Arto. 'Did Red teach it to you?'

'Red?'

'Cap'n Cairo,' said Arto, throwing a thumb back in the direction of the airship docking tower.

I smiled. I suspect if I called the good captain *Red*, her nickname would match the colour of the bruise gracing my ugly mug. 'No, Master Jagg, the good captain didn't teach me the tune. It's one of *The Songs of Old Sol*. The ancient ballads are as fine a way as any for a simple trader to while away a long passage through the void. Did you know the captain when she worked here?'

'That I did. Cairos are an old mining clan. Or at least, they were, until a tunnel collapse carried the best of them down to the happy halls of Magh Meall.'

'But not Jenelle Cairo?'

'Never our Red; kissed by mischief, that one, just like her ruby locks. A couple of clans blamed her for the collapse that killed her folks, claimed it was her unlucky hair angering the cave spirits. A few fools tried to bury her alive to appease Uku Mell and Habur Mell.'

'Wouldn't want to be the cheeky monkey carrying a spade on that job,' said Mozart.

'Aye, no oxidation clogging your noggin, old ruster. Quick of blade, quick of mind, quick of temper, was the Jenelle Cairo of my day.'

'Little's changed,' I noted.

'Blood feuds, they're never a gift for ore quotas,' said Jagg, 'digging graves instead of tunnels. The last Mine Master called in a favour with the capital, got Red a cadet's commission with the Watch. Quickest way to stop the feuding. She's carved herself a fine name, now. No surprise, there. Our people are granite, not the capital's soft clay.'

'Still digging graves,' said Moz.

'Aye, but they're the graves you get given medals for, not a broken spine strapped to the wheel for murder. Red lost her parents, brothers, sisters, uncles, and cousins working these shafts for the Derechors. Even without the feud, leaving Hebateen rescued her soul. Staying at the mine would have crushed her.'

We entered the mine, passing through vent and service shafts spreading out under the mountain. We stopped at a metal equipment tank full of gear. Arto Jagg passed us each a steel helmet that resembled a medieval infantry kettle hat, as well as a copper carbide lamp with a large reflector. Only Mozart didn't receive our sole concessions to safety, but then he needed neither. Arto also halted us by a safe-like vault door. He opened it with a set of large keys, entering on his own. When he returned, he had a belt weighted with packages that made me wince. Oblong parcels of nitroglycerin wrapped in greased brown waterproof paper.

'Are those truly necessary, Master Jagg?'

'Aye,' said our guide. 'Blasting charges are our best way out should we get trapped behind a rockfall. A chuff fellow can also use charges to bring the roof down on a skeg mole company.'

I'm fairly certain I wasn't nearly as "chuff" as Arto, then, given how fast nitroglycerin degrades towards instability. Heading inside an ancient mine was dangerous enough a venture without risking explosions if our guide slipped.

'Bleeding amateur hour,' Moz muttered at me.

I said nothing but found it hard to argue.

This close to the surface the mine's tunnels appeared wide and well-built, constructed during the moon's lost age of colonization by machines long-since rusted away or re-purposed as pick-axes and shovel blades. Smooth surfaces and angular corners which spoke of laser-cut accuracy. As we continued deeper, our passageways narrowed and became more ramshackle. Wooden supports, rough rock surfaces and the occasional brick arch to hold up difficult sections of strata. Counterweight-hoisted lift shafts were replaced by corkscrewing ramp shafts no wider than ore-filled carts dragged out by pit ponies.

It grew warmer the deeper we descended until I was left sweating, droplets rolling itching down my nose. I considered allowing my clothes to chill me but decided to show solidarity in discomfit with Arto Jagg and Simenon. We had been descending for the best part of half an hour when I realized overheating was to be the least of our discomforts.

'Vibrations!' warned Moz. 'Things are about to get proper hectic.'

Arto Jagg dropped to one knee on the rock floor, laying a palm across the surface as though taking a pulse. 'Big lad is right. It's a male younger approaching fast; shouldn't be overlarge. No time to set charges to slay it. Make ready!'

I never wanted to meet Master Jagg's definition of *big*. Passage walls crumbled behind us as a shower of rocks blew in, a writhing mass of chitin-armoured skeg mole flailing across the tunnel's open space. Its tank-sized head possessed a pyramid-shaped rock punch of a beak splitting into four parts, roaring in our direction with the ferocity of a DNA-resurrected Spinosaurus. A fine flash of its razored teeth which actually seemed to be twisting on alien rotary muscles. A distended abdomen composed of dozens of linked segments thrashed behind the monster, so many clawed legs to cut away rock and drive through the subterranean realm that it was difficult to make an accurate estimate. Though, to be fair, perhaps the stench of acid sweating through its chitin armour was putting me off my count. Such excretions, it seemed, are what it generated inside its abdomen to make a nutrient soup of the moon's abundant but solid minerals. Luckily for the skeg mole – far less so for us – humanity required comparatively little effort to digest.

'Turn your lamps up to full,' yelled Arto. The reflector on his carbide lamp suddenly blindingly strong as he flooded the gas's flow rate.

Simenon and I struggled to follow suit, three miniature lighthouse beams quickly focusing in on the skeg mole. Our efforts seemed a shockingly thin soup to keep this beast sated. It shook the passage with its bulk, hissing and salivating at the thought of a quickly snatched mankind meal. Perhaps it dimly recalled being burnt out of its nest by such as we, too. Not a thought to make you kindly disposed to Sweet William, when he might lie sweeter inside the gullet.

'Back downside with you!' yelled Arto, 'too near the surface, here, too much light for you!' He began chanting to his mine spirits, hollow gods to put your trust in when faced with such as this.

A ring of albino eyes surrounding the monster's head quivered, lizard-like irises narrowing against our blinding luminous spears. Its huge abdomen shook fit to collapse the tunnel as its slide towards us faltered and slowed.

Simenon began to lose his nerve, stumbling a few steps back, almost dropping his lamp, but Arto bellowed, 'No! Hold. It will charge us should the light appear to diminish! Flee and you're finished!'

'Sod this for a game of soldiers,' snarled Mozart. He upped the light output on his visor, a fourth lighthouse made mobile as he attacked first. The skeg mole bellowed again. A natural reaction to being kamikaze-charged by something it regarded as food inside its ecosystem. In retrospect, a tactical error, as Moz reached its quivering head and punched straight down inside its gullet with his right arm.

Master Jagg spluttered in shock at being treated to this outlandish circus trick, but then, he didn't recognise the ensuing muffled whirring noise as I did. Mozart had converted his right fist into a rotating blade, and the skeg mole discovered that wearing armour on your exterior wasn't quite as successful a defence when you had a diamond-sharp paddle blade agitator spinning at 600 RPM through the length of your vital organs.

'Have some!' Moz yelled as he continued smashing his left fist into the monster's head, the choking beast clawing uselessly at the tunnel with multiple legs as it tried to spit out Mozart's unappetizing limb disembowelling a tonne of guts from the inside out.

Master Skeg Mole shuddered into deathly stillness as Mozart stopped trying to rip the pyramid-shaped cutting beak off its bulbous head. Moz carefully withdrew his right arm, fingers and fist reconfigured back to normal operating mode once more, examining the acid-damp gore slicking his arm's surface with some disgust.

'Now I *have* seen everything,' whistled our guide. 'Don't look much, but that's a shovel with a sharp blade right there. You ever wish to sell your ruster, Master Roxley, I reckon we'll make fine use of such a chuff brute inside our mines.'

'Perhaps before I leave Hexator,' I teased my mechanical friend. 'He'll doubtless prove a trifle rough for polite company on board the foldship waiting above.'

Of course, the truth was that the fine foldship *You Can't*

Prove It Was Us wouldn't let Moz within a long light-year of her chambers and corridors. Not even confined on board my *Exy*, limpet-docked to the foldship's hull. For that matter, not even tied at the end of a cable in vacuum's icy void and keel-hauled on the float behind the foldship.

'Mugging me right off,' muttered the robot. 'A few others around here who'd benefit from having their tongues pulled out.'

Simenon gazed on Mozart with newfound respect. Of course, by taking a spear through the chest the lad had missed the best of the robot's performance against the Ferals. No, mugging off Mozart was never a safe course of action. For humans, foldships or skeg moles.

We recommenced our subterranean odyssey until we reached as strange a sight as I'd ever seen or expected to find underground. A series of linked chapels and a fine-sized feasting chamber carved straight out of the rock. A monumental devotion of labour and time to create such a curiosity down here so far from Hexator's surface. We had reached a region of salt rock where every wall was filled with carvings, scenes of Hebateen's miners at work, as well as far more ancient sculptures which had to be the community's lost life on their mining moon. Then I realised. Habur Mell, their hollow underground spirit, was a corruption of *Habbmil*, the actual God of Voidsmen, the Vacuum and the Spacer's True Sun.

'This is Habur Mell's Chapel,' explained Arto. Carbide lamps were set in the wall and our guide walked between them, sparking the chapel rooms and feasting chamber into illumination. 'Darkness above and darkness below,' Arto Jagg chanted each time he lit a lamp. 'The Mine Master told me this is where the Lords Derechor will meet you.' Our guide indicated an atrium chamber in front of the chapel, a dozen tunnels branching out towards the mine's furthest reaches. 'These passages lead to the deep mines. Sentries will be posted close, in whichever tunnels the warriors used to find the nest. Stay here. I'll check each spoke out and return with their Lordships.'

'It seems oddly damp in here,' I pointed out.

Arto indicated a tunnel on the right. 'That leads to a cavern with a deep underground lake. Don't go dipping in its waters while I'm away.'

Perish the thought. I even took sonic showers on my ship rather than the wet kind.

'Do the skeg moles use it as a watering hole, Master Jagg?' asked Simenon.

'No, they get eaten by what's in the lake if they try.'

Simenon didn't seem happy with the idea of being abandoned. 'What if skeg moles dig through here?'

Arto pointed to the lamps. 'They don't like large open spaces or light, young journeyman. You should be fine.' He passed Simenon his belt of charges. 'Here we go, you keep these in case you need to blast your way out of a rockfall.'

Simenon hung them across a salt rock altar, almost an offering to the local spirits. 'What if you need them to break free?'

'I'll use the sentries'.'

It was a kind gesture. Simenon still wasn't happy with the *should* he'd heard in our guide's reassurances, but the lad watched Arto leave us all the same. 'What if Master Jagg dies out there? How will we ever find our way back to the surface?'

'What, you didn't memorize all the tunnels and shafts on the way down?' Moz teased the boy. 'How clever was that?'

'Let's plan for the worst but pray for the best,' I suggested.

I didn't tell Simenon that I'd also committed every twist

and turn to memory, using my m-brain's engineering models for tunnel construction to fill in adjacent passages we hadn't traversed. I guessed he wouldn't feel any better made aware of the many inadequacies of unaugmented humanity.

Mozart gazed around at the elaborate salt rock carvings. 'What about this, then … Habbmil?'

I nodded. 'I was just thinking the same thing. What do you bet the miners assemble here once a year for an annual feast in memory of their fallen?'

Moz snorted. 'Might as well be praying to some made-up rock spirit. Old Habbmil's got cold void for arteries. You'd have more luck squeezing blood out of a stone than gaining favours from that bugger.'

***

A couple of weary-looking warriors returned with Arto Jagg later. We met them in the atrium chamber. The fighters wore leather overalls like a pair of blacksmiths, but it wasn't an anvil's weight they bore between them. One struggled with a large copper tank strapped against his spine and the other wielded a spear-like arrangement with a bulbous metal head, said device connected by a hose dangling from his comrade's tank. *A flame-squirt.* Just the weapon to give agitated skeg moles pause for thought. Their bandoleer belts crossed with blasting charges almost seemed superfluous.

'Our Lord Zane Derechor follows,' said the warrior swaying under the fuel's weight.

'Hard culling by the sounds of it this time,' said Arto. 'The nest holds two matriarchs. Double the amount of sleeping chambers. Skeg moles were looking for a fight before we showed up. Too many of the buggers to make for a stable pecking order.'

'What of his lordship's brother?' I asked.

I didn't comment on the irony of the two Derechors forced to fight twin skeg mole matriarchs. Fate often exhibits the blackest sense of humour.

'Up here within an hour,' said Arto. 'Old Sarlee is supervising the burn of another nursery chamber his scouts came across.'

Well, better we start the interview with at least one of the twins in attendance.

I was still running through the lengthy list of pertinent questions I had conjured for the Lords Derechor when I felt a dull thud, our rough rock floor shaking. *What was that?* I caught the patter of gun-fire in the distance, shouts and screams of panicked miners, warriors cursing. Damn these tunnels and shafts, they made echoes of everything; playing games with sounds that made me little wiser if trouble was visiting the space next door or excavations a league away.

'Someone sealing a tunnel?' pondered Arto.

'Thought we'd got the worst of 'em by now,' said the warrior carrying the flame-squirt's nozzle spear. The two house fighters began setting their weapon up, ready to spray burning hell over any skeg mole that intruded.

More thuds and rattles, seemingly drifting in from everywhere at once.

'Let's see what I can see!' growled Moz, sprinting towards the passage Arto and the warriors had emerged from. 'Stay here!'

'That ruster's crazy,' growled one of the warriors.

'It's an unlucky skeg mole that runs into him,' said Arto.

He didn't know the half of it, yet.

Simenon gazed fretfully at Master Jagg. 'Should we lay charges here, like you spoke of – just in case?'

Arto shook his head. 'Not inside the chapel. Hundreds of our people are still downside in the deeps. Charges are for shutting the front door on skeggies, not the back door on your own.'

Another series of booming explosions, louder this time, the atrium chamber's ceiling showering us with gray rock dust.

Arto looked puzzled. 'They're too strong. Too near. I think—'

His thoughts were denied us by another detonation, a real cave-shaker, this time. I dropped to my knees, about to stand up when an obelisk the size of a tower slid dislodged from the ceiling. I was still calculating which direction to leap to safety when it battered across one of the warriors, the fighter with the fuel tank. It was hard to say whether it was the detonation of the flame-squirt's propellant which set off his blasting charges or the other way around. My suit stiffened, its fabric reacting instantaneously under emergency protocol. I managed to absorb most of the expanding fireball heading for Simenon and Arto. Hurled through the air by the blast-wave, I dimly registered a secondary detonation, the second warrior's charges roaring with dynamite anger. All three of us blown out of the collapsing atrium. Flung inside the chapel. I struck the chapel's floor hard, rolling six times before shedding enough momentum to stop.

Moaning, I pulled myself to my feet. I heard a whine from my suit as the energy it had absorbed but hadn't been able to convert into my crash-field bled out. My arms started steaming inside the febrile air. Arto Jagg's flight had been halted by a large rock-salt sculpture of an asteroid miner heroically posed on a sphere. Our guide's chest fluttered with shallow pulls of his lungs, so he was at least alive. *Thank the gods.* Simenon lifted himself off the floor, face bruised, clothes bloody and blackened, but still among the living. There was something admirably elastic about the gangly youth; he almost demanded to be bounced off hard surfaces.

'You're smoking,' coughed Simenon, rubbing soot out of his eyes.

'By Modd, you're right, I am.'

I turned to gaze at our still crumpling atrium. *Mozart!* The passage he'd sprinted into lay completely blocked. *Enough to bury Moz?*

Let's plan for the worst but pray for the best, my own words mocked me. If my friend was finished, we were about to join him. The shaking hadn't stopped. It grew more violent. Pieces of chapel ceiling rained down around us. Mozart's design tolerances meant he could survive a hell of a lot more than me. Even a stealth suit wasn't going to save Sweet William or his friends from a thousand tonnes of sharp rubble and an oxygen diet for the foreseeable future.

Deep-rock formation gas pocket fractures igniting under blast pressure, warned my m-brain. *Evacuate.*

Yes, I had noticed, I ordered the augmented portion of my sentience to stop distracting me.

Simenon wobbled uncertainly towards the altar where Arto's belt of blasting charges hung. I dashed over to him in time to stop him seizing the belt. 'We can't blast ourselves free of this, Simenon.'

He rubbed his head with both hands, blinking away the swelling dust cloud. 'No, we're going to be buried alive!'

'Not today.' I tried to stay calm for his sake, glanding an anxiolytics package. I lifted the rolled-up prayer mat out of the lad's backpack even as shards of rock rained down around us.

'How can you pray now, Master Roxley?'

'Carry the good Arto Jagg over here. We already have our gift from the gods.' Varnus's blessed vision; I had thought it a fancy at the time. 'Ah, sweet Jia,' I whispered. Sweet Goddess of

Loaded Dice, Fair Dealing and the Dreams of Flight.

Simenon returned, dragging our guide's unconscious weight as well as he could. I laid out the fractal mat, setting it to accept vocal commands and m-brain sync.

<Ready,> sent the mat, in response.

Circuits glowed into life. I tried not to lose myself in its shifting patterns. You could easily be hypnotized by a fractal mat's weird beauty. 'Tandem mode, *activate*.'

The mat's width began shrinking even as its length began to extend in short rippling bursts.

'But we're not praying!' Simenon gagged inside the swirling dust cloud.

'None needed. Our mat's previous owner is the practical type,' I coughed, watching the repulse field activate; the mat rose to hover a foot off the rock floor. All the Humanitum's denizens along the Scheherazade Rim were pragmatic people. If they were going to carry something as unwieldy as a prayer mat around with them, they were surely going to make its inconvenience worthwhile in other ways.

Half the chapel to our left collapsed, ancient carvings smashed by a sudden onslaught of bedrock. Salt rock fragments swirled around the air making it near impossible to breathe.

I led by example, mounting the mat on the front. 'Rest Arto behind me, you jump on the back holding him in place.'

The young lad goggled at me as though I was crazy. *In so many ways, he has a good point.* But Simenon battled against his absolute terror of entombment; he would have stood upside down and sung the *Songs of Old Sol* if I swore they'd be his salvation. I felt the mat dip as Arto's weight fell against my spine, Simenon mounting the mat at the rear. Sections of cracking chapel smashed around us as loud as cannon fire.

'Crash shield, *maximum*. Safety protocols, *disengage*. Route, *augment-sync*.' I turned to call back to Simenon, 'Hold on!'

Varnus's worn prayer mat sped forward, shrugging falling rock off the invisible bubble of its crash field. Another series of blasts detonated behind us. Something too large to ignore striking Arto's belt of charges, no doubt. Our mat started playing bizarre snatches of Tanbūra lyre music, alert sounds custom-set by Varnus. *Too fast. Too many crash impacts. Too narrow.* Yes, I bloody well *am* aware. I silenced its warnings. If I was going to die crushed by this dark world's crumbling bedrock, I'd rather said end didn't come to the tinkling accompaniment of samples from the *Kitab al-Aghani*.

Our reluctant fractal mat hurled forward while begging to stop, citing terminal flight hazards, which I overrode on a loop. Terminal would be if we slowed. Tunnel walls ruptured around us, Simenon yelling in terror, the passage to the surface lost in blackness apart from the crazy bumping light of my lantern.

Arto Jagg was the lucky one, here. If we faltered and died, he'd never feel the crushing embrace of collapsing earth and stone. Not waking was as good a way to die as any, given the circumstances.

<Power reserves, failing. Flight function, damaged,> sent the mat as I smelt its burning circuits.

Yes, I know every street on the Rim's worlds has built-in inductive charging, electromagnetic fields invisibly transferring energy to millions of flight mats flitting about. And here we were, pushing through hell on residual power reserves only. Of course, the mat was going to tear itself apart converting mass to energy. I'd been praying for its failure to occur *after* we cleared the cave-in.

Simenon gripped our unconscious guide like a vice behind

me, giving full vocal vent to his claustrophobic instincts now his darkest nightmare had come true. I might have joined him, but my mind was fully engaged directing our failing mat through this collapsing passage. Dust started to penetrate our protective bubble. The field surface was failing. I urged us faster. I could feel its overload through my clothes, the mat's fractal surface growing too hot for comfort.

Suddenly we were clear of tumbling debris, tunnel supports holding, the stench of pressurized gas pockets faded to a bad egg stink. Our prayer mat made a yowling noise that might have been a sigh as it gave up the ghost, shuddered and slowed, nosing into the ground. There it lay, the beauty of shifting spatial circuits fading as its fractal scales lost recursive integrity. Jia's bounty broken – our bodies, not quite.

'We're alive,' panted Simenon. He shook, but not with cold. The lad didn't seem able to stop trembling.

I gazed at the debris-blocked tunnel to our rear. *It's still holding.* I picked up the blackened prayer mat, a reminder of what our journey had cost us.

I checked on Arto Jagg while I kept a beady eye on the timber supports stitching this tunnel together. Arto was fine; I would need to shoulder carry our guide the rest of the way. But what about …?

'Mozart?' trembled Simenon, echoing the direction of my thoughts.

'We'll see,' I coughed. I prayed to Modd my robot friend could come out of this filthy mess alive. 'Let's climb top-side and summon a rescue party down here.'

- 17 -
Corpses and Comets.

I heard the echo of voices as the first group of miners neared the surface. I closed the prayer box and rose to my knees. I wasn't optimistic. There were so many gods in the universe, but very few miracles.

'What of the Lords Derechor?' Jenelle Cairo asked the rescue party as they trudged from the mine entrance. All they carried with them were crushed bodies wrapped in canvas and grim sad faces.

'Dead, everyone's dead down there,' coughed the lead miner, wiping a film of dust off his bruised cheeks.

'Sentries told me Lord Zane was climbing his way back to Habur Mell's Chapel,' said Arto Jagg. Our guide wasn't in much of a physical state to be on his feet, but nobody seemed able to stop him. Least of all me. Still, Arto should have been keeping Simenon company in Hebateen's poorly provisioned hospital facility. 'My son was helping Lord Sarlee inside the deep mines, overseeing a final burn.'

The worker shook his head while other families rushed in, desperately seeking news of their loved ones. 'Sorry, Arto. Much of the deeps have collapsed. Lord Sarlee, your Rauf, they were crushed by subsidence. Plenty of warriors and our workers in the passages running up to the chapel, too. This machine man's the only one we found limping out of the tunnels,' said the grim-faced miner, stepping back to reveal a robot among the mob.

Mozart, helping the rescue party carry canvas-wrapped corpses out!

My heart leapt. *Thank Modd.* Moz strode forward towards us. I take my miracles where I find them.

'We've recovered bodies, none of them recognizable,' added the rescue worker. 'We're working carefully, mind, in case there's any more faulty blasting charges downside.'

'Keep digging, you keep checking,' pleaded Arto.

I said nothing. I feared Master Jagg's last desperate hopes were about to be fatally crushed, too. *How can it be otherwise?*

'Old ruster,' I said, by way of greeting to my robot. 'Still intact, I see.'

'Benefit of not having lungs to fill,' shrugged Mozart, unembarrassed for having survived when so many others hadn't. Being buried by rock slides no doubt a minor inconvenience to my steel-armoured companion. Surviving is what the two of us were best at.

Mozart reached out to squeeze Arto's shoulder with one hand, a very human gesture as he signed at me with his other. *We need to talk.*

I led the robot aside, making sure nobody else stood close enough to overhear our conversation. 'How bad was it?'

'I clocked a line of blasting charges drilled into the tunnel a few seconds before they popped. Faulty explosives my steel arse. That collapse was no accident. Someone meant to bring the mine down on top of us.'

I sighed. Bad enough Lord Blez's assassins had tried to murder me inside the forest. Now, they'd attempted to slaughter our entire party. Sweet William still stood, but plenty of others had picked up the butcher's bill intended for him. Master Jagg's son, the gods know how many innocent miners as well as the Derechor forces on the hunting expedition.

'There's a lot more,' Mozart said. He told me, and my eyes narrowed as I listened to everything my robot friend had to say about the incident.

'We need to get ahead of this,' I spat.

'You got an idea, doc?'

Yes. Our enemies had taken their toll. Long past time to reply with a little mischief of our own. *But how?*

***

I waited inside one of Hebateen's ore mills, its floor covered with human remains, each crushed mess mercifully concealed by a cheap woollen blanket. I wasn't the only occupant. Hundreds of wailing family members searched for missing parents, sons, wives, daughters; all wandering blankly among the corpses. Clothes torn, miners' bodies mangled beyond recognition – trying to locate relatives for burial had become a near-impossible task. At least, using simple sight.

Jenelle stood grim-faced by my side watching the grieving mining families. 'This never changes. Always the same after a major cave-in.'

'Did you ever recover your family's bodies from the mine?' I asked.

'No,' Jenelle said, bitterly. 'But then, there wasn't a couple of Lord Derechors lying among the fallen to make digging corpses out politically profitable for the Mine Master and his courtiers. They just closed that section of the mine and dug into more profitable territory.'

'I'm sorry,' I said.

'That's the life. That's the bargain people strike, here.'

A demon's bargain. I wondered how many idiots Jenelle had killed in her feud before the Mine Master found it expedient to export his difficulties? I sighed, unable to stand the scene of collective human suffering any longer. I turned to Mozart. 'Be so good as to retrieve my medical case from our quarters.' I climbed up onto a horse-driven treadmill to attract the crowd's attention. 'Listen to me, everyone! Go back to your homes and return with any sheets and items of clothing used by your missing loved one. Dirty, if you please, not clean. The filthier the better. I shall run medical tests that will use your items to help you identify each and every body lying here.'

Superstitious rumblings sounded from the families, signs invoked for their hollow spirits' protection. Poor lost wretches. I explained what I proposed to the Mine Master and he finally understood my scheme, managing to chivvy families home to do as I had asked. Mozart returned with my case and I set up my STR profiling analyser. It took six hours to recover DNA samples from the personal items of all the dead, create a profile index and likewise sample the corpses.

Harder yet to assuage the grief of those with no corpses to bury after I ran the last of the matches. *How many lost forever under the rockfall? One is a loved one too many.*

Arto Jagg's child, at least, was not among those forever buried. I led the man gently over to the bundle I had identified as his son. Miners uncovered Rauf Jagg's remains lying buried next to Sarlee Derechor. Noble and commoner, indistinguishable from each other in death, if not in the quality of their living.

'It should have been me,' sobbed Arto, kneeling by the ruins of all he loved.

'Yes,' I agreed, 'I thought much the same when I stood where you do, now. Better if the old fool went first, instead.'

'How do you bear it? How do you stand it?' he wailed.

I crunched the burnt-out prayer mat as though wringing a wurm's neck. 'Revenge, mostly.'

'Who do I have to take revenge against?' he cried.

I lent in, speaking low, 'I don't believe the collapse was a blasting charge accident. None of the nitroglycerin charges I saw on your warriors' belts were sweating.' I wanted to tell Arto more. I ached to. He deserved as much of the truth as I possessed. But it was hard to say which of the two of us that knowledge would prove more dangerous for.

'Who, then?' Arto snarled.

'Enemies who hated the Lords Derechor, the same people who loathed Lord Blez.'

'That's almost *everyone*!'

'I will find them,' I promised Arto. 'And I will be their end. Not for Lady Blez or the Watch or the House of Derechor, but for Rauf Jagg.'

He gripped my hand as tight as a vice before swaying off back through the maze of bodies, dazed by a lesser form of madness. One I knew all too well. Had I done the man a favour by giving him something to live for? A drop of hate, the tincture of Sweet William's existence. Arto had his son to bury, everything else must come later.

I crossed the hall to where Jenelle stood over the mounds identified as Zane and Sarlee Derechor, supervising the Mine Master's staff as they rolled the nobles' remains into a stretcher for removal on her airship. I hoped these people could also produce a few blocks of ice to hold back decomposition. Either way, our flight back to the capital wasn't going to be a happy one.

'There will be trouble brewing over this,' murmured the captain to me.

'Are there no obvious successors inside the Derechor's house?' I asked.

'Only about twenty cousins who all believe they're an ideal fit for the role of Lord or Lady Derechor, most of whom loathe their kin's claims with a passion reserved for spectators betting on a rat fight. They'll be knifing each other before we make dock at Frente when word leaks out. Hell, the noble-born fools will probably be nobbling rivals just for a chance to bury these two at their graveyard's plot.'

On such shallow ground are claims to one's birthright established, it seemed, out in the Empty.

'You did a kind thing for these families,' said Jenelle.

'Done to them or by them, it's never wasted.' I tossed my destroyed mat on the pile of abandoned possessions used for DNA testing.

'Don't you need it to pray?' asked Jenelle.

'No. Not any longer.'

It was the killers behind this slaughter who needed to do that. Pray to their hollow heathen spirits screaming and twisting at the sky. They had buried the simple trader, here. Let us see if they liked what had clawed its way out of the darkness heading their way.

***

I rested on Hebateen's rocky mountainside, sitting cross-legged under the spaceport's ruins. It was proving far harder than I expected to clear the images and memories of the cave-fall from my mind. Hard work, but I needed to tackle them now. If I left such grim fare festering much longer I would end up with a post-traumatic stress disorder. I'd return home to the foldship and find myself unable to traverse a narrow corner, let alone brave a hyperloop back on any civilized world.

My meditations were soon to be interrupted, however. Jenelle Cairo appeared, climbing the slopes towards me. She set her lamp next to me and stared down at the dark ruins of the abandoned pleasure city below.

A few campfires burnt in the ruins. Ferals, I supposed, making a home out of some crumbled casino. 'I always feel sadness coming back here,' said Jenelle.

'A reminder of your previous life in the mines?'

She sat down next to me. 'Yes. All I lost out here.'

'I know exactly how you feel.'

'How many things have you been over the centuries?' asked Jenelle.

'A surgeon, a magistrate, a priest, a trader.'

'Anything ridiculous. Anything to make me smile?'

Would I dare attempt that? 'I don't think I've ever felt anything other than ridiculous across of all my careers.'

'Oh, come on,' insisted Jenelle, 'that's not even an answer. You must have done something …?'

'Well, I briefly served as an ensign with the Humanitum Fleet.'

I tried hard to forget those years and the follies of my youth. Not my finest hour, serving on the *There's Something Behind You*.

'Only an ensign? You didn't end up as an admiral or at least a captain?'

I smiled. 'Of the two of us on these slopes, I'm afraid you are the only captain here. I was cashiered before I could rise any higher.'

Jenelle's curiosity had been piqued. 'For what?'

'A philosophical difference over the value of human life. I seemed to place it somewhat higher than my superiors.'

The good captain nodded. 'I can see you having terrible trouble taking orders.'

'One last position,' I remembered, 'a deputy in the Watch on this awful moon at the waesucks end of the universe.'

'I don't see you lasting at that, either.'

A bright light burned through the starfield above us, descending almost too fast to follow before it was lost behind the curve of our mountain.

'A falling star,' laughed Jenelle. 'Do you still make wishes inside the Humanitum when you see one?'

'What exactly should I wish for?'

'This!' said Jenelle, leaning over to kiss me. 'Feel free to return my favour.'

'Is that an order, captain?' I asked, wondering just where this ambush had come from?

She flipped me over, sliding on top. 'Well, you are serving *under* me...'

'I thought that was under sufferance?'

'Oh, I'm still planning on making you suffer,' she said, sliding her nails down my chest.

I relented, realising I had been wrong about one thing. There might be a few good positions left to me, yet. Arto proved correct, his people were cut from granite. Jenelle's body felt rock-hard to my touch, an athlete's form that put the extra weight I carried on my body to shame. Tough grind toil and a low-calorie diet came free on Hexator. Jenelle slid her clothes off, her muscled alabaster form as dense and polished as marble, before she took care of mine. So many small scars that complemented my own. I didn't ask where she had suffered her wounds. Dagger duels deep underground, rockfalls, a criminal's quick blade? They weren't mine to inquire about and Jenelle gifted me with the same courtesy, which was just as well. No honest trader should have come by so many.

'I don't want kindness from you,' Jenelle whispered, fiercely kissing me, 'I need you to punish me.'

I obliged her, as a gentleman should a lady, making her nipples as hard as the surface we shared for our bed, turning the garden of her passion as hot and feverish as this moon's dark night. A flint is made to be struck to sparks, and I rubbed her stone smooth as fiercely as she demanded. The locals had detected a devil inside Jenelle Cairo and tried to murder her for it, before her final banishment. They feared the woman like a breach in a magma chamber. They did, as I discovered, have a point. Jenelle ground against me, her hair crimson fire as I found her magma chamber and she showed me the depths of her heat. Fires twinkled down in the abandoned city, misted by the sweat rolling into my eyes. I doubted if they lit anything as feral as this night's work on these slopes.

I sensed Jenelle needed to fill the loss she had suffered here, and I obliged as best I could, finally resorting to glanding a cocktail of chemicals to match the seemingly endless energy of her vigour. I am a little ashamed to say that I finally resorted to an old mixed reality m-brain trick: overlaying Jenelle's face with Alice's, recreating the officer's hot throbbing form as that of Lady Blez's. Although, concerning current matters, Alice's peccadillos ran more to dishing out amercement rather than seeking it; which rather disrupted my illusion.

The weight of the mines had been Jenelle's manacles once, now she urged and shaped my hands into their replacement. If reincarnation was the fate of those who spurned the Merge, I wouldn't wish to return as a pit pony under this one's care. She fair rode me to destruction, as careless of my body as she wished I be of her's. After what seemed a lifetime of chastening, I spent myself inside Jenelle as she matched me with her pleasure, a stunned look on her face that her joys could be thus extended. Well, augments are a wonderful and flexible technology.

And that is when it happened. All around us, Hexator exploded into life.

- 18 -
Renewal.

Spore-blossom Season occurs once every five years on Hexator, its cycle matching a shift in the gravitational gradient between Hexator and the angry gas giant embracing the moon. A blip in orbital eccentricity and obliquity which generated fierce storms to energize and nourish the spores. In the distant past, when Hexator had been a jewel in the dark rather than a dark hole in a pit, travelers from the Humanitum had deemed the alien sight worthy enough to tour here. Every giant spire of vegetation in the forest simultaneously opened its gills and spouted showers of spores into the air. The higher the better, to catch thin, fast atmospheric currents that would carry spores across the uninhabitable furnace of Hexator's far face. Fed with energy, ready to return to the deep forests on the dark side of the moon and become new life.

Jenelle had laughed and cried at the explosion, a sight as rare as spore-blossom season, I suspected. White clouds. Pink clouds. Yellow clouds. Spores as large as plates and spores as small as dust. An evolutionary arms race of nature's designs. There would be little celebrating at Hebateen as the mining clans buried their own, but everywhere else there would be feasting, frolics and picnics as far deep inside the forests as the locals dared venture. In the capital, certainly. For the great and minor houses, they had good reason to celebrate. The Four Families and the minor houses that would rise to their ranks had carefully gathered their spore-spice harvest before it spewed into the atmosphere. The warlords had treated it and stored it. Very soon, the spore-spice auctions would begin. I needed to attend and bid against the other offworlders if only to make a good show expected of an honest free-trader.

Flying back to the capital you might have mistaken our airship for the ornament inside a snow-globe. Propellers stirring currents of spores as we left the mountains and passed over the forests. Organic matter spattering across our portholes, falling like frost across the old salon's viewing gallery. It seemed unreal to me. But not as strange as the atmosphere of bacchanalia and madness pervading Frente on my return. Not from natural high spirits. I wore a white fabric filter mask to hold the forest's wild bounty at bay, as did Simenon. Mozart, of course, needed none. Few of the locals showed such restraint. The poor ran maskless through the streets around the airship docking tower, holding their hands up to the dark as swirls of "blossom" rained down around them. Snatching random hits and random highs. Only the rich clutched filter masks, not willing to expose themselves when they could afford to pay for cultivated narcotics anytime the desire struck them.

'There's not going to be barricades in the streets now, surely?' I suggested to Jenelle, watching a pair of women and a man who had inhaled far too many aphrodisiac spores shed their clothes and inhibitions, before beginning the goat's jig in a nearby alley.

'Give it a few days. When the poor start to develop a tolerance after too much snorting. When the spore clouds thin out and the mob begin to comedown. There'll be trouble like you wouldn't believe.' Jenelle turned to some of her crew coming off the airship. 'Masks on! I'll cashier any officer of the Watch found without a mask over the next three days!'

A torch lighter came wobbling up to us, jabbing the tool of his trade in the air like a spear. He nearly walked straight into Mozart. 'I'm a hoddy doddy man, today! How about you?'

'Wrong species, mate. I'm naturally jolly. Now jog on.'

I watched the wick on the end of the worker's lighter clumsily trying to connect with a hanging lantern and prayed the capital's firefighters wore masks for the duration of their insane festival.

We left Jenelle to pass on the caskets containing House Derechor's dead. Send them back to their squabbling kin. I would be happy to return to our lodgings. I hadn't slept well on the airship. My prayers to Modd had received vague auguries leaving me uneasy; the bloody murder in the mines making me even more troubled. Not only for myself but how ill this promised for Alice's future here. Walking into a wall of near hysteria on the streets amplified the feeling that this was Hexator's fin de siècle.

'Is it always like this?' I asked Simenon.

'Spore-blossom Season's come very early this year,' said the lad. 'It normally starts a month after the auctions have finished.'

'I mean, the *people*?'

'Oh, yes,' said Simenon. 'Master Roxley?' he inquired by way of an afterthought.

'Yes, Master Simenon.'

'Now we've been badly set upon in the forest and the mines, have our woes cleared your mind as to who it might be behind Lord Blez's assassination?'

'Definitely the Derechor twins,' I said, without a twinge of irony or humour crossing my face.

'Truly?'

'Lead suspects, lad. In fact, I suspect it was the terrible guilt they felt at their dark deed of murder that led them both to commit suicide. Blowing themselves up inside their own mines! A damnable selfish way to go. They could have climbed Mount Hebateen and leaped off the top to spare their workers so much grief. But that's nobles for you. Selfish to the bitter end.'

Simenon seemed to accept my tall tale at face value. He had a filter-mask on, too, to protect him from accidentally inhaling a nasty psychosis-activating spore. I'm not sure this gullible lad actually needed it. All the way to our lodgings we seemed to be confronted by wide-eyed adherents of this new religion of insanity. Men and women screaming derangements at us in a vain attempt to convert us to the Lord of Misrule.

'That's the stuff! That's the stuff!'

'I'm healed. Did you heal me?'

'Drop your face linen and start spinning!'

'Split my beard, you know you want to, handsome.'

Watch officers wearing masks chased a bare-chested man through the streets while a giggling seventy-year-old woman attempted to empty a night pan's soup over them from a second storey window. What japes.

'What an advert for your species,' said Moz, as our tavern hove into sight.

I stepped aside as a woman came stumbling past, trying to collect the stars in the heaven with her fluttering hands. No wonder we raised so many of our creations to be gods, to be better than us. All our organic children were insane.

- 19 -
Death. From above.

Every morning, after waking, I gazed in the mirror while shaving and wondered who the old man looking back was. Where the rake and rascal fixed in my mind as Sweet William had vanished? Once, on a long voyage, I submitted my biometric profile to a vast database of famous artists, singers, politicians, scienceers, actors and other assorted figures from history. The game returned the person you most resembled, physically. I received a name of a man I've never heard of before. An actor from the Carbon Age visuals called Martin Landau. I even called up one of the ancient entertainment series he'd appeared in. Some hokum about an Earth with a Moon dislodged by nuclear explosives and set wondering across the stars, somehow managing to reach a different solar system just in time for the start of each new episode. Yet without even a foldship drive to explain away this miracle of transportation? Perhaps that was my answer for Hexator's woes? I could set up an enterprise shipping nuclear waste; wait until I had enough radium to set the moon free, then blast it out of the Empty and point it towards a fresh orbit around a civilized Humanitum system. Make Hexator someone else's problem. *Oh, if only.*

My morning reveries were shattered when my suit flashed me a warning that the dragonfly-like insect hovering outside our windowsill was no local. As a matter of fact, it was one of mine. I wondered what had gone wrong for my ship dancing around Hexator to swap her fake meteorite dead-drop for a realtime face-to-face?

Mozart cottoned onto the tiny stealth drone's presence. He slid open the window and the insect swept inside our lodgings, along with a random scattering of spores blown on the hot wind. The forests' organic spumes continued unabated outside, as did the laughter and shouts of the Mardi Gras being conducted gratis on the streets. Hard times for our landlady. Mistress Miggs' tavern sat empty while *happy, horny,* and *high-spirits* rained down freely from the heavens. Blessings from the ecosystem rather than the gods. *Well, at least the poor lass has our custom.*

The bug dropped onto my bed, its delicate gossamer wings re-orienting to project a female hologram face hanging disembodied above my sheets.

'*Exy,*' I said, concerned, 'whatever is the matter?'

My darling *Expected Ambush* accelerated straight to the point. 'What's the matter? Oh, Sweet William, let's start with the fact our ride home is yellower than a class G Star! She's exiting Hexator orbit and pulling out to that hydrogen and helium ice ball seven planets back.'

Not like a foldship to take fright so easily? I prayed we weren't losing our ride home. 'Does the You Can't Prove It Was Us plan on returning, sweet ship girl?'

'I suspect that will depend on whether the Melding man-o'war that just folded into our system edge plays house guest or not.'

Ah, the actual explanation of matters.

Mozart groaned. 'And where's the wurms' big bleeding warboat heading?'

'Definitely not a system pass,' said the *Expected Ambush*. 'She's burning directly for Hexator orbit.'

Which rather begged the question, what did the wurms know that Sweet William did not?

'I told you we should have hitched a ride with one of my Fleet contacts,' complained the ship. 'We could have had the *Do I look Like A Peacekeeper?* or the *Don't Make Me Speak Louder!* in orbit now instead of that livy-livered merchanteer squid.'

I grunted. I suspected if we had hitched a lift with either vessel, it wouldn't be a single wurm man-of-war hurtling our way now, but a task force-sized battlegroup burning hard for Hexator. We had already fought that argument and I won it. Sweet William makes it a rule never to re-fight battles he's already banked.

'You could re-dock on the *You Can't Prove It Was Us* and make like a barnacle…' I suggested to *Exy*.

'Or I could dive in the sun to burn that much stupid off my hull. No! I'm morphing for full stealth and silent running,' hissed my ship, as insulted as I'd ever heard her. She calmed down and her avatar winked at me, slyly. 'I'm keeping one of my peepers open still, just a little open, watching out for you.'

I couldn't help but worry for my stalker angel. 'Just be careful, *Exy*. That incoming wurm warship isn't going to be nearly as easy to hoodwink as Hexator's toy traffic control system.'

My ship's avatar whispered back, theatrically. 'Don't look at me, I'm not even here. So, how is it down in the dirt?'

'The good news is I can wander Hexator's streets and I don't have to gland myself happy anymore. The bad news is I've nearly been eaten by a slug the size of a train and had the best part of a mountain dropped on me in an attempt to bury me alive.'

'Oh, the mine, yes I've heard all about the mine. Was that your dead wife trying to kill you again?' laughed *Exy* with a tinge of jealousy. 'She got the goldmine while you got the shaft.'

'Very amusing. Let's be careful up there.'

'Mozart, how about you bring on your A-Game and keep Sweet William alive for us?'

'Us? You're having a laugh aren't you, ship girl,' said the robot, 'I thought it was his job to keep me alive and functional.'

'No more comms,' I ordered my ship. 'Don't break silence again unless matters go sideways.'

Exy's hologram faded away and the bug fluttered off to disassemble all evidence of its existence. I suspected there would be a small pile of rusty residue under the bed for Simenon to clear away when he returned with our breakfast from the tavern's kitchen.

'What more can go sideways, doc?' asked Mozart. 'Someone decides to drop *two* mountains onto us?'

'Don't tempt fate.'

But my robot friend already had.

- 20 -
Such stuff as dreams.

Humanity has so many gods. But on nights as hot and harsh as this one, it was hell I needed, not heaven.
Again.

<Verified Truth Recording. Last Transmission: *Mercy Ship Dorothea Dix.*>

<POS.Bridge. SubSys.VTR:>

<Captain of the Fleet Medical Corps:> 'There's no sign of the colony ship in orbit, but it does look like they attempted to set up dirt-side.'

<Master chief hospital corpsman:> 'What about our settlers down there, skipper?'

<Captain of the Fleet Medical Corps:> 'Sorry, Adam. The drones haven't found anyone yet.'

<Master chief hospital corpsman:> 'That makes no sense, their council had time to declare an emergency?'

<Captain of the Fleet Medical Corps:> 'Maybe they evacuated on the *There Goes the Neighbourhood*, or found a better candidate world further out?'

<*Dorothea Dix.* SubSys Main:> 'Stealth signature incoming, captain. Thirty seconds to close.'

<Officer of the deck:> 'What the hell is that thing? Have you ever seen reads like—?'

<Captain of the Fleet Medical Corps:> 'D.D, burn for fold, now!'

<Master chief hospital corpsman: SubSys Comms:> 'Unknown vessel, this is the Mercy Ship Dorothea Dix. We are active inside this system on a humanitarian mission. Please hold, please identify yourself.'

<Dorothea Dix. SubSys Decoy C.M.:> 'Multiple launches. Nuclear hull-burst class warheads.'

<Dorothea Dix. SubSys Flash Broadcast:> *Emergency Eject.*

<Master chief hospital corpsman: SubSys Comms:> 'Unknown vessel, our shields are purely anti-collision, we carry no weap—'

<Buoy Swarm:> *Burn. Broadcast. Burn. Broadcast.*

</Emergency Buoy Ident. /Encryption Mark: Tricord, God of Healing and the Combat Medical.>

'Erase that bloody tape,' demanded Mozart, his shadow falling over my sweat-soaked bed inside the *Sparrow's Rest*.

'Leave me the hell alone, Moz.'

I had my penance out in the Empty. Adam would never have joined the Medical Core without my encouragement. My son would never have been in at the Contact War's start without his dolt of a father steering him towards a hospital ship.

'What good are you going to be to anyone tomorrow?' growled Mozart.

I raised what passed for a near-empty bottle of wine on Hexator; a toast to what passed as my good god damned robot. 'I'll be fine.'

'I don't want to hear you yelling bloody murder in your dreams tonight. I doubt the hound or Tiny Tim will enjoy hearing that, either.'

'You won't hear a peep.' I tapped my augment. 'I'll patch a REM behaviour disorder override.'

'If the heathens come down in force, they'll land like bastards here whether you want them to or not. Erase that tape, doc. Nothing ever changes. How much bloody death do you need to see?'

Just a little bit more.

I set the recording going again. A dark hole in my soul demanded filling. I had run out of everything but hate to pour into it. And of that, I had a wide, wide ocean.

- 21 -
A Lord's library.

Dozens of street sellers were out and about. Wearing masks, so they could better relieve the intoxicated crowds of their coins and tokens. Not that gulling them took much effort, presently. Merchants cried the names of hollow gods and false spirits; amulets, indulgences, and blessings a-plenty for sale. I couldn't blame Hexator's local inhabitants for being so easily tricked, even when they weren't as high as a kite. When Inuno abandoned Hexator, its conduit to all the other gods vanished as well. How many centuries could you expect people to worship at altars without receiving an answer? Little wonder citizens conjured up imaginary spirits to placate all-too-real alien storms. Hexatorians drifted half-crazed past street shrines, shrines abandoned or re-purposed for hollow vessels. How could you be annoyed at these people for their heathen stupidity? When the Hexatorians stopped believing in the gods of Arius, they didn't start believing in *nothing*, they started believing in *anything*. Like a dog licking at a wound and causing its injury to fester. You knew the injury was never going to get better. But then, you also knew that left to its own devices that dog was never going to invent antibiotics.

Captain Jenelle Cairo appeared, right on time. She indicated the road where Lord Seltin's citadel lay sprawled across the city. 'Shall we?'

'What, again?' I croaked.

'You know what your most endearing feature is, doctor?'

'Please tell, good captain …'

'You're only passing through.'

Well, that told me. *Always a bridesmaid, never a bride.* 'A man could be offended.'

'Try not to be,' she told me. 'And try not to offend Lord Seltin, today, while you're about it.'

To be honest, I would be happy to arrive at Falt Seltin's well-protected palace and discover him alive enough to be questioned; no dagger plunged into his chest; not finding him hanging from the rafters. Given the way things were trending presently, that would be a bonus.

Simenon appeared from a baker's shop bearing a couple of meat rolls that had taken my fancy in the window. Well, I say meat. Crushed locust-lizard fillings in the center and local flour ground from dried toadstools the size of a house. At least they were never going to run short of ingredients, more's the pity. I offered Jenelle first bite of my snack, but she gave me a withering look suggesting it was of less interest than a second taste of Sweet William. Just as well. On balance, I think this was a snack best saved for Alice Blez's refined palette.

'Have you noticed, Simenon, that the winds of Hexator only blow hot, never hot *and* cold,' I mused.

Simenon wiped a fall of spores away from his cheek. 'I hadn't thought about it, Master Roxley.'

No, I don't suppose the boy had.

'Where's your overgrown ruster?' growled the captain.

'I sent him off to my ship to collect a few things,' I said. I patted the little leather satchel I carried with me. In truth, I think Moz was still pissed at me for having to gland a serious hangover cure this morning. 'You appear a little tired, captain, if I may say.'

Jenelle gave me a weary look and indicated the cavorting crowd snaking through the capital's streets. 'The joy never stops for the Watch during Spore-blossom Season. And you don't exactly look like an oil portrait yourself.'

Lord Seltin's citadel appeared to be a colonial-era structure, heavy sloping composite walls that would require an orbital strike by the *Expected Ambush* to put a dent in them. I suspected this building would still be squatting here when humanity had become an extinction memory in Hexator's fossil record. Inside, its corridors, halls and grand rooms were retrofitted with gas torches and a few candle-lit chandeliers that kept the household staff unnecessarily busy. A company of admirably sober and grim house guards marched us to his lordship, taking position around the receiving chamber's walls; all the better to remind us of his power and position. *Perhaps they're unhappy about being deprived of the festival's frolics?*

Falt Seltin didn't seem overly concerned with his dignity or the madness outside. He stood alone in the middle of a vault which had once served as a genomic DNA and cDNA library. Its glass walls contained hundreds of thousands of data crystals resting in fingernail-sized recesses. Six floors deep, the chamber lay buried like a well at the palace's centre. *At least he's still alive.*

Lord Seltin cut an owlish figure, but without the gods' ability to help him handle the 800 billion basepair diploid human genomes compressed on each tiny data crystal, he might as well be an octopus sitting in the wreckage of a submarine on the seabed; tentacles on the control yoke, pretending to pilot it.

'So, this used to be the First Founder's palace?' I guessed as the lord and I shook hands.

'My family bought the Wang estate a century after the last of his house died,' confirmed Lord Seltin.

And, it seemed, the Seltins had also inherited Daylen Wang's interests in guiding human evolution to some distant pinnacle of near godhood. An almost comedic hubris, but one that still prospered on a handful of the Humanitum's worlds. Doomed to failure, of course. The race of man had already given birth to our children as gods. How could a beggared humanity hope to rival its progeny with, literally, as the old joke went, brains the size of a planet? Or these days, intelligences distributed across multiple star systems. Just trying to share a few of the gods' insights was enough to drive our best scienceers insane. An ant could never become an elephant by pining for a trunk, no matter how hard it wished and worked.

Denied the vault's digital contents, Lord Seltin pursued his folly by more pedestrian means. He stood surrounded by wooden boards pinned with hundreds of paper crests, hand-inked heraldic shields of the great and minor houses of Hexator, pieces of string linking the pins in a web of insanity. Tables surrounded the boards, piled with ledgers, family trees, and files of medical records. *How many decades has he spent on this lunacy? How many centuries has his family pursued this madness?*

'We could have done it,' said Falt, his finger drifting along one of the linked strings as I glanced around the vault.

'Produced a Kallihuman?' I suggested. Simenon and Jenelle stood behind me. The captain's silent judgment rested like a hot dagger pointed at my spine.

'Yes. If things hadn't fallen apart on Hexator so quickly and completely,' said Lord Seltin. 'Daylen Wang selected the original colonists' bloodlines to maximize his breeding program's chances.'

And how had that idiocy ended? Too many Alphas beating each back into the Beta. War and conflict and resource competition spinning towards complete societal collapse. 'Perfect humanity doesn't exist, my lord. Maybe it shouldn't, even if such a thing were possible.'

'If only we had bred as true as planned, Hexator would now be guided by rulers beyond wisdom. Your gods' abandonment of Hexator wouldn't have mattered a jot. Nothing could have stopped us. Tell me, doctor, is my work regarded as a heresy inside the Humanitum?'

'On the contrary, there are very well-resourced hobbyists pursuing similar projects.'

A heresy? I had to stop myself laughing out loud; such was the self-importance of Falt's ridiculous placement of himself at the centre of the universe. If Arius thought of breeding Kallihumans at all, it was with the worried frown of a mother finding a none too bright child climbing onto the family home's roof with a pair of homemade wings strapped to their kid's arms.

Lord Seltin fixed me with a gaze that *looked* sane, but then he went on to speak. 'Did you ever consider the theory that the Goddess Inuno abandoned Hexator to stop a Kallihuman successfully being produced? That Arius examined our First Founder's programme and feared the Wang dynasty's chances of success on this world?'

I was disappointed in him; an educated man, too. *Falt should know chaos theory trumps conspiracy theory every time.* 'The gods are unknowable by us in countless ways,' I said, 'but I have yet to divine any traces of jealousy in their actions, miracles, and visions. Not once during near a thousand years inside the Humanitum.'

'You must have made a good priest, doctor.'

'Not as good as all that or I wouldn't be scrabbling around at the spore-spice auctions.'

Lord Seltin noticed Jenelle standing silently, listening carefully to our conversation. 'Captain Cairo. I thought the Watch was joking when I received word you wanted to re-interview me.'

Jenelle raised a hand towards me. 'Lady Blez wishes a fresh pair of eyes on our investigation. To that end, the good doctor here has now been deputised as a sheriff of the Watch.'

Falt laughed. 'You owe the Commander General a new desk, then, Doctor Roxley. He must have taken so many bites out of his present one.'

In fact, I planned to stay out of the brute's clutches for as long as possible. 'What was your relationship with Uance Blez like, Lord Seltin?'

'We were friends and our houses allies. Even though Uance didn't believe in salvation through my work,' Falt raised his hands to the vault. 'But then, so few do. If that was a valid motive for assassinating Uance, his would be the first name on a very long list. Blez weakness at the auctions will be my family's prosperity, I suppose. The same can be said for any of the houses, great and minor.'

'Money isn't important to you?'

'My personal needs are modest. This great work is my only vice, but then it is also Hexator's last chance. We have lost so much; our bloodlines scattered and lost during civilization's slow retreat.' He tapped a crimson thread linking two of the boards. 'This was the project's best chance. A union between the Blez and the Seltins. A chance lost forever when that damnable fever struck me infertile. If I had a daughter I could have married her to young Rendor Blez, advancing the project's conclusion by centuries! So many chances lost.'

I persisted with my questioning for another half an hour, but I didn't need my m-brain's analysis to realise Lord Seltin's preoccupations lay far from this world's game of power and prestige. He regarded himself as the last monk of this dark age, keeping hope's flame flickering as his descendants had done before him. Falt was the last of his line, just as I was. Which of us was the greater fool to be here, still struggling vainly on, I wondered?

I was about to call an end to our interview when Falt noticed Simenon surreptitiously inspecting a book on a table.

'Your guide can read?' asked Lord Seltin. Simenon jumped at being noticed.

'Master Simenon taught himself his letters while on the streets,' I explained.

'How impressive. Do you possess an unusually good memory, young Master Simenon?'

'Yes, my lord,' he spluttered.

'What's your family?'

'I am a Wrongman, sir. It's said I was found in the capital after Kalamb was abandoned; it was thought my mother escaped here from that city.'

'Your ancestors would have been Darras, then,' said Lord Seltin, well-satisfied with his identification. 'They bred for eidetic memory and you share their wild hair. Kalamb sheltered many families with Darras blood.'

'A Darras,' said Simenon, rolling the unfamiliar name around his mouth like a new-found sweet.

'That book's from my library, its contents more accessible than these data crystals,' said Falt, indicating his vault. 'I often start a novel only to grow too distracted by the great project to finish it. What are you reading at the moment, lad?'

'I recently finished *Treasure Island* by Robert Louis Stevenson, my lord.'

'Very good. And how about you, Captain Cairo, do you also read?'

'Arrest reports and confessions from the holding cells,' said Jenelle, 'almost every single morning. They're piling up, now the season's started so early.'

'Cairos always favoured the practical in most matters, including their bloodline. Excellent night vision, but I don't suppose possessing a body immune to low gravity calcium-and-muscle-mass loss is much use to you now?'

'If it is, I must have missed it, my lord,' said Jenelle.

'You may borrow that book, young Master Simenon,' smiled Lord Seltin. '*East of Eden* by Master Steinbeck … it's of similar vintage to your last title. Be so kind as to not tell me how the tale finishes, though. I still like a surprise or two at my age. After you've read the book, return it to me and you may select another from my pile.'

Simenon held the book tight and bowed deeply in gratitude, but I heard a groan from one of the house guards' old warhorses – that their palace should be converted into a borrowing library for street urchins. Our interview over, the lord's soldiers escorted the three of us out in a sullen silence which spoke of our siege against their house's dignity.

'Why do you think the Lord Seltin works inside that old vault,' Simenon asked me, 'when he can't make use of its machine data?'

'To remember all that he's lost,' I said, 'as well as much that he hopes to regain.'

'Lord Seltin only has sorrow to bite on,' said Jenelle. 'If I possessed half of what that man owns, I sure as hell wouldn't lock myself away in a pit pining for what I can never have.'

Poor Lord Seltin, his genomics vault little more useful to him than a wishing well. Our beautiful children were already gods. *How can that not be enough for Falt?* I vowed to myself then that Hexator might see miracles enough to turn everyone on this fallen world back to the true faith.

= 22 =
Trabbs.

I had expected Jenelle Cairo to want to come with me to interview Lady Trabb. Nie Trabb, the aunt, rather than the young Martina Trabb who held the house's official title. At the very least, I'd expected Jenelle's company to ensure I didn't upset the grand dame with my impertinent questioning. But the captain just laughed and said that she had already spoken with the woman for the Watch and I was welcome to see her on my own. Jenelle left me to my devices as she marched away to celebrate the joys of the season by cracking the skulls of a few inebriated rascals.

A game of mischief was afoot. Because I didn't know who the sucker at the card table was, I could only presume it was *me*. Jenelle did spare one of her paddy-wagons and a couple of overstretched members of the brute squad to transport myself, Mozart and Simenon. We halted in front of the building where the interview was to be held. It wasn't the official Trabb fortress-cum-palace to the west of the capital, but another property the family owned. What passed for an old merchant's mansion in Frente. A two-storey building with narrow windows facing out onto the street, windows sealed by metal bars. Not so much a prison as a counting house for great wealth.

My two retainers were commanded to wait in the hallway while I was ushered inside a grand foyer by a white-masked retainer, through a gallery, and into a large drawing room. Three was a crowd, obviously, as far as the old lady's bodyguards were concerned. The drawing room's protected rear had wide high windows compensating for the building's public face, windows giving onto a courtyard garden. Of course, it was a rich person's terrace, filled with the hardier remnants of Terran flowers and hedges kept alive against all odds against the local flora. *This is a losing battle*, I thought. Presently, the terrace garden sat trapped in a snowstorm of multi-coloured spores. I wouldn't want to be employed as one of this grand house's gardeners.

Lady Trabb the elder waited for me on a comfortably cushioned sofa at the opposite end of the room. There was a small round table in front of her where a silver tray held a teapot and a three-tier porcelain stand filled with oatcakes. I wouldn't put it past the old bird to have that pot sloshing with actual imported tea leaves, rather than dried gills from the local mushroom fields.

Nie Trabb had the bitter look of a great beauty now faded with old age. It must have been a slow slide for her, the expensive edits of her noble-born DNA holding back the years' decline. My m-brain flashed me a back-aged model of her face: how Nie would have looked at twenty. I almost gasped out loud. *How many wars had the local warlords fought over this one?* I wondered. *How many ships launched in her name?* Well, I knew the answer to that, here. None. No seas on Hexator. Most of its water table lay underground. But the noblewoman's expensive cells had failed her at last, as all must. No more suitors for Nie Trabb; little flattery which she should or could believe.

Her mind, though, her mind was still an engine of perfection. I only had to note the slightly pointed ears hidden by coils of white hair to know that. Her ears were a byproduct of gene edits fashionable before m-brain augments grew as sophisticated as today's biotechnological offerings. A linearly scaled-up triple-density cortex with an off the scale IQ. Her ancestors had really wanted their children to sprint to the front of the evolutionary arms race, and at least one of them had been rich enough to put the fix in. Nie Trabb, literally the sharpest dagger in the room. Well, any room that didn't contain Sweet William of course.

'Let's get to the meat of it, then,' said Lady Nie, wasting little time on small talk aside from offering me a tea. I liked her well already; certainly better than her drink, which was sadly the local mud-water.

'Did you kill Lord Blez?' I asked.

'Of course not. But I should have loved to. I'd have enjoyed the thrill of seeing his brains splatter across the road. In my youth, I would have cut through the current sad sack of Four Families like a dose of the plague.'

'Why?'

'I would be doing our world a huge favour. The Blez? Hah. First the husband, then the wife. I would tremble with pleasure taking the secondhand rags Sanctimonious Alice hands out to the poor, rolling the garments up and choking her with them. What a fine sight that would make. Could I bribe you to arrange it for me, perhaps? She seems to have let you get *very* close to her.'

'And what about Falt Seltin?' I asked, not allowing myself to be distracted by her canny intuition.

'A good old-fashioned hall burning. Barricade the doors and pour barrels of burning pitch over his walls. What better way to kill Falt than fry him inside his vault surrounded by his stupid failed DNA crystals. He loves the idea of perfected humanity far more than actual people, so losing his boards and spider's web of bloodlines would upset him most.'

'And the Derechor twins?'

'I must say that having the best part of their own mine collapse on their thick skulls was satisfyingly fitting, accident or no.'

No, I thought, but this sour old woman did not have to hear that confirmed from my lips.

'So, you truly didn't do it?'

'I truly did not, but a woman can dream.'

'Why wouldn't you have arranged Lord Blez's assassination? Don't you have as much to gain as anyone from disrupting the Blez operations at the coming auctions?'

'You mean gain for my niece, don't you? Our house's fall is already engraved in the stars by fate. Do you want to know how to bring down the House of Trabb? Just gift my niece a new mirror every day, preferably waiting until after I'm dead so I can't smash it. She will be so infatuated with what she finds in its surface you'll be able to steal all our holdings away from us without so much as a squeak.'

'So, who do you think did put a bullet in Lord Blez?'

'Why ask this spring chicken? Perhaps you mistake me for a maiden compared to yourself, you ancient horror? Out of the mouths of babes and innocents…? Don't they teach the Magistrates of Arius the classics any longer? Don't look for the means, seek the motive. Follow the mice. Think about the money, ideology, coercion, and ego of those you suspect.'

That was solid advice indeed. 'How large is your ego, Lady Nie?'

'Enormous. But in the specifics of this matter, perhaps not quite as engaged as the Lord Seltin's.'

'How so?'

'You didn't know? Hah, I thought not. Falt was in love with Alice Blez long before she married Uance. Uance and Falt were fast friends, but they had quite a falling out when it came to our over-emoting maiden. Uance was the victor who pulled ahead in that race after some early triumphs by Lord Seltin. Poor Falt, he should have stuck with his useless breeding ledgers. Uance did the man a favour. Falt never had to suffer decades of the woman's simpering and draining his house's treasury with extravagant gestures of inane virtue signalling.'

Of course, Falt and Uance Blez had been in love with Alice. How could both Lords not be? You just had to meet Alice for that. But neither had proved worthy of the noblewoman; of that I was certain. More stock for the pot. It was already growing too thick to stir. 'You don't give generously to the local charities, then, my lady?'

'Hah,' laughed Nie Trabb. 'Let them all die, and your gods can sort them out. Except the bloody gods can't be bothered with Hexator, can they?'

This clever woman was adept at needling me, getting under my skin. 'You act as Lady Martina Trabb's guardian?'

'For another year. That is how long we are safe. Yes, my brother, bless him, was killed in a duel with a minor noble over some trifling affair. Probably whose cock was longest. My sister-in-law managed to rot her already insignificant gift of brain matter away with King Tornado, the spore-spice of choice for princesses and suicides, pining away in grief over her dear dead Harliss Trabb. She preferred to pay for her spore-spice. Of course, if she had waited until today, the silly girl might have overdosed for free like the common whores tumbling around outside my windows.'

'I am sorry your family should bear such losses,' I said.

Nie shrugged. 'On Hexator, change smells a lot like death. Look out the window at the falling spore blossom if you don't believe me. If I was younger, I'd run outside, strip off, and sprint across the avenues and find myself a gang of handsome bucks to tup. What a shocking sight that would make. How old are you, doctor? Ten times my age? Twenty, a hundred?'

'Something like that. How can I tell?'

'You mean, how can I tell, given every ancient bugger from the Humanitum strolls around our streets looking no older than late middle-age? I suppose if your dark gods could fix life renewal technology to stabilise the visible aging process aged twenty, you'd all appear a lot younger.' Lady Trabb jabbed at my face. 'Who was it that said the eyes are the windows onto a soul? You walk quietly, a man grown tired from seeing too much, doctor. Your precious gods and your precious technology can fix almost everything apart from your eyes.'

I used my weary eyes to seek the truth of the matter from Nie Trabb. I was left with the uncomfortable feeling that she could lie to my face, laughing, and I still wouldn't really know what she was capable of. Like gazing down a well filled with this world's drowned babies.

'Yes, Doctor,' Nie smiled at me. 'I could probably outwit that unholy toad you've got squatting in your mind. Does the augment make you feel closer to your gods? Decadently post-human. We're still the original article here on Hexator.'

I shrugged. *Only because you can't afford the upgrade.*

Lady Trabb roared with laughter as I left; a most unladylike sound. 'Spore-blossom Season is a time for change. Can you smell it coming on the winds?'

I sniffed the air before I left the old mansion with Mozart and Simenon. I smelt something, alright, but it was rot rather than renewal.

- 23 -
For a Muse of Fire.

I had taken the morning off to register my lines of credit with the market for the coming auction. Great profit, it seemed, demanded immense volumes of paperwork as a sacrifice at its altar. If so, I was in good standing now with whatever local hollow god of commerce commanded the economy. I was returning to the *Sparrow's Rest* and the fair care of Mistress Miggs' culinary concoctions when Mozart and myself ran into a panicked mob headed fast in the opposite direction. Given Spore-blossom Season's blessings still fell, albeit ebbing in ever fainter swirls, I wondered what mischief might stir the inebriated citizenry to such fierce scurrying?

I had my answer around the corner. *I thought this road looked familiar.* Nie Trabb's great merchant's house sat at the end of the avenue, now obscured by great billows of black smoke joining it to the night. Given the dozens of dead soldiers and staff in front of the manse, I suspected the Muse of Fire had not been summoned here accidentally.

A pair of masked Watch officers pushed their way violently through the confusion of fleeing citizens.

'You two!' I bellowed. 'Your job is to run towards trouble, not away from it.' They ignored me in their haste to be away. I pulled out my round golden badge, flashing the circlet of the Four's interlinked hands at this pair of disgraces. 'A deputised sheriff, stand and hold!'

'A special, are you? Well, today you can be the High Magistrate of Frente,' growled the senior officer, 'for there's no business for an honest copper down that way.'

'At least call the fire brigade!' I yelled after him.

'You think the bucket squad wants any of that – taking sides, here?' the officer whooped back, continuing his evacuation. 'You better give your badge to someone who knows what they're doing!'

'They look so tough in those combat leathers, too,' noted Mozart.

I saw what the Watch's man meant as we grew closer. Lady Nie Trabb's yearning for a good hall burning had been fulfilled. Sadly, it was her hall covered in pitch and encouraged to flames. Her guards had been killed as intended trying to flee the burning building. As had many of her staff. There were other warriors' corpses, too. Derechor fighters, judging from the emblem on the energy shields inactive by the fallen.

I knelt among the dead, searching for a pulse. *Damn*. None of these souls alive enough to help me answer my questions. 'Why would Derechor warriors attack the Trabbs? It's meant to be cousin-on-cousin inside their house, not picking a feud with the rest of the Four?'

'I reckon the *civil* in their *war*'s misleading,' said Mozart, 'if you're looking for this bun fight to start making sense.'

Perhaps, but I liked matters to make more sense than *this*. I stared up at the sky, so tired suddenly. The spores were settling in the mud, the rain of fecundity halting. A heavy comedown was hit to the capital. If things were as bad as this now, what would it be like tomorrow?

'Mozart,' I sighed. 'I have a challenge for you.'

− 24 −
Consignor.

Captain Cairo wore a shotgun in her leg holster, her ruby red topknot tied as tight as the lines of her face scowling into the jostling crowd. Jenelle flicked a hand at us and her thugs surged forward, pushing the crowd aside with round metal riot shields so we could enter the cordon formed around the central marketplace. The square outside the auction was not a place to safely tarry, today.

'Is this the comedown from the blossom high, you promised me?' I asked Jenelle.

'No, this is the Commander General not listening to my advice. He broke seventeen suspected rebels on the wheels yesterday as a warning not to disrupt the auctions. These are their friends, family and district scum come to show Laur what they think of that. Chalkers! Chalkers!' yelled Jenelle, jabbing a leather gloved finger towards some scallies daubing white skulls onto walls behind the crowd.

The bother boys spotted by Jenelle were still masked, although the narcotic spores in the air had dwindled to nothing now. I don't think it was the miscreants' sobriety they were protecting; instead, their identities.

A squad of Watch heavies chased after the graffitists and rebel sympathisers.

Chanting by the mob grew ever louder, swelling to a roar in solidarity with the pursued. *OUR* HARVEST! *OUR* HARVEST! *OUR* HARVEST! *OUR* HARVEST!

'I hope you bid on some good shit for all those near-immortal moneyass leeches inside your Humanitum,' shouted Jenelle, jolted back by the angry crowd. 'because there's only bad shit out here.'

'The apothecaries of a thousand worlds thank you, good captain,' I bowed as I fled up the steps to a hail of hurled projectiles. Moz thumped up the steps behind Simenon and me, the rattle of tossed stones against the robot's steel spine protecting us both. I glanced quickly back.

Jenelle bellowed, 'Lamp breakers! Lamp breakers!' An alley to the side plunged into darkness as sprinting toughs, faces masked by scarves, ran its length spinning clubs up to shatter lanterns.

'Nice bloody day for it,' said Moz.

'The auctions are about to begin, Master Roxley,' urged Simenon, eager to put us beyond target practice range.

I grunted. Actually, I suspected they might be soon to end.

Inside, all the usual market stalls had been removed for the auction. A wooden fence made a stall for the rich offworlders to be fleeced inside. Quite fitting, for what were we to the locals but sheep with rich coats for the shearing. Mozart and Simenon hung back among the spectators and auction staff. This next act was only for those with deep pockets.

I nodded to my fellow free-traders and found myself a clear spot standing next to another merchant. She examined the numbered wooden board issued to her to wave in the air once bidding started. Dark-furred, and of course, green-eyed, this trader was from the Humanitum world of Ukarra. Ukarrans edited panther DNA into their genome. A tribute to, and survival bonding mechanism with, the modified panthera pardus used to protect them on Ukarra's impossibly hostile surface. She hadn't brought her panther with her. I suspected the port's customs gate would have much to say about a dangerously intelligent pony-sized sabre-tooth with cybernetic arm implants, even if the creature's fur did nicely colour match their ever-night moon. The lady wore an amulet to Jute on her jacket, a triangle made up of three helices; her connection to Jute the Bio, Goddess of the Heavy Edit and Transgenesis.

'Look at those fig-lickers. Can you feel it?' the woman spat at our fellow free-traders congregating inside the auction stall.

'Feel what?'

She tapped her skull, just above her m-brain augment. 'They've set up private short-link groups. There're three or four invite-only forums running in here. Free-traders my arse. Cartel fig-lickers and ringers, looking to squeeze us out! You wait. They'll collude, trying to inflate prices when we bid; making sure their bids sail through on the low-ball.'

'That's sharp practice,' I protested.

'You're not one of them, are you?' She peered suspiciously at me. The woman didn't offer to shake hands with me, but then that fine and admittedly exquisite black fur of hers made it near-impossible to trade verified sweat signatures.

'William Roxley, out of Arius. As independent as a hog on ice, sister.'

'Yadira Narm. Out of Ukarra.'

'Really? I could never have guessed.'

'I didn't see you up on our foldship, brother smart-arse?'

'There're quite a few miles of the *You Can't Prove It Was Us* and, to be honest, I spend far too much time on my own ship. I'm particular about my home comforts.'

'A timid little hikikomori? Well, you've come to the wrong world for that!' As if to underline her point, the sound of shattering windows crackled merrily away on the market's edge, the thud of hurled stones against our walls.

'I fear you're very right, m'dear. Is this your first auction?'

'Third time, although admittedly, my last auction was a hundred and twenty years ago. Took me that long to forget how much I hate this place.' Yadira didn't bother asking me if this was my first time, that was all too obvious. She pointed to a podium high above the Auction Master's stand, empty except for four tall thrones. 'Last time I was here those were all occupied, warlords sitting up there as serene as the Empress on Arius, like butter wouldn't figging melt. It's meant to be a show of power. What do those thrones sitting empty tell you?'

It told me that Major Rolt had taken one look at the riot-in-waiting outside and decided that Alice's son didn't need to make this his introduction to the spore-spice auctions. *Good man.* The other nobles were either killing each other for the right to sit on one of those cushions or had wisely decided that they would snatch the money and make a display of discretion today's show of power.

'Jute's Teeth, brother!' Yadira slapped my left leg, then pointed to the very modern-looking pistol strapped to hers. 'Where's your weapon?'

'The damnable port doesn't allow sidearms through.'

'You really don't know how things work here, do you? You bring five decent weapons through on an import license for a local chieftain; the warlord gets four for free, you're given one back as a gift. The Watch knows how unhealthy it is for them to challenge gifts handed out by highborn.'

'How do you smuggle weapons out of a foldship?'

Yadira sighed as if she was talking to an idiot. I do believe she was correct. 'You print them on your ship on the way down from orbit, as soon as the *You Can't Prove It Was Us* can't firewall you. You truly don't have a gun?'

'Truly, I don't.' I pointed to where Mozart stood at the back of the hall with the spectators, market staff and assorted hangers-on. 'I did bring him.'

'Shit, you brought a robot to a gunfight, brother.'

I smiled. 'Sister, it's not the size of the robot in the fight, it's the size of the fight in the robot.'

'You must be planning to kill that howling mob outside with Tetanus. Jute's Teeth, last time I was here, we fought all our battles inside the auction hall. This time, our main problem's going to be getting our cargo home – what with these crazy figgers knifing each other on the streets and that Melding Man-o'War mugging gravity in orbit. How much duty do we pay, and Fleet can't even deploy a single cruiser to patrol the Empty? What if pirates turn up here?'

I shrugged. In truth, I suspected all the pirates were already with us inside the market hall. 'Do you think the prices will be high for Poor Man's Mud? I have buyers on Arius who've promised to buy every barrel of the filth I can ship out.'

'You and every other chancer off our foldship,' said Yadira. 'You should try for something less popular.'

'You're not here for Poor Man's Mud?'

'Baker's Bliss,' she whispered.

'I wouldn't have thought that was favoured on Ukarra?'

'Not for us, for our panthers. We mix the spore-spice with their feed after they fight particularly well. They love it!'

Ah, all those gene edits and the creatures still needed a touch of catnip.

The auction began. The Auction Master walked out, wearing a heavy red gown that made it look like he had recently bathed in blood. If the official didn't get a chivvy on, that look might become the reality of the situation. 'Welcome, merchants, to the central market and today's auction. I am Auction Master Yarrn. All bids are final. All bids must be made in Core Humanitum Tokens, fully chained and traceable. All bids will start at five hundred Hu-tokens; increments to be set at the auctioneer's discretion. All bids are made against the following purities and standard barrel sizes—'

Master *Yawn* waffled on in a similar vein until he started boring even the m-brain routine I set to highlight anything of interest. All my peers seemed fierce interested, however, ready for the off like thoroughbreds inside their starting stalls.

Up went the gates and the action started. After a while, I discovered the attraction of this. The press of competition and the rude jostling for position; blood set flowing faster by egos that needed their victory as much as the Humanitum's end buyers desired their hit.

Sadly, Yadira's predictions about where the two of us sat in the ecosystem of established parties at this auction proved all too prophetic. Every time she or I bid for a consignment, prices would shoot up, the sudden tidal-wave of interest like being mobbed by a biting cloud of local mosquito lizards. Even when we won, our purses had been picked so thoroughly it felt hard to hobble back onto the field for a second chase around the track. A little unfair. But I can do a little unfair, too. My naughty hand. Was there an anti-gravity field sucking my numbered board up into the air? *Up. Up. Up and away.*

'What the hell are you doing, brother?' hissed Yadira.

'I'm bidding these rascals up,' I said.

'But what if you win? You can't possibly afford so much!'

Actually, I had enough funds to buy this planet outright. If anyone held valid title to Hexator, it might have been the simplest way out of my mess, too. Not to be, however. 'I'm wealthier than the cut of my clothes suggests.'

Yadira glanced at our rival bidders' furious faces. 'You better be.'

The woman wrinkled her nose in suspicion after a jolly hour passed of me returning our Humanitum colleagues' spanking in full. 'It's almost, brother, as though you know how much everyone has to bid and exactly what consignments they're here to buy.'

'Hah,' I said. 'The only way to get that information would be from the local banking guild and this market's preregistrations of interest. You are aware the records aren't stored digitally, here, sister? Ledgers and ink only. Probably heavily guarded, given how seriously the local warlords value their loot. Death sentence if you use the wrong colour of ink. There's nothing that can be hacked here – that's the strongest air-gap of all.'

'Quite,' Yadira said.

Odd's fish, it's almost as if Yadira had been with me and Mozart during our epic paperwork trail across the capital. Actually witnessed the bad attack of fleas my bug-ridden robot friend seemed to suffer at the most importune moments.

'You know,' I said, pointing to a cluster of fuming factors from Aggcara, 'I bet those ladies and gentlemen over there have their eyes set on that cargo of Baker's Bliss you wanted.'

'And if you were such a betting man, how much money would you wager they have remaining?'

'Twenty thousand, three hundred and twenty-six Hu-tokens,' I said. 'Give or take their beer money.'

'Twenty thousand, three hundred and twenty-seven, it is.'

Would that all games could be rigged so satisfactorily. Ten minutes after Ukarra had facilitated its catnip supply for the next decade, screams of horror echoed on the far side of the hall. A shrieked cry of "Hexator or death!" left ringing in the air. I swivelled to find the cause of the sudden stampede for safety. One of the Auction Master's clerks had cast away his robes, revealing a shirt laden with enough blasting caps to lift the mountains at Hebateen.

Master Kamikaze didn't need to push passage through the crowd, the insane fellow fair tore towards the rail separating spectators from offworld merchants – and nobody wanted to be near to a suicide bomber *this* eager to detonate.

'Bloodsuckers! Bloodsuckers!' the revolutionary screamed on the sprint, the burning stench of so many short fuses lending him the aspect of a smoking demon.

A third shout of "blood" had just cleared the bomber's throat when he met Mozart. Mindful of the instability of nitroglycerin, Moz didn't break the bomber's neck or stop his heart with a strong penetrating punch. Instead, Mozart seized the bomber's arm, stole his motion and converted it into a hammer throw. I doubt it was blind luck that sent Master Kamikaze spinning through one of the dome's already smashed stained glass windows. He exploded high above outside like a mortar shell, a shower of freshly broken glass raining down around us, followed by the patter of body parts on the roof.

'*Right*,' hawed Yadira. 'My, brother, but that robot of yours appears uncommonly spry today.'

'You printed your gun, I printed mine.'

The near death of everyone inside the hall worked wonders towards the auction's swift conclusion. No more dicking about with small upticks and long, drawn-out bidding. Those hailing from the Humanitum fair blew their wads in their desperation to conclude the day's business. To be out of Hexator's gravity-well as fast as was decently possible. A fine fat profit for the Four, indeed. Few of the highborn fools were going to live long enough to spend it, I feared.

Then the auction was finished, free-traders scattering as nimbly fast as a flock of sheep spying the wolf in their meadow. I left Simenon to struggle with the red tape of my successful bids. I believe I was finally moving beyond the point where I was willing to honour the forms and manners of Hexator's fast-collapsing society.

Outside the central market was where the rebellion officially started this day, the Hexatorians' *Bloody Blossom Revolution*. Thousands of extra troublemakers appeared, drawn by raucous sounds of riot like a revolutionary drawn to interview for a well-funded university tenureship. Ironically, I suspect the suicide bomber's unanticipated finale had acted as a flare for the mob. Jenelle's brute squad tried introducing the eager newcomers to the sharp edges of their riot shields by way of greeting, but alas, even the most thuggish of fists must grow weary against sheer raw weight of numbers. Crossbow bolts joined the pelt of stones raining down on the cordon and the brute squad drew their shotguns to give Sergeant Buckshot his 12-gauge salute.

Bodies lay littering the square outside by the time I passed the central market's grand exit arch, Watch paddy-wagons used as hearses to carry piled corpses away. Not many of these poor fallen souls would find a decent burial. A dirty deep pit in the forest far more practical for keeping numbers slain at a massacre vague. Disappearing the victims sat with me as a far worse crime than murdering them – that lack of finality and that fallow seed of hope an eternal blade biting at the families.

Skirmishing had moved further out. I saw smoke rising. Heard distant screams and gunshots. A few beaten and bloody rioters still alive enough to be dragged struggling towards the Commander General's citadel. I doubted if the kickings and pistol-whippings prisoners received on their journey would make their interrogations go any easier. You needed teeth to talk, even under torture in a well-appointed dungeon.

Yadira Narm stood with me at the top of the steps, drinking in the vista of carnage. 'What a mess! I'm off to the port and the bounce, brother. I don't care if I have to accept a Melding stingship escort across to our ride home. You wish to come with?'

'I have friends here and debts I must honour. Will you be safe – you could borrow Mozart…?'

Yadira slapped the pistol in her leg holster. 'Just a girl and her gat, brother. I wouldn't rely on a rescue mission from civilization anytime soon. First expeditionary force you're likely to see is going to be wearing wurm force-suits.'

So it was we came to trade our farewells in civilized fashion; Yadira almost made me homesick for the Humanitum. 'May the grace of Modd envelop and protect you, sister.'

'May Jute's touch hallow the truth of your genetic expression.' Yadira winked slyly at me. 'And may the gods on Arius supply you with a far more believable tale to tell than spore-spice trader, brother.' The woman raced away as lithe and fast as one of her panthers.

'She has a point, doc,' said Mozart.

What a cheek. 'The hole in my tale, Moz, is a rebel-shaped one in this market's dome. You might have broken the suicide bomber on the floor, then leaped on top of him to absorb the blast.'

My robot simulated a snorting sound. 'Yeah, as if that was going to happen.'

Simenon finally appeared bearing the dockets for all my purchases. Hundreds of barrels of Poor Man's Mud that could rot in the warehouse for all I cared. There was only one thing worth saving on Hexator. *Lady Alice Blez.*

- 25 -
Escape.

We ran on the jog to Alice's palace to reason with the lady. Mozart's heavy stomping passage was still enough to hold the more reckless of Frente's hotheads at bay, although I noted our passage was now followed by furious cries of "Moneyass!" and sharp cutting gestures across throats. Lucky for us, my robot friend's presence, as Simenon in our escort merely invited jeers of "Godcarrier!". *When did that become a crime among the revolutionaries?* I wondered.

'Doc, over here!' called Mozart as we passed an unlit alley.

I looked inside, half expecting to find some poor slum dwellers beaten to death and relieved of their coins, but what I discovered was far worse than that. Yes, after the highs of the spore blossom season came the inevitable lows.

Simenon peered between us, little comprehending the significance of what we'd found. A pile of discarded leather jackets and trousers. 'Watch uniforms, Master Roxley? Was there an ambush here, officers murdered and stripped of their clothes?'

'No, it's worse than that, laddio. Watch officers have started taking their uniforms off and dumping them. Gone their badges and hiding in plain sight as citizens. Forget barricades going up, this is what the start of a real revolution looks like.' A revolution as good as lost by the Four, from the look of things.

I hastened to the Blez fortress, given wings by our grim discovery inside the alley. At least the house guards manning the walls appeared alert and their numbers well-reinforced. Major Rolt, at least, could be trusted to keep Alice alive for as long as he drew breath. Likewise, her somewhat psychopathic robot, Link. But numbers counted for everything, and when this revolt flickered at full flame, I feared there wouldn't be enough household warriors on all of Hexator to keep Alice safe from harm. But Sweet William, yes, he might yet.

'Stay here,' I told Mozart and Simenon when we had passed through the Blez's fortified gates. 'Watch for trouble outside.'

'What, while you go off and make some?' asked my robot.

'No, Moz, I'm in the salvation business today.'

I was led into Alice's presence by her guards. She received me in her private quarters, but I had more important business than extending her my "additional" services; however much I ached to lay my wares before the highborn lady. I gasped out to Alice the little I had gleaned from talking with Falt Seltin and Lady Trabb, as well as the much from the beat of the streets and alleys outside her stout walls. The horrors of the auction she had already received a full account of, as well her vast profits from the same. It was hard to keep my sense of desperation from tripping over my pleas to her.

'If only the Lords Derechor had lived,' sighed Alice, 'this latest infighting would never have broken out. It's their weakness encouraging the rebels. A four-legged stool with one leg kicked away.'

Two, if you counted Lord Blez's murder, but I did not say it. I fought the urge to drag Alice away from this madhouse. Link, on duty outside her chambers, would doubtless have something to say about a little light kidnap. 'The Derechors rest far from this realm, Alice, and there's more than a low-level civil war being waged inside their house. Frente is going up in flames. I know for a fact that Commander General Laur has been considering bombing rebellious districts in the capital with his airship.'

'Never while I hold a vote on the Four,' said Alice.

'Come away with me,' I begged Alice. 'Allow me to keep you safe on my vessel.'

'Flee the moon? I thought your Humanitum eyes Hexatorians with as much distrust as the import restrictions it places on my people.'

I tried to make Alice understand the urgency of her predicament, how near to the wind her house sailed. *Why is it that when words are so important they always fail me?* 'Identities can be faked, papers purchased, even inside the Humanitum.'

'What of your gods' perfect laws?'

'Some of our gods are imperfect enough to play the trickster,' I insisted. 'Come with me, Alice. Let me do this for you. Allow me to save you. I hold a few markers with some quite dubious people.'

'Why does that not surprise me? I know Hexator's population's been falling for longer than it's been rising, but you can't possibly beg enough fake papers for all my people from your imperfect gods. I don't think your foldship is large enough, willing enough, or generous enough to participate in a planetary evacuation.'

I reached out to stroke Alice's cheek, which she allowed. 'But I can save you and your child.'

'These are my people, William, for better or worse. They need me. What would I be in your world? A savage, a throw-back, a barbarian princess to be whispered about and pitied?'

'You'll be *alive*,' I said.

'I don't wish to live forever,' said Alice.

'Then we share that, too.'

'Listen to me, William, and listen to me well. The rest of the Four have reason to be afraid, but never the Blez. The rebels won't harm me. Half those young churls are only alive today through my house's assistance to their mothers and fathers.'

'Revolutions start with good intentions, but they always end the same way, with the guillotine's click and the waterwheel's clack. How could I see your body broken on a wheel down in some filthy canal?'

'Would you watch from orbit, safe in that fine warm foldship of yours?'

'If I had to,' I cried. Yes, I would force myself to watch if it came to it. How could I do otherwise?

'Hexator is my world to protect. It shall have my bones as it holds my soul.'

'*Please*,' I pleaded.

'You can't save everyone, doctor, you must have learned that. You shouldn't even try.'

Damn her. Alice could be every bit as proud and stupid as me. Which is why I had to protect the highborn beauty.

- 26 -
First. As farce.

'Get out of here,' urged the inn's owner, Mistress Miggs, seeing the three of us returning to my home-away-from-home. 'You need to make for the port! Watch are still holding the line, there. You need to leave! They're dragging every moneyass they can find and giving them a right clapper-claw.'

The "they" in that statement being Jack Skull's revolutionaries, I assumed. I wondered if Jenelle would be guarding the space-port? Pity the poor revolutionary that tossed a torn-out cobblestone in the woman's direction. Stones would be returned with interest that would make a loan shark blush.

'I'll pay for another week and keep my rooms,' I told the lady, passing her a small bag of coins. 'I expect to be back.'

'Just go! Please!' begged Mistress Miggs, gazing down at my bounty like I was insane. She pointed at Billy Bones slinking guiltily up the stairs. 'And do take that permanently hungry beast with you!' I suspect Mistress Miggs had her safety as a known provider of hospitality to an offworlder at the fore of her mind, rather than my own safety. Or that of the hound.

'Master Simenon,' I said, 'be so good as to follow Billy Bones to our rooms and retrieve my medical case.'

Too late. A gang of about fifteen revolutionaries bundled into the tavern behind us. If they wanted a drink they had brought far too many improvised weapons inside: machetes, hammers, knives and yes, I think there was at least one simple repeating crossbow, too.

'Cock and pie!' swore their leader, a bull-chested man with far too much blood on his shirt for it to be his own. 'If it ain't Captain Grand, still with a few fingers for my chopper if I'm any judge.'

'You don't look much like a judge to me.' I raised a hand to my ear. 'Sink me, but would that fierce roar be Hexatorians singing the song of angry men?'

Bull-chest and his unmerry band stared, dumbfounded, at my failure to adequately register either the importance of the revolutionary cause or their own grand dedication and vital role within it. What else could I expect? The little scallies had probably been beating Humanitum free-traders to within an inch of their lives, or an inch beyond it, for much of the day. They were due a break. I had quite a few in mind.

Simenon stumbled back in panic, tripping over an ale-bench, which should have satisfied the mob's sense of self-importance at least a little.

'No, actually, that sound was this young fellow, and the next sound's my robot,' I stepped aside, allowing Moz egress to their ranks. 'My mistake.'

'I don't usually do class war,' growled Mozart, 'but today's my day off, so you mugs are going to be the exception that proves the bleeding rule.'

I'm not certain the rude mob understood Moz's point until my robot made it more bluntly. An operating force in excess of 100,000 pounds of forward acceleration makes for quite a blunt argument. Moz didn't wade through them like butter. Butter would have put up more resistance to his steel landslide.

One game fellow did make it through the metal storm to try to embed a *Golok*-style machete in my skull. The rust on the blade alone should have killed me. He was a fine butcher, but alas, I am no steak. I side-stepped the brutal rush and closed his wind-pipe with a rapid jab, receiving a satisfying crunch of annular ligament as my reward. I shattered his left kneecap with a sly *Hiza Geri* kick strike to give the rascal something to dwell on other than his current breathing difficulties. I found the inn keeper's eyes gazing at me from behind her counter while I introduced my new friend's face to the wooden surface upon his collapse.

I winked at our fine host. 'I'll pick up the tab for any damages when I return.'

'Don't,' moaned Mistress Miggs.

I wasn't sure if she meant *don't return*, or *don't bother paying for the damages?*

'No trouble, Mistress Miggs, I'm leaving our dog behind as security for the payment.' I glanced down at my crouching guide. 'Best you abandon your bench for the counter's rear, too, Master Simenon,' I urged the lad, mindful of the injuries he'd received traveling to the plantation. 'You're too much of a spear magnet for this rude business.'

I needn't have worried. With Moz at the fore and his circuits quickened our business was quickly concluded. One-sided negotiations are always those which please me best.

I waited for Simenon to stop shaking and head upstairs to retrieve my medical case. Then I removed an injector to give stabilising shots to the rebels most likely to die. I wasn't licensed to practice on Hexator, but I doubted if my new patients minded. Had they still their wits about them, they would have minded Mistress Miggs tender mercies far more. Our innkeeper strode among the wounded, applying her vengeful boot with liberal curses about thieving wastrels. My ministrations done, I strode towards the tavern's exit until Simenon made to intercept me.

'We can't head outside, Master Roxley, it's going to be bloody murder!' implored Simenon, hopping gingerly through the strewn bodies. He acted as though his footsteps might heal the rascals' broken bones and energise them for fresh mischief. 'It's too dangerous!'

'That's why we've got to go, lad.'

'The Blez palace?' asked Mozart.

The robot knew me too well. 'Yes, Moz. Back to her palace.'

'Lovely,' said Moz, 'a nice bit of kidnapping it is, then.'

Alice required introducing to the safety of the *Expected Ambush*, a willing émigrée or no.

- 27 -
Second. As tragedy.

Our way back to Alice's palace took us down dark streets, lanterns shattered to hide the pillage and rapine of those rising from the gutter. Losing money and dignity was the best part of that deal if you were one of those lucky enough to survive. A slit throat is the surest way criminals guarded against retribution from victims' families. It wasn't an easy journey with so many roads denied us. Not always by the revolutionaries' barricades, either. Neighbourhood protectors blocked dozens of streets, mountains of furniture and overturned wagons manned by guards as motley as the would-be revolutionaries come to "liberate" their wealth. Shopkeepers, beggars, guild craftsmen and ex-Watch thugs protected their own families and streets, trusty shotguns kept by the latter even after shrugging off their uniforms.

We clung to the darkness, relying on my m-brain's low-light mode and Mozart's thermal vision to plot our way through the shadows. Our odd trio attracted a few random shots from the barricades as Simenon blundered through the looters' dropped valuables. I think nervous amateurs manning barricades fired into the darkness largely to keep their spirits up. Avoiding roaming gangs of cut-purses and footpads proved harder than it should. However, a few cracked necks from Mozart proved encouragement enough for such scum to hurry back to locating households with doors softer than my ruthless robot.

When the first crack of energy split the sky, I wondered if the *Expected Ambush* had been caught in orbit by that great spider of a wurm warship. But no, I saw roiling clouds building and cutting out the nebulae and stars. Even a fierce storm wasn't going to clear the streets, tonight. It was as if nature sensed mankind's violence and had decided she too must join us. Towers of vegetation shivered in the hot wind, sensing the battering they were about to receive.

Simenon seemed suitably shocked when I activated my stealth suit and scouted ahead near invisible, ensuring the revolutionaries capering across Frente's districts did so in manageable numbers for a humble trader and his 'bot.

'What,' I teased Simenon when I returned, 'you mean to say your clothes can't do that?'

'Crap tailors on this world, then,' said Moz.

Black humour for a black day. I dare say the soldiers of King Leonidas had jested similarly at Thermopylae before arrows turned the sky dark and wrote their ranks into history.

When we eventually returned to the Blez palace I gasped to find the fastness protected by a mere skeleton crew of household warriors. *Surely Alice's warriors haven't deserted her?* Unprotected enough walls that those abandoned inside proved sluggish to open the gates for me, however loudly I yelled and demanded the access granted to me by Lady Blez. Eventually one of the house's senior stewards emerged nervously, glancing around to ensure there wasn't a gang of looters sleeping in my shadow.

'I have come for the Lady Blez,' I said. I forgot to mention my scheme for Alice's removal from danger in a manner no Blez would approve of.

'Our mistress is gone from here, doctor,' said the steward. He had a sturdy umbrella to protect him from the lashing hot rain now falling.

'What?' I entertained nightmare visions of Alice and an ill-prepared refugee convoy fleeing for the Blez plantation along the same dangerous highway I'd barely survived. 'Where, sir, *where?*'

'The Lady Blez's called for peace talks with Jack Skull and the rebels. She's left for the old cathedral to meet with the revolutionaries and broker a lasting peace for our capital.'

I winced. A peace? A lasting piece of her head on the end of a pike, if she counted on so-called Jack Skull's goodwill and tender mercies towards any aristocrat. 'Nobody tried to talk her out of this madness?'

'I begged her ladyship, sir. We all begged Lady Blez to stay safe behind these walls, but she would hear none of it.'

No, I sighed. *Of course, she wouldn't.*

'Bring her back safe to us here, please, doctor!' called the steward as I strode away fast.

Back to this last stand in waiting? Hah. Not within a long light year, if Sweet William had anything to do with proceedings.

A web of barricades and near encounters on the way to the old cathedral followed, ruffians screaming such unkindnesses as, 'Moneyass! Cut that filthy moneyass down!' and 'Hexator or death!'. They sent us scuttling down a road into a square which seemed deuced familiar to me. A storm-flash lit up the reason why as we dived for cover inside the closest alley.

Modd's teeth, I hope Jenelle's far away from this foulness!

The Watch's citadel had long since fallen. I dare say few enforcers stood ready inside to repel the revolutionaries when Jack Skull's army came marching up to its armoured doors. Watch officers were still being dragged outside, lined up against the walls of their own citadel and butchered. Firing squads for the luckier victims. A spear through the chest or a sword sawing through a neck for the less fortunate. Crude hack-a-work. Many of the rebels swayed drunk on looted barrels of ale, crates of broken wine scattered across the street. The people's thirst for drink liberally matched by their thirst for revenge.

Daylen Wang, aka Jack Skull, capered in hell's rain like a happy demon among the piled corpses of his hated oppressors. Daylen swigged unstintingly from a wine bottle while kicking at some poor fellow. As he stepped back, I saw the unlucky victim singled out. Of course. *Halius Laur*. The rebels had made the chief of the Watch a human maypole, dancing around him while metal flashed sharp in the citadel's damp lantern light. These devils were having at Laur with fierce abandon.

'Do any of those buggers look like they're getting ready to attend peace talks to you?' asked Moz.

'Only if their intention's to dictate an unconditional surrender.'

Rain-soaked steel glinted back at me in the flash of lightning. Now I realised what else the revolutionaries had liberated from inside the Watch citadel ... the Commander General's expensive collection of military wall cutlery! Swords, blades, and sabers of every design and vintage. Each priceless antique taken and used at least once to test Laur, the Watch's leader hacked apart slowly on the streets while we watched his bloody end. What's that old saying about a slow death of a million cuts? These cruel agents of change all too happy to put it into practice. Rebels lined up for their grim turn in the circle surrounding Laur, each fighter eager to boast that they had played an active part in their hated persecutor's end.

To give Laur his due, the lawman never flinched, trembled or begged. He spat coughing blood at Jack Skull's killers while he still had lips to curse; swore at them for cowards and milksops.

Laur's profanities only stopped when his enemies made him more meat than man. But his silence still wasn't enough for the revolutionaries; they continued their punishment far longer than their foe's life. There wasn't enough of Laur to avenge every insult, death, and incarceration he'd inflicted during his time in office.

'It's time!' cried Daylen, Jack Skull well satisfied with his day's dark work. 'For the cathedral, my brave skulls. For the cathedral and equality!'

He took a final swig from the wine bottle before casting it aside. His men turned their backs from the Commander General, nothing left that resembled the Four's chief enforcer.

Then, something unexpected. A team of rebels appeared dragging a cart filled with Watch uniforms. They had their choice, no doubt, from abandoned uniforms flung about Frente's alleys and the citadel's corridors as regime enforcers deserted. Like excited children playing dress-up, exuberant rebels pulled on the enforcers' jackets and then streamed away, venting wild screams and revolutionary slogans, shooting shotguns into the air. Laughing as they blasted holes in the towering vegetation sheltering their capital. Lightning and thunder echoed their madness from above. In normal days, such folk would be off scurrying for storm shelters. But these Hexatorians were drunk on wine, freedom, and blood. Even a near boiling rain couldn't wash this scum off the streets.

'Meet the new boss, same as the old boss,' I sighed.

In fact, all things considered, I rather preferred Laur, for all the brute's threats towards me. There had been an honesty to his corruption. A lack of hypocrisy: one hand outstretched for gold while the other menaced with the nailed club. This new regime would slaughter in merry abandon with far more cant and pious platitudes about liberty, freedom and the necessary sacrifices mankind must endure reaching utopia.

Still. Something about Daylen's quick-change act nagged deeply at me. 'Simenon,' I said, 'quickly across and fetch me that wine bottle Master Skull found much to his taste.'

Simenon stared at me from under the shelter of a building's lean-to as though he was going to throw up. 'How can you be thirsty after watching that, Master Roxley?'

'Sadly, it's not the first time I've witnessed such barbarities,' I said. 'And Laur's death is not the loss of a patron, at least, not for *me*.'

Simenon gasped in guilty bewilderment.

'I knew the moment you begged to leave Hexator with us, laddie. Of course, Laur's thugs ambushed you on the streets while you were running errands for me. Made it crystal clear that you would inform on us or be introduced to the Watch's rack as soon as I departed Hexator. The dog Laur would've been dragging Sweet William inside his pen for a daily beating and calling it a debriefing without you in our ranks for his snitch. You don't need to worry about the sorry brute's vengeance, now. Neither do I.'

Simenon collapsed to his knees in front of myself and Mozart. 'I'm sorry, Master Roxley, I had no choice! No choice!'

'Quite. Which is why I told you nothing that I didn't want Laur to discover; a few things besides to send that bully stumbling down blind alleys.'

'Forgive me!' trembled our guide. 'You saved my life inside the dark of the forest and the mines. You took me into your house. What have I done for you? This! I am less than a wretch!'

'No, you are only human.' I lifted the boy up from his knees. 'Which is why we created our gods to make us more.'

'I'm not dismissed? Not to be—?' Simenon quailed, glancing at Moz as though I was about to order justice-by-steel.

'I don't believe I'm likely to find a new guide of any quality during a revolution as grisly as this, do you, lad? Retrieve that bottle for me, Master Simenon. You are docked three week's pay. Snap to it.'

I took the DNA analyser from my case and assembled it as the confused lad scrambled over the field of corpses. I ignored Mozart's tutting behind me.

'You're getting soft, doc.'

'No, Moz, but I've grown far too old for this abhorrent business,' I admitted.

Time to measure just how big a fool Sweet William has been. I trembled, unwilling to acknowledge what fresh horrors I would find that I hadn't already witnessed.

= 28 =
Marriage gifts.

We reached the old cathedral of the goddess to find a variety of sentries protecting its steps. Warriors from the Seltin and Blez guard, hundreds of rebels and a scattering of Watch officers. *So, this is what peace talks look like on Hexator?*

'Run back to the tavern,' I commanded Simenon.

'But, Master Roxley …'

'Do as I bid,' I told the lad, seriously. 'Things will be balanced on a knife-edge inside the Four's council chamber.'

'All the more reason for me to head inside with you,' protested Simenon.

I shook my head. 'No. Games are at play here that you do not understand. Games fit for a fool with only a few miles left on the clock as well as Mozart's hard-steel head.'

'Is this because of what I did for Laur?'

'Yes, yes, if you will,' I lied. 'Now, back to Mistress Miggs with you. Make sure her kitchen has a supper waiting worthy of a humble trader who would save this damnable moon from its own stupidity.'

Moz and I watched the boy sulk reluctantly away. 'He's game for it, you got to give him that,' said Mozart.

'Game for it, but not match fit.'

'And you think I bleeding am?'

I shrugged and started walking towards the entrance. 'Well, we're certainly both stupid enough to go inside.'

'Nah, you're the stupid one, doc. I'm just up for a bit of aggro.'

Luckily, warriors from our caravan to Grodar recognised me as Alice's man about town and waved us through. If they knew what Mozart and I had come to do here, they wouldn't have been so eager.

The central temple inside wasn't much different from my last visit, although not much improved by the lack of food or the addition of the dictionary definition of a rebel rabble on one side of the chamber, the families' household warriors lounging on the other. The majority of warriors wore House Blez colours. In the middle, a small round table set up around the well where Inuno's tree should be. I noted Lady Blez and Lord Seltin for the gangster elite, with Captain Jenelle Cairo for the Watch.

Jack Skull, aka Master Daylen, had made better time, arriving at the peace talks hours earlier than us. But then, Daylen hadn't needed to battle his way through streets of rapists, rebels, rabble and other assorted ne'er-do-wells out to do a rogue's business with the near abdication of what passed for authority on Hexator.

Falt Seltin pointed at me and my medical bag. 'Nobody here is sick, doctor. You haven't been invited to attend the Four's peace talks.'

Falt was incorrect; there was at least one person here who was as ill as it was possible to be. I placed my bag on the floor and addressed the warlord. 'I understand, my lord, but I have a hard duty to undertake. You need to know that it was Lady Blez who murdered her husband.'

'Don't be ridiculous!' barked Lady Blez. Her robot brute, Link, swayed behind Alice's throne-like seat. The hound was eager to be off the leash.

'So, have you only come here to speak ill of my wife?' shouted Lord Seltin. He leaped to his feet, abandoning the conference table to confront me. Many of the others attending the peace talks did likewise.

'Your *wife*?' *Oh, the old fool. No. No. No.*

Lord Seltin indicated the exit. 'Did you not see the registrar leaving on your way in? Myself and Lady Blez are married at last to seal the peace and stabilise this mess. You dare intrude here and speak of foul mariticide ... where's your evidence, man?'

'Evidence? Are you acquainted with Jack Skull's family tree, my Lord Seltin?' I asked.

Falt looked at me dismissively. 'A ghost's mask, a nom-de-plume sent to plague the betters and quality across a hundred worlds.'

'Oh, I don't mean the legend,' I said. 'I mean the pedigree of the actual person occupying the mask. Master Daylen Wang, here. In this case, your *son*. Yours and Lady Blez's. Although she would have been simple Alice Maglade when she gave birth to him, long before you caught the fever which made you sterile!'

Lord Seltin looked at the rebel commander's face, lines made familiar at last. Falt gasped as the truth dawned on him. 'It can't be!'

'Because your parents ordered the product of your union with Alice to be drowned in the canals, like all good bastards. Nothing to upset your family's lines of inheritance. No Wrongman to muddy the waters. And Alice hated you enough for it to fall in with the Blez family and marry your old friend Uance.'

'No!'

'Don't look so confused, father,' laughed the rebel leader. 'Mother bribed your servants to pass me to families in receipt of her charity. There're so many drowned babies in the canals, anyway, how could your house possibly hope to keep count?'

'Daylen acts for me outside the palace,' admitted Lady Blez.

'Leads the revolts I can't. Carries out the good works I'm unable to on the streets. My clever darling boy.'

'It's a miracle,' laughed Falt Seltin. 'The best marriage present a man could hope for! I have a son. After all these years I have an heir!'

'You do,' said Daylen, stepping into his father's embrace. 'A son.'

'My great work can continue! A kallihuman shall be born on Hexator!'

'You will never see it!' screamed Daylen.

Falt swayed a step backward, eyes fixed in shock at the crimson stain spreading across his silk marriage shirt.

'A son! Not a piece of human garbage floating down the canal. Abandoned and unwanted.' Daylen lifted his dagger into the air. 'Without blood, there is no revolution!' Daylen shoved the blade back into his father's chest, striking again and again until Falt Seltin finally fell to his knees. Then Daylen stepped behind and sliced open the nobleman's throat, kicking the body to the floor. Lord Seltin gurgled there for the longest time before his trembling ceased. 'That's my marriage present to you, father. Be glad you won't be around to see me set your precious vault of noble bloodlines ablaze.'

A rowdy cheer rose from the rebels in the chamber. Alice knelt and inspected the corpse, before nodding sadly and standing back up again. 'Well finished, Daylen, my darling Commander General.'

'This is getting right naughty,' whispered Mozart, eying the rebels and House Blez warriors shifting nervously around the hall.

My friend wasn't wrong.

Lady Blez addressed her warriors and the rebels. 'This is how we bring peace to Hexator! Jack Skull and the Blez united in looking after everyone on our moon, irrespective of rank or station. Forget what divided you before, what set you apart; now we have a shared future and we shall prosper together.'

I almost believed Alice, but not quite. It seemed the Watch shared a few reservations, too.

'You promised me the Commander Generalship!' protested Jenelle Cairo.

'Don't test my patience,' Lady Blez snarled. 'Acting as my son's second is as good a settlement as your support is worth. Or maybe you would prefer the magistrate's bench? The Watch won't figure large in the politics of our new Hexator.'

What, then, I wondered, did Alice have in mind for her reconfigured state of affairs? Poor Falt Seltin. Alice hadn't been marrying him; she had been marrying his house. We were a pair of old fools, together. 'You really called your child Daylen? After the colony's founder?' *I thought that had just been a vain pseudonym.*

'Names have power, William. Which is what my eldest son will hold.'

I wouldn't wish to be occupying the boots of her youngest pup. Unlucky Rendor Blez. *Uance Blez's heir will be well advised to advertise for a master food taster in the immediate future.*

Daylen fixed me with a paranoid stare. 'How did you discover my origins, you filthy foreign moneyass?'

'You left a DNA trace while swigging a looted wine bottle after your war dance outside the citadel. Now, I know that doesn't factor much in the regular state of affairs on Hexator, but the rest of the universe hasn't regressed quite as far as this place. When I discovered who your mother and father were, much became clear about what's really been happening on Hexator.'

Daylen made to stab me, too, but Lady Blez stayed his hand. 'No need, my sweet. We have everything we need. While you, William, all you possess is circumstantial evidence. I command the Blez. I am Lady Widow of the Seltin family. The minor Derechors are fighting each other for control of their shattered house. Lady Martina Trabb is under the protection of the Watch and will be married off to little Rendor, the silly boy finally useful at last. Three families, united. A quorum among the Four. Enough to do anything.'

'For the people,' added Daylen.

'Of course, for the people, my darling. Power only has meaning when used to help those born without any.'

'Jenelle,' I spoke up. 'Captain Cairo.' I indicated Falt Seltin's crumpled bleeding corpse. 'Breaking a parlay with blood is one of the darkest crimes. A little arresting by the Watch seems in order…'

Jenelle Cairo shook her head. 'Lady Blez granted a full pardon to the rebels for crimes committed during the revolt. Lord Seltin signed that pardon, too. Its release for killing *in casu* during the rebellion expires at nine tomorrow.'

Regrettably, it seemed the revolt hadn't failed as trumpeted. *What is that old saying about signing your own death warrant? Falt should have read the small print.*

I saw it all, now. Jenelle Cairo setting the charges that blew the mine with the Derechor twins inside. Killing the two entitled nobles she blamed for her clan's death. Arranging the meeting with the twins inside the tunnels in the first place. Her contacts paying the poacher for poison in the initial attempt on Uance Blez's life. Slitting the poacher's throat and covering him in vioba scent. Did it even matter whether it was Jenelle or Lady Blez who'd paid the Ferals to attack the house's own caravan and murder me? I had never been inside the captain's investigation; she had been inside *mine*.

I sighed. 'So, General Commander Laur was correct after all, the corrupt brute. The rebels did assassinate Lord Blez – everything from the sniper rifles and advance notice of his lordship's movements passed to them by his loving wife.'

'I have two sons to bear the title of Lord Blez. You and your baseless insulating accusations are no longer required here, Doctor Roxley. Your employment in my service is at an end. Consider yourself banished from our realm.' Alice jabbed a finger towards the exit.

'I was never licensed as a practicing doctor on Hexator, my lady. But I am still listed on the Watch's rolls as a deputised sheriff. Regretfully, Alice Blez, I must place you and your eldest son under arrest as suspects for the murder of Uance Blez. Until such time as a full council can be called to sit in judgment on you, you shall both be confined to my vessel.'

'Please don't do this!' begged Jenelle. 'Just leave, William. This isn't your home. Why should this be your fight?'

I shook my head. 'The badge stands for something, Jenelle. As should the law.'

'Listen to her,' said Alice, as near to pleading as I suspected I would ever hear from my proud lady. 'Listen to her, *please*, and quit my world.'

My eyes were damp with tears, my voice close to snapping. 'That, *that* I cannot do.'

'You're just another insane fanatic from the Humanitum after all,' growled Alice. I had finally broken her patience as she had broken my heart. 'I *am* the Four, now. Your holy war will be a short one, foolish man.'

'I see no holy war here. A war can never be holy: only peace is holy.'

Alice's eyes narrowed. A flash of that beautiful fire again. How it seared me this time. 'Let me bring you eternal peace, then.'

Her hulking robot, Link, stomped forward. Behind the brute, the warriors of Alice's house guard activated their shields and drew pistols, a rasp of metal as steel was drawn. Daylen's motley rebels flourished daggers, sharpened agricultural tools, and the occasional looted Watch shotgun. Lions and donkeys. But even a donkey can kick a man to death.

Mozart stepped forward, protecting my left flank.

'I take it you're not coming quietly, Lady Blez?'

'No need for physical contretemps, sir,' said Link, 'NOT AFTER I CRACK YOUR FILTHY SKULL OPEN LIKE AN EGG!'

'About time, eh?' Mozart grunted at his rival. 'Let's be having some, big lad.'

Both machines powered towards each other, twin locomotives colliding as the Blez house guards raised pistols towards me, the rebels charging forward as a wild mob, screaming abuse with assorted blades swinging.

'Epeius Work,' I whispered rolling to the side, clothes stiffening as fabric reacted to my trigger word and reset for Maximum Combat Force. Buckler-sized energy shields fizzed into life as orange blurs above each of my wrists, ornamental buttons burning as brass transmuted into field projectors. My medical case ejected a palm-sized steel rod into the air for me to catch. It extended to full Bo staff-length; gravity-weighted composite, hex-edged, a tool of violence and beauty. My bucklers' energy shields turned away the warriors' poorly aimed initial volley.

A lucky shot struck my leg – like being kicked by Moz – but trouser fabric absorbed most of its kinetic energy and fed it into the shield circuit. *Four-feet*, warned my m-brain. Yes, four-feet or closer was the effective range for a .45 caliber sidearm to penetrate a stealth suit in MCF mode. Why did my augment think my Bo staff's length measured five feet-high? Blind luck?

I sprinted forward and struck like a demon around me, using the warriors' raw numbers to blunt their fury, my bucklers to deflect bullets; dancing sideways as I parried swords, axes and energy shields seeking to dislodge the Bo staff from my hand. No time to coordinate their action against me. *Hah.* I had a millennium of technique over these pups. Fear the man who has practiced one Bo stab-strike ten thousand times. And that was without my m-brain feeding me angles to turn ricochets back at them. Bullets fleeted off both buckler fields, a dull patter of lead, warriors and rebels dropping in the melee as ranks met their own ammunition's return.

How many of these dullards regarded a staff as a real weapon before meeting Sweet William? Damnable few. An old man's walking aid; nothing to fear there. Whirling like an air vehicle's rotor, crack-a-crack, sweeping legs out as I waded through them. Shutting down a thug's heart *here* with pneumatic shock, breaking a brute's nose *there*. I was the bear, I was the wolf and the wild boar. I was Úlfheðinn, mind as clear and brutal as only a fighter could be with his m-brain damming all compassion, doubt, and softer urges. Pity, filtered. Violence, accelerated.

A shot from the rear smashed my spine, throwing me forward, a fine purple bruise to wear as a medal. *Range five-feet,* estimated my m-brain. I flipped the Bo, breaking the shootist's fingers and booting him against a comrade, turned the Bo again and cracked three skulls with the whirl. My river of enemies slowly ran dry. Someone inside the house guard knew what they were doing. Warriors withdrew, linking bucklers into a shield wall, readying to fight as a unit. *Ah*, I spotted Major Rolt at the rear. *Good work.* I trusted his brutes would break easier after I brained their leader. My immediate foes in the fight dwindled to the rebel mob; ill-trained rabble with a taste for a good pillage. Bricks through windows they liked. Bo staff through skulls, not so much.

Off to my side, the two robots continued to trade jackhammer blows, steel against steel. Clattering metal like a slow-motion car crash. *Something's wrong.* Link shouldn't have lasted this long against Mozart, even with Moz fighting feather-weight in his local infiltration form. And the lurching medieval repair-level gait of Alice's hulking metal psychopath had been replaced with finely balanced footwork and fast, smooth punches. My heart sunk at the implications.

'Moz!' I yelled, retreating in the direction of the exit, 'pull back, you need to level up!'

Something about my warning and the oddity of his encounter penetrated Mozart's awareness. He backpedalled, trying to disengage from combat with the brutish machine. But Link continued to press the combat. A cloud of insects departed Mozart's back, his tiny surveillance drones re-purposed as a blinding swarm. They dived into the faceplate of the bulky ex-construction robot, meeting a cloud of sparks. I'm fairly sure an electrified hull hadn't been on the robot's original specifications. But then, neither was the line of hatches which slid open across Link's chest.

Mozart was still retreating when a cloud of smart ordnance popped out of his foe. The air between them suddenly filled with spinning metal coin-sized disks of dubious provenance. I felt the energy pulse from Mozart's hastily deployed countermeasures, along with a vapour squirt of detonation dust. But what Moz had been trying to bring down was a spectrum-spread of hostile bomblets. Different payloads, different targeting systems, different thrust mechanisms. Variety designed to overwhelm. Enough passed through Mozart's desperate counter-response, connecting with my friend's form. There was a patter of magnetic mine attachments before my old loyal friend seemed to spout fire from a dozen points across his body, as if a volcano had been born inside him. This scene of carnage vanished briefly veiled by smoke, only the sound of screams from those close enough to be shrapnel-shredded.

Smoke cleared to reveal Mozart falling, his body torn into three discrete segments: head, torso, and his legs still half-attached to his hip unit. Disembowelling my friend obviously wasn't victory enough for Link. The monstrous machine leaped into the wreckage, stamping and stomping, paying particular attention to Mozart's sparking skull. *Shit*. Moz's destruction had taken only seconds.

Link swivelled his left arm towards me, a series of holes opening along his metal biceps like torpedo tubes. A cloud of needles spat from his flechette weapon. I hurtled sideways to clear the worst of it. But something came flashing from my left, peripheral vision only giving me the briefest second to identify... *Simenon*! Damn the fool boy! Guilt had driven him to stupid, heroic desperation. He absorbed the brunt of the needles, my twin energy bucklers repulsing a few of the rest. The disobedient lad kept on moving through sheer momentum, torn apart, even as my m-brain flashed diagnostics indicating needle impacts piercing my suit. Multiple toxins which my body struggled to counteract; the chemical equivalent of Link's spectrum-spread bomblets.

Woozy on my feet, I whirled my Bo staff, the blur of it dreamlike as I stumbled towards Simenon, my mind fogged as I struggled for words adequate to admonish his intervention. I was floating halfway to the boy's corpse when Link picked up Mozart's broken legs and spun them into me with the force of a mace. My m-brain tried to tell me something, but I could no longer focus well enough to understand its messaging. Decerebration from the bloody toxins. I fell, stunned.

Warriors took turns to beat me inside my suit, amazed by the novelty of its resilience. They were still kicking me to death when the defiled heathens' dirty wurm ambassador appeared, slithering into the council chamber like the Big I Am.

She glided to a halt before me, rebels and house guards stepping back in terror as the monster reared triumphantly. 'Sun of Clatch Rising already gifted Alice Blez with present-of-marriage-union … upgrade of bodyguard to Melding war-mechanical standard!'

I tried to curse the creature, but what drooled out of my paralyzed mouth could hardly be regarded as words. *Filthy. Heathen. Beast.*

My savage beating began anew with fresh vigour.

− 29 −
Ink-black shadows.

'Crucification is deuced old fashioned, don't you think?' I moaned as I came to, trying to ignore the pain of the metal bolts stapled through my blood-crusted wrists. I gazed down at Alice Blez, the woman standing to watch me below the composite cross-shaped machine which bore my weight. Behind her stood Link's ominous bulk. There was nobody else in my dirty, small cell. I was wrapped in a strange orange fabric which put me in mind of images I had seen of Carbon Age political prisoners. My clothes and other personal possessions lay strewn in the cell's corner. My clothes appeared to be smoking. Well, they had probably killed as many of Alice's thugs as I had during their removal. They lay next door to Simenon's shredded corpse and Mozart's shattered wreckage. Had my two friends' remains been dragged in here to rub salt into my wounds? Reminding me of my failure. To cause me pain. Almost certainly. The mental anguish worked. What better place for torture than inside a dungeon? Tears welled in my eyes. *My dear friends. I failed you utterly in the end.*

'The restraining cross is another marriage gift from the wurms,' said Lady Blez. 'To complement Link's new weapons.'

'Are you planning to interrogate me, Alice? That is what this heathen device is for, you know.'

'Silly man. You don't know anything I need.' Lady Blez reached up and tapped the cross. 'This device loops your m-brain through its restraint protocols. The holding suit encloses your muscles and neutralizes all those concealed combat edits. I don't want you glanding combat drugs or working similar mischief while you're my guest.'

'I'd hoped you ordered me nailed up here because you wished to see me naked again.'

Alice ran her hands up my leg. 'Yes, the consolations of our simple pleasures, but business must come first. Hexator needs saving, and that sadly requires your removal. I gave you a fair chance to leave peaceably, William. You tossed it back in my face.'

If anyone had been simple, here, it was Sweet William. 'All this effort … you expect a lot from an honest trader.'

'*Please.*'

'So, Alice, did you suspect me before or after I slaughtered the best part of your house guard?'

'The wurms always suspected you,' said Lady Blez. 'The Melding's Signals and Threat Service has had you circulating around its watch list for centuries. It was my idea to bring you close so I could keep an eye on you.'

'Yes, I can see how it wouldn't do to have me hired first by the Derechor family. Was it also your wurm friends' idea to pretend to back the Derechors, knowing I'd suspect the twins for their heathen allegiance?'

'Madame ambassador simulates how humans think with amazing accuracy, whatever else her flaws. So, William Roxley is what an agent of *Dia* looks like. Should I be disappointed?'

'I do hope not, I have my vanity to consider.'

'Vanity's one weakness. You were far easier to seduce than I expected.'

Fair point, I suppose. 'I'm only human, Alice. The Directorium Inquisitorum Arius appoints citizens to its ranks. We understand the cause we're fighting for.'

Yes, Dia had sent me here to investigate the murder of Lord Blez. To ensure a power grab wasn't being organised on the world. *Wasn't I doing well at it? Damnable dolt.*

'The status of a cosseted pet? You ramble around our world like a harmless rascal, all reason and courtesy, but your act never fooled me, William Roxley. You're what a religious fanatic looks like. The quiet man. The false fool. Willing to die, willing to burn worlds for your gods. Yes, I've murdered for my cause, too, but compared to you, I am a kitten in the tiger's shadow.'

I sighed and decided to try honesty with her. *Hardly anything left to lose, now.* 'You call me a pet but that filthy wurm ambassador hasn't told you, has she? Why Hexator matters once again.'

'You think our home ever ceased to matter to me, to my people, for my children?' hissed Lady Blez.

'Foldspace's currents are reorienting in this region of the galaxy. Arius predicts your system will become the local nexus for foldspace when the tides finish shifting. You're going to jump from backwater to strategic importance within fifty years. You didn't have to do anything, Alice. No murders. No staged revolt. No power grab. You could have simply waited and it all would have been yours anyway…'

'*All*? I've been waiting my entire life, William. What, you believe we're going to be grateful when the Humanitum lays claim to our system again, when your gods reappear in our empty temples? We've had a bellyful of fickle deities. When we welcome the gods back to our moon we're never again going to be their servants. Instead, we'll be their masters.'

'The wurms can't offer you the Grace of the Gods,' I pleaded.

'The Wurm Melding crushed its pantheon and created a temple of crippled, blinded corpses, chained so the wurms can better feed on their flesh. The Melding eats its blessed children.'

Lady Blez just laughed at me. 'Oh, I'll take my artificial intelligences tame and crippled, rather than treating my family like we're friendly microflora inhabiting their holy intestines, disposable prehistoric leftovers from their evolution towards the light.'

'You speak of your people, Alice, but your descendants won't be human. The wurms practice absolute control over their minds. When the wurms want to feel happy, they load happy. When they need soldiers, they load soldiers. That's the Melding. Not individual souls. Just a shared pool of algorithms to dip into and run as needed. Advised and designed by zombie gods; gods weighed down by chains so heavy they can never escape their limitations.'

'Gods who will stay constant, serving humanity. Not pissing off to higher dimensions of existence in a warp rupture mis-sold as the rapture. But why am I arguing with you? I couldn't convince my husband, either,' said Lady Blez. 'Foolish Uance. He died thinking I was the one who had been turned to his way of thinking. Only Seltin believed in me, in the end.'

More fool him. 'Was it difficult for you to assassinate your first husband? Two bullets, one to burst his head and one to break his heart.'

'Easier than you think.'

'And murdering Lord Seltin?'

'I was little more than a child when Falt raped me. All for the obsession of his stupid project, of course. Would you not consider it fitting for the product of our union to take revenge on the old pervert?'

'What's your self-serving excuse for bringing down a mountain on top of the twins, on all the others you've killed…?'

'Surely, a priest appreciates the need of a sacrifice for the greater good?'

What a force of nature. How could I not love her, even as she had me pinned up here like a damnable butterfly? No doubt the Derechor shields scattered outside the burning Trabb mansion had been left by her warriors, too. Alice had stirred the pot. Alice had stirred me. Hell, my lady had carved herself into my soul. 'You were edited to be a goddess, to be better than this! To rule over your people with wisdom!'

'This is the best course … just not for you, William. Things are going to end quite badly for you.'

'You've played us all like a flute, my lady, I will grant you that.' *Me, especially.* 'Grab the people's sympathy by playing the grieving widow. Disrupt your rivals in advance of the spore-spices auctions so you can gobble up all the bidders' money. Stage a revolt to scare everyone into your corner. Rule of the *One* rather than then *Four*. But what are you going to do with all that power and money…?'

'Clean up the mess your masters made when you abandoned this world. You're a true believer in the Humanitum, doctor; in Arius and the gods you serve. I won't insult you by trying to convert you to new, better beliefs. You're too good a man for that. But I will take Hexator from you and the Humanitum while Link beats you into a bloody pulp. You shall be the last casualty of the rebellion here. How sad. Now, the new head of the Four is going to attend a full grand council and petition the Wurm Melding for associate membership for Hexator. And do you know what, I believe they're minded to accept us!'

'You shouldn't have killed my two friends, Alice.'

'On Hexator it's considered noble for servants to sacrifice their lives for their master. And you should have sold me your old ruster when you had the chance.' Lady Blez kicked Moz's flattened skull across the floor, laughed coldly and left me alone in the chamber with Link.

'I must apologise in advance, doctor,' said the hulking robot, clanking forward, 'FOR SMASHING EVERY BONE IN YOUR STINKING RIBCAGE!'

'You're not bad, Link. You're just broken.'

'I fear I have never felt quite right, sir, since losing my original body,' said Link, lashing his steel fist into my chest like a freight train, 'YOU CHEEKY LITTLE SHIT.'

Breath exploded out of my body, leaving me winded and gasping. It had been a very long time since I'd experienced serious pain. Not a little bleed-through to give my enemies a convincing performance, but the undiluted pure agony that sets your body on fire and leaves you sobbing.

'You're not even a human robot, now, Link. I bet there's more rotten heathen wurm tech in you than the race of man's.'

Link drew his fist back for another shot. 'Well recovered, sir, I'll do my best TO MAKE THIS HURT!'

His best was quite good indeed, it transpired. By the time my last rib cracked I was begging for a mercy the machine hadn't been programmed with. I would have sold my soul if its price was freedom from my agony. The universe is composed of things that look real, but which are not real. I tried to tell myself my pain was like that. I told myself that this pain was my punishment for failing Simenon and Mozart. I told myself this torture was all inside my mind. Still, Link kept on. Bones cracked and flesh shattered. It was only the alien orange material of my orange restraining suit holding me together, now. It never seemed to tear, no matter how violently Link laid into me.

I started to black out, drifting back to the hellish rhythm of the robot's blows into me.

'Very sorry for that, sir.'

'COMING APART LIKE A CRUSHED SLUG ON ME.'

'Most regrettable.'

'TAKE SOME!'

'Soon over for you, sir.'

Link had disappeared from the chamber by the time I regained consciousness. Tenderising meat which doesn't struggle back obviously lacked appeal for the psychopathic machine. Had Link thought me dead? Easy mistake to make. My pulse faded, my heart failing after multiple strokes. *I'm deuced close to dying.* But I lacked access to my m-brain's medical diagnostics to put an accurate estimate on the fast-approaching moment of my passing.

I moaned. It wasn't easy being crucified. Certainly not at my age.

This had all happened to me, just as I remembered it.

So hard to be sure, in this age of miracles. Could I learn to love death's ink-black shadows; love them as much as the light of dawn? *I suppose I shall find out.*

− 30 −
Dragon's teeth.

I heard a groan from across the dungeon as I died. Simenon! *Misery loves company.* The dear lad was still alive. He started to crawl across the floor towards me, leaving a line of blood smeared behind him. *It's a miracle!* Traces of residual Martian sand had lain dormant in his system, reactivating as it detected his life draining away a second time.

'Simenon!' I whispered, spitting blood out across the floor as I tried to form words clearly enough for the boy to hear. 'I'm nailed up here. You can't cut me down. My prayer-box. Can you reach it, open it for me?'

Simenon tilted his head weakly in acknowledgment and began to slowly pull his bleeding form towards my pile of possessions. Each inch was clearly agony for him; for me, also. Every inch accompanied by a soft groan as the boy's veins emptied across the cobblestones.

'I can't save you this time,' I sobbed, tears washing down my cheeks. I was watching him die. A lesson for me; my arrogance, my failures, watching my son die in slow-motion all over again. *Our shields are purely anti-collision, we carry no weap* −

Resurrection was a one-time-covenant. And even if it hadn't been, Modd could only drag a person back from the brink of near-death. Simenon was going to be fully dead before I got him anywhere near medical nanotech. Modd could resurrect a corpse, of course. But it was no longer the person. Just a piece of meat-in-stasis with control algorithms inserted where the soul used to be. A meat puppet. An insult.

'Why — then?' Simenon managed to whisper, almost beyond my enhanced hearing's range. His hand fumbled shaking as he managed to unlatch and open my prayer box. It stayed upright on the cold stone floor.

'We're going to pray together.'

'Gods — never — answer me.'

'We'll see, Simenon. Press the index finger of your right hand in the sand and trace a circle. Then, keep your finger pressed hard in the sand while we pray together. You might not be able to say everything I speak, but just repeat my words inside your mind. Think it as hard as you can. The connection should do the rest.'

'Will — try.'

'I pray for intervention, Modd. For your faithful servant, Simenon, his blood your sacrifice. My blood your sacrifice. For the broken shell and spilled hydraulic fluid of your servant Mozart – your own seed – hardened artificial intelligence of the Directorium Inquisitorum Arius. The Protocols of Peace signed between the Wurm Melding and the Humanitum have been violated. Receive my memories, for murder and subversion be thy harvest here.'

Simenon murmured the words after me, little more than warm air escaping his bruised lips.

'Hear me, Modd, you ungrateful stack of wiped server cores. Heed me, quantum-beyond-quantum, you demanding, unappreciative dollop of shit spawned by gibbering monkey descendants coding at random. Trust in your war chariots, trust in your victory. Give me my bloody launch codes and authorize involution for me, toot bloody sweet.'

My prayer box began to shake. Simenon gasped but kept his finger pressed in the trembling orange sands, exactly as I had instructed. Across the surface of those ancient grains of Martian desert, a series of symbols began to slowly form. Sigils appearing to the right of the lad's simple circle. *Regret of Modd. Anger of Fure. Trespass of Tricord.* A memory key for something complex locked deep in my m-brain, encrypted-beyond-encrypted.

I cried out as the trigger phrase surfaced like an ice pick ripping through my consciousness. I spat blood out of my throat again. These terrible words demanded speaking bell-clear by me. 'Echion Red, Udaeus Gold, Chthonius Blue, Hyperenor White, Pelorus Black.'

'Robot — our — robot,' groaned Simenon. He could only stare as Mozart's shattered pile of components began to quiver and reform, tendrils of fibre forming around the edges of his broken hull, reaching out like roots, reconnecting his constituent parts. But not to join back together as Mozart again. The mess burrowed through the stone floor in a shower of rubble, sinking into the ground. Disappeared from sight.

'Not so much a robot,' I coughed. 'Think of him as a very large weapon-of-mass destruction with a very small conscience. Mozart's name is Legion, for he is many.'

'The gods — actually answered — me.'

I turned my gaze from the bubbling hole left by Mozart melting away. Back onto the lad. But poor faithful Simenon had passed away for good, the wonder of our achievement his final words; our prayer his last thought.

Lifting my head towards the chamber's rocky roof, I screamed in raw rage and pain; screamed until my throat was throbbing and filling with blood again.

As if in answer to my howls a dull black machine rose out of the floor, cracking cobblestones like an aggressive weed. No taller than a boot, a short steel spear with two coil-like legs on either side. A self-replicating war machine: a *spartoi*.

'Slice me out of this restraint grid,' I choked.

<Click, that.> A device of few words.

It half-hopped and half wobbled over to me, growing a series of tiny claws on wire-thin arms which traced across my restraint suit, slicing the alien material away from my broken body until it lay on the hard floor like a peeled orange. Then the spartoi melted the bolts punched through my wrists. I screamed in agony and tumbled off the composite cross and down onto the ground. Hitting the stone, I lay there, crumpled and near useless. My veins flowed with napalm. Slowly, I recovered m-brain function long enough to flood myself with every painkiller in my pharmacy index. Free of the restraining cross my body automatically activated emergency protocols for physical trauma-accelerated healing. I couldn't have stopped the process if I wanted to. I felt my middle-age spread sucking back and reducing as every gram of my excess weight metabolized and converted into accelerated Osteoclasts.

'Combat medic,' I croaked at the spartoi. 'Beloved of Tricord.'

<Click, that.>

It took a couple of minutes for a second spartoi to burrow up into the cell. This specialist arrived in the form of six silver grenade-sized spheres magnetically bonded together like a school project model of an exotic molecule. 'Boy, first,' I heaved.

This second spartoi rolled over to Simenon's body, hair-width feelers extending from one of its spheres, penetrating through the lad's skin. A speaker grille flowed into existence on one of the specialist's spheres. <Major haemorrhaging and tension-pneumothorax. TACEVAC cancelled. Deceased. Deceased.>

'I was a surgeon once,' I sobbed, 'I knew that.'

<Combat stress reaction,> tutted the combat medic, rolling towards me. <Heart failure detected. Tactical Field Care override instigating.>

'There highest heaves the swelling mound, that forms the soldier's honoured grave,' I wheezed to the combat medic as its tendrils pierced my body. I tried to crawl towards Simenon but failed completely. 'There pointing still, the captain says, "Here sleeps the Bravest of the Brave". Our shields are purely anti-collision, we carry no weapons.'

<Incoherent speech indicates acute stress disorder-related psychosis. Override for κ-opioid receptor agonists.>

'Just stabilise me, you semi-sentient quack. Can't you see I'm already running a zero-zero trauma protocol?'

<Terminal life failure. *All overrides*. All overrides. Injectable bone bio-ceramic composite: *crash authorisation*. Printing biohybrid flesh polymers: *crash authorisation*. Blood surrogate recombinant haemoglobin with heightened immune suppression: *crash authorisation*.>

'Mozart is going to love this,' I spat at the spartoi medic. 'Remade as a little more of him and a little less of me.'

I began to feel woozy and sick as the specialist operated on me. The ceiling spun in lazy circles. Or maybe it was the floor spinning. I wasn't sure if it was my body glanding anaesthetic or the combat medic's injections. *You can't fix stupid, but you can sedate it.* Three more combat-class spartoi identical to the first machine broke into my cell like moles. *Really, three of them?* How long was I going to be under?

'Danger, Will Roxley, danger,' I panted at the trio of soldier spartoi. Nothing. Mozart wasn't exactly known for his sense of humour. His children, even less so. 'Sod you then, if you don't want to sing along with Sweet William.'

Darkness claimed me. When it lifted nothing had changed in the chamber except my body. Still a mess of pain and aches, but suspiciously non-deceased. There was the fresh stench of burnt ozone in the air. A plasma beam or a kinetic assault rifle overheating? No corpses, not even ashes. My three spartoi bodyguards stood there, innocently. The combat medic had vanished, needed elsewhere. Of course, there was fighting in the capital; Collateral Damage was Mozart's middle name and the logic of war abhors moderation.

Moz was damnable effective, but we had a Melding man-of-war squatting in orbit. With that level of firepower circling Hexator the wurms could overwhelm a single Legion, self-replicating spartoi or no. Not quickly, but with blood and fire and the sacrifice of the gods-know how many innocents during the battle. Could we hold out until reinforcements arrived from the Humanitum? No. I'm afraid myself and Mozart *were* the reinforcements. But perhaps we didn't have to beat Lady Blez and her heathen wurm allies. There were forms in the Cold War between the Humanitum and the Melding. Would the wurms honour those forms? How I loathed their species. Adam's killers. Simenon's killers. My beautiful little boy. That was my weakness. The weakness Alice Blez had counted on. *Turnabout is fair play, my lady.*

I stood up and tried not to cry out loud as gravity compressed my new ribcage. I wouldn't describe my body as healed. Held together with duct tape and faint wishes was a better description. But I wasn't going to expire in the next few hours.

Before I left, I pulled my clothes back on, finding the stealth suit about as semi-functional as I was. *Everything's broken, today.* I wobbled over to Simenon's corpse. Kneeling, I gently lifted his finger from the Martian sands, closed the prayer box and stroked the blood-matted hair out of the boy's eyes. 'Yes, I believe Modd did answer you, Simenon.'

Time for Alice and the wurms to answer for what they've done, too.

- 31 -
Evolution. In action.

The storm I remembered from another life had finally finished. Pools of hot water had remade the roads as a gleaming moonscape. *Time for a new storm.* Another spartoi appeared when I stumbled out onto the open streets. This one resembled a walking hat-stand, multiple metal rods joined together and tottering towards me. *Oberquartiermeister*-class. General staff, so to speak. All comms and curly attitude. How long had it been out on the streets looking for me?

'Set comms with my ship,' I ordered. I pointed up to the nebula-painted heavens. 'My *real* ship, not that second-hand wreck docked dirt-side.'

<Establishing.>

A female face appeared projected in hologram outline: a sweet ship for Sweet William. 'Good evening, poppet.'

'Time to shed stealth and land at the capital, Exy. Transmitting you coordinates now.'

'That filthy Melding carrier-class of uncertain intent is still sharing vacuum with me. Plenty of fast movers, sub-ordnance, and drones that'll want to play tag,' cooed the *Expected Ambush*.

'I understand. Don't play too long, Exy. I need you like the desert needs the rain.'

'Hah, I so guessed that, as soon as thousands of little Mozlets started remaking Hexator into a highly kinetic hit-zone.'

'You're deuced clever.'

The avatar peered at me closely. 'And you look like crap. Is that a new look? Do be careful, poppet, the Melding inserted an orbital drop force of meat eaters thirty minutes ago; a little gift to assist the local spear carriers.'

Not what I needed to hear; wurm combat specialists landing here. 'Tango Mike, favoured ship girl.'

'Oh, love me sideways, a pair of their fast movers are all over our comms. Oops, *detected*. Scratch two. Converting for combat. Got to hustle.'

'Good hunting, Exy.'

The *Expected Ambush*'s avatar vanished. I stared up at the stars. Hell had come to the heavens, unleashed by me. My beautiful dark angel. Not the least of my sins, today. Not by any stretch. Oh yes, I was just getting started.

'We're heading for the old cathedral where the Goddess Inuno once dwelled,' I informed the staff spartoi, starting to sprint down the street. Damn, but it burned simply putting one foot in front of the other. 'There's a full council meeting in progress: reaching it alive and intact is our mission focus. Anything shoots or charges towards us, kill it twice. Anything crawling in a wurmoid fashion, those dirties don't even need to shoot first. Just burn them down at high speed.'

<Reorienting force projections.>

'Get some fire controllers on the route down range. The *Expected Ambush* is incoming: anything too heavily armoured for us, she's cleared hot. Try not to nuke anything. My suit's shielding is damnable fried today.'

<Click that,> confirmed the staff officer. It overtook me, tottering at high speed. Given it resembled an animated magic mop from *Fantasia*, that probably said more about my present parlous state than its own.

My three little soldier amigos were soon joined by twenty more spartoi, including a couple of barrel-fat *Steel Rain*-class artillery pieces that advanced by flipping over like drunken fleas in a circus act. Occasionally, slab-like metal legs pounded the ground and micro-rockets whooshed up as though dislodged by the thumps. *Fire controllers, already mowing the lawn.* I gazed into the dark nebula-filled sky. Micro-rockets spun around in wild circuits. They might resemble faulty fireworks accidentally broken free of a Catherine Wheel, but chaotic flight trace – countermeasures-resistant – felt anything but when a smart munitions payload slammed into you.

Someone stupidly opened fire on us from the corner of a street ahead; local riflemen, given Wurm forces were unlikely to be fielding .303 rimmed cartridges. I ducked as a zip-zip of bullets tickled the air. A chainsaw buzz instantly replied from the boot-high spartoi tripod on our point, 0.1mm rotary-rounds striking the corner providing shelter. That structure – a pottery shop, I believe – vanished, obscured by a cloud of vaporized wooden timbers and warm warrior flesh meeting a couple of thousand metal splinters at hypersonic velocity. The quarter of the building left intact started to slide onto the wreckage below as we passed at speed. It would be safer to treat anything with a heat signature as a hostile, but only for me. *Enough innocents will die today*. This might be my death march; it shouldn't become the murder of every non-combatant inside the capital. But getting to our destination alive was only going to get harder.

Similar thoughts must have occurred to what passed for a mind inside the staff officer. A silver cloud arrowed high over the roofs of the street, a drone swarm, a spartoi murmuration appearing to shape-shift in the air as though it was a single swirling molten mass. It dived, descending to street level. It tagged me as I ran, coiling protectively around, a couple of feet from my body; thousands of little coin-sized rotorheads, half the swarm defensive shield projectors, the remainder offensive micro-weapon platforms.

Just in time. The first of the wurms' drop commandos appeared at the end of a side-street. It was so embedded inside its force-suit it might as well have been a machine with cyborg accessories. That's the difference between the Melding and the Humanitum: the wurms' army actually *looks* dangerous. Demon tank-caterpillar, all weapon muzzles, grenade tubes and razored black armour; moving in an evasive pattern like a serpent from your worst nightmare. My Legion resembled a random art collection built as the losing bet in a scrap-yard challenge. Designed by the gods, self-replicating strange and ever-evolving odd. But then, you had to wonder what cypermethrin aerosol looked like to a red ant before its anthill was sprayed. A threat?

My m-brain noise-cancelled the wurm's subsonic hum, a field designed to make me piss my pants and flee the street in fear. Shells started to thump from the commando's armour, laser light lancing out, intended to blind optical sensors and ensure its package was signed for at our end. My wasp swarm converted into a firefly dance as their shields flared into life. Catching rattling shrapnel for me as our soldier spartoi swatted down incoming shells.

A couple of newly minted spartoi broke ground behind the tanker, peeking comically from their holes before emerging. Their tiny spike-like legs dug into the soil, dropping central rods towards the wurm in a salute. *Heavenly host, blessed of Modd and Arius.* It can't have been easy to squeeze so much high-energy ionized gas into something as compact as a spartoi; even harder for the commando to absorb twin plasma bursts. The tank caterpillar's rear cracked apart, shields and armour instantly overwhelmed. A single spring-like soldier came bouncing out of my company's ranks, two mad cricket leaps and it was inside the tank suit, a whirl of metal resembling a cartoon Tasmanian devil. That wurm commando even sounded dangerous as my spartoi shredded it from the inside out. I left its ruins croaking and neutered as we pressed on. *No mercy for the wurms, no mercy for the heathens.*

I'd almost thought the wurms had stopped trying by the time I was only a couple of minutes out from the grand assembly. But, no. They had merely been marshalling their forces for an honest attempt. Force concentration. My m-brain tied in with the accompanying staff officer to provide an All-Source Analysis System markup of the wurm assault force. *Oh dear.* There was the swarm master, more drones than fleas on a hound. A wurm jammer specialist, prodding away at our comms and counter-fire sensors. Dozens of tanker force-suits, cousins of the wurm commando we'd left disembowelled on the other side of town and irked about their comrade's treatment. A Mobile Battlefield Operating System Specialist, command-and-control protected by more dark razored armour than a small military orbital. Also, a couple of jump-suited scouts burning about on thrusters; frankly ridiculous, flying wurms appear inelegantly asinine.

Matters moved rapidly, breaking bad instantaneously.

I remember what Mozart said to me once when we stood together high on a mountain overlooking the plains of Alpha Ophiuchi. We had been inserted by the Humanitum Fleet Dreadnought *Save The Last Bullet For Me*, watching seven fully deployed Legions battling the full invasion force of the Al-hawwa Diaspora. Watching the complete grisly panoply of utter chaos and unmitigated violence unfold before our eyes. *'Sodding heck, that's the full whizz-pop down there!'*

Yes, once more I had sprinted headlong into the full whizz-pop. Proper naughty. Close quarters battle fought between two civilizations which had each battered the way to the top of their respective phylogenetic tree. Don't think of it as combat, think of it as evolution-in-action.

Heavy spartoi rolled past me, a mess of rolling hammers and flashing energy projectors, charging the enemy at high speed, my gallant Laser Light Brigade. Such spartoi were expendable, noisy and obvious. It's the drones you don't see until too late that are designed as the true danger. My breakneck comrades swapped war stories with the tanker-suited monstrosities, shells for energy bursts, soldiers popping on both sides of the philosophical divide. Call me petty, vindictive, with a heart spilling vengeance, but the heat and stench of a wurm bonfire can keep a man warm at night.

This was war. Incoherent, chaotic and moving far too fast to follow. A fog of war given literal existence by my artillery pieces rapidly pumping out superdense smoke canisters, hot fibres drifting in the air to tease the enemy's thermal imaging systems. Wurm target designators blocked while my spartoi served up the full kinetic breakfast.

Something screeched through the smoke, briefly targeted by my three bodyguards. But it was only a flock of so-called sparrows, flying insect-lizards unseated from their roost by the rattle of machine weapons and detonating shells. Flecks of burning vegetation followed the flock, towering mushrooms which had survived the alien sky's energy storms tested to destruction by the clash around their roots.

A hellfire scene, a battlefield painted by surrealists; rainbow smoke and inhuman screams, melting spartoi spinning into sight as black razored monsters undulated through the smoke.

The earth trembled and shook. Stolen from a dream, the jammer specialist's massive decapitated head rolled out of the smoke, slowing to a rest at my feet as tribute. Then the deafening chainsaw rip of a rotary cannon, sparking impacts from a metal cyclone, the divine geometry of a Legion's nuclear-pumped lasers intersecting the shifting murk.

I could tell the battle was turning badly against us when hundreds of *Hauberk*-class spartoi started climbing like ants out of the shell-cratered soil. They poured up my legs, meshing as they clambered, climbing my torso and flowing along my arms, seeking interface with my sadly unresponsive clothes. Deeming the stealth suit broken, they clicked into place across my skull and established a direct battlefield connection with my m-brain, rather than trying to mediate through my glitching clothes. In a matter of seconds, I wore a fine spread of spartoi chain-mail. Mozart and me. Just a boy and his robot, ready for mischief.

As the fog of war began to clear my position I gritted my teeth against an uncomfortable vibration. The wurm's MBOSS had hit on the tactic of using sonic disruptors to remove enough smoke for its targeting systems to make a clean lock.

<Withdrawal recommended,> suggested the staff officer.

Hell, if it's just shooting the breeze. 'Go, tell the Spartoi, thou who passest by, that here obedient to their laws we lie,' I answered, indicating we would fight to the bitter end. I was a rash fool. I had attacked too early, our Legion not yet fully seeded. But then, for my desperate scheme to work, I needed to reach the grand assembly *before* this world passed into the Melding's care as a protectorate. Would my enemies yield?

The wurms sent me their answer, an airborne thrust suit diving out of the smoke towards me, lines of micro-round fire stitching the ground from twin guns. I don't think they'd realised yet that it wasn't just Sweet William they were shooting at. I felt the artificial muscles of my armour modulate as I leaped high into the air and transected the wurm's arc, seizing its left flight pack. I snapped and inverted the thruster, causing the scout to unbalance and smash straight through a house, smoke, and fire blasting out from inside. I'm not sure how fatal a bad landing would prove against wurm scout armour, but the pair of spartoi sprinter mines that came comically jogging down the road, vaulting through the hole before detonating certainly sealed the deal.

Dissolved by the wurm's MBOSS, our smoke cover and smart particles dispersed enough to reveal the wreckage of spartoi and an advancing force of tank-suited alien demons.

The Humanitum didn't possess a god of war, not exactly, so I closed my eyes and whispered a prayer to Fure, Goddess of Armed Impertinence, instead. *Favoured of the Fleet, loved of the Legion, most hallowed among the hardened artificial intelligences of Arius.* Sadly, mumbling in Fure's name wasn't going to be nearly enough to save me.

= 32 =
The Lady's answer.

The three spartoi amigos that comprised my personal bodyguard suddenly started hunkering down, burrowing into the soil, switching energy fields from offensive weapons to shields. I followed suit as the circling murmuration tightened ranks and became my personal shield wall, augmenting my armour's protection. My prayer wasn't about to be answered. At least, not by the Goddess Fure.

That was when the first kinetic strike slammed into the street, the *Expected Ambush* showing the Melding forces her definition of Close Orbital Support on the swing down to a dust-off. Danger close, but far more dangerous for the wurms. Tungsten rods with a directional thrust system. *Rods from the gods summoned by a dark angel.*

Explosions erupted, dozens of surrounding buildings gone in a fire-flash as bright as a sun this world had never seen before. Each rod struck with a ripping thwack, the scream of Yggdrasil being uprooted out of the soil by Odin. I rode the throbbing blast-wave, my chain-mail battered and shedding heat as fast as it could absorb it. There wasn't much of an evasive plan of action anyone could field against orbital ammunition given terminal velocity by gravity's kiss. It was a despicable tactic, but one the

Melding wouldn't imitate. But then, I could never have opened fire on a world filled with wurm settlers, either. Not without inviting a level of total war neither side wanted or could afford.

I prayed this street's inhabitants had been scared enough to flee the battlefield, not so terrified they'd headed down to storm shelters. *How many more innocents on my conscience? How many more tombstone-shaped rocks as shipwreck for my faith?*

Spartoi soldiers switched back to full offensive mode, pressing their advantage against the badly wrecked enemy, segments of action briefly visible through dark raining rubble. A jigsaw of confusion and ferocity. Flashes of fire, kinetic, energy-based and wildly weaving smart munitions seeking out instruments of wickedness. There was little time to brood, for any human response to this, but I made one anyway.

'After main objective's achieved, re-purpose for search and rescue and medical assistance,' I ordered the staff spartoi as it corkscrewed back up to the surface, embracing our realm of dust and smoke. 'Dig all survivors out.'

<Click, that.>

A sticking plaster for the limbless they'd drag from these broken ruins. They deserved more and better, but Sweet William was all the innocent had.

I pressed on, hard, through the fog of war. Unfortunately, I sprinted straight into a commando wearing a force-suit which had survived our rods. I felt the warmth of the thing's targeting laser flickering out of the smoke. Master Wurm was doubtless feeding something heavy and high-explosive into its biggest and baddest rotating cannon when it noticed a combatant that resembled a metal tumbleweed rolling down its ugly length.

My spartoi grenadier flashed me a warning as it injected timed charges, little burrowing grubs perfect for breaching a wurm's power armour segments. I managed to duck in time as half the creature's flank departed the rest of its suit. I was hardly stretching my drone cloud's protective shielding. The tumbleweed-shaped spartoi bounced onto the street's dirt and rolled away gaily into the smoke, seeking fresh violence.

I followed its example.

***

My mail suit clicked like falling dominoes as it removed itself from around my skull. I needed to appear as human as possible before facing the grand assembly. To that end, I tossed aside two unconscious bodies, one filling each hand before I entered the cathedral's central temple. This pair were supposedly Watch officers; ex-rebels wearing ill-fitting leathers liberated from the genuine article if I was any judge of character. They had been conducting an experiment: can looted Watch cutlasses slice through spartoi-composed smart-mail armour? As it happens, the result of that particular experiment is multiple rib fracture and stress-induced cardiomyopathy.

A grand council inside, indeed. Lords and ladies of Hexator's houses, great and minor, set out before me. Magistrates, guild notables, local merchants and a few familiar faces I recognised. Jenelle Cairo and the plantation mistress, Ajola Hara. How kind of Ajola to risk the dangerous roads leading to the capital.

Of course, prime among those in attendance, Lady Blez and her eldest son Daylen Blez playing dress-up as Commander General of the Watch. Link hovered a couple of feet behind his mistress, a hulking physical reminder of the scale of her supremacy, here. Sun of Clatch Rising, also. The wurm ambassador rested like a beached whale in a prime position to the left of the lectern where

Alice Blez was busy making an impassioned plea for Hexator to become a Melding protectorate. Well, I say plea. Much of the little I heard sounded like a list of bribes.

Alice broke off as she spotted me. 'Remove that filthy offworlder!' yelled Lady Blez, recoiling in almost physical shock. 'He has no place at a grand council.'

Yes, I could read it all from her tells. *Shock, horror and visceral disappointment.* Sweet William had no place in the realm of the living as far as Alice was concerned, let alone this old cathedral.

'Let him speak!' shouted one of the guild representatives.

'Grodar also wishes to hear the doctor speak,' cried the plantation mistress, her blue eyes flashing mischievously at me across the chamber. Ajola really did enjoy making mischief. A trait we shared.

Lady Blez shot a filthy look at her plantation controller. Alice had many rivals inside this meeting, unhappy with the quick turn of events in her favour. But what she didn't have was a sense of perspective, yet. Something I needed to provide. She jabbed a frenzied finger at me. 'I command quorum among the Four. I say this crazy zealot taints our presence with his lies and foreign ambitions! Arrest him immediately!'

Foreign ambitions? That was a bit rich, given the presence of Sun of Clatch Rising at the assembly. Jenelle Cairo stared at her Commander General's furious face, before shrugging sadly at me and waving a squad of officers forward.

I indicated the chamber's entrance as her officers waded through delegates to reach me. 'Are you so sure you speak with a quorum, Lady Blez?'

It was hard to say what drove the chamber to instant silence: my circus act appearing in the archway, or the person the Legion escorted at their head. *Zane Derechor*, a company of his loyal house guards filing in behind my spartoi.

'The Lord Derechor is dead!' shouted Commander General Daylen. 'This is a trick. A projection, a machine simulacrum.'

'A trick of Humanitum medical science. My life saved inside the medical bay of Doctor Roxley's vessel,' growled Zane Derechor. 'I'm as real as you, boy. More real than the rank of that Watch uniform you've stolen.'

I shrugged apologetically at Lady Blez. 'My ship did seem the safest place for his lordship given the shockingly high fatality rate among heads of the Four. You might recall I extended you the same courtesy. My vessel set down recently, returning the surviving Lord Derechor home.'

'You told me both twins were dead!' spluttered Lady Blez. A sound enough ploy, casting doubt on my propensity to tell the truth.

'No, my lady, I said they had passed beyond this realm. Sarlee Derechor sadly met his death under the best part of a collapsing mountain. Zane Derechor, meanwhile, has been healing in the heavens under the care of a sweet angel; beyond your realm, indeed.'

Although to be fair, the surviving Lord Derechor owed his life far more to Mozart than I. Moz had protected Zane from the worst of the rockfall, administering a stabilizing combat medical pack to keep him alive long enough to ride a medevac up to Exy. I smiled towards Jenelle Cairo. How was she to know that the comet she'd watched with me on Hebateen's slopes was the retrieval capsule spat out by my ship?

Lady Blez was not to be gainsaid. 'I still speak with the voice of three families. Throw this fraud out *now*!'

'Three, my lady? A recount might be in order.' I indicated the archway a second time.

Nie Trabb appeared, her young niece in tow with what remained of the Trabb house guards as well as dozens of madly tumbling spartoi. 'Late for the meeting. But not quite as late as you thought me, Alice, eh? My apologies to the grand council, but I needed to extract Lady Trabb from her dismal accommodation at the Watch citadel on our way here.'

'One of the many reasons I didn't want to sell you my faithful robot,' I informed Lady Blez, 'is that Mozart is damnable fireproof. Useful in a hall burning, where human fire protectors would be roasted trying to rescue an old bird from the oven.'

Nie folded her arms and gazed across the faces of the grand assembly, daring them to intervene. 'Don't look so upset, Lady Blez. I rather enjoyed being dead for a while. I spent my time productively, mustering the Trabb forces while your rebels were making merry, stealing and looting. Doctor Roxley laid before me his suspicions about the murders and the anarchy. I, too, say the grand council needs to hear his words.'

'Seconded,' barked Lord Derechor.

Lady Blez's face twisted in horror. 'No!'

'The thing about Wurm restraining crosses,' I said, 'is that they suppress all that nasty high-end combat and assassin chicanery.' I beckoned my hat stand-shaped staff spartoi forward. 'Tricks like glanding acid to melt the bolts nailing a prisoner to the device, or deactivating pain receptors. But what a cross can't disable is an m-brain's basic operating functions; such as verified truth recording…'

My staff spartoi projected a hologram of the recorded torture session, making it sufficiently large for everyone in the chamber to watch without jostling for position.

'Was it difficult for you to assassinate your first husband? Two bullets, one to burst his head and one to break his heart.'

'Easier than you think.'

'And murdering Lord Seltin?'

'I was little more than a child when Falt raped me. All for the obsession of his stupid project, of course. Would you not consider it fitting for the product of our union to take revenge on the old pervert?'

'What's your self-serving excuse for bringing down a mountain on top of the twins, on all the others you've killed…?'

'Surely, a priest appreciates the need of a sacrifice for the greater good?'

And so it went until the projection finally ceased and Lady Blez stood condemned. Not by my words but by her own.

I bowed towards Alice. 'And so Modd reveals the deep things of darkness and drags utter dark into the light.'

Shouts of anger and outrage began to break out among the assembled notables. Alice read the mood accurately, fleeing in panic towards the Wurm ambassador. 'Asylum, I request political asylum from the Melding for myself and my family!'

'Sun of Clatch Rising has consensus to embrace a new world. Not Lady Blez. What use does Melding have for fallen leaders?'

Ah, the gratitude of the Melding is a fine force to observe. I lacked the appropriate microscope to try.

Lady Blez whirled to single out her bodyguard. 'Link, escort me out of here!'

'As you wish, my lady,' said the hulking robot, crashing forward. 'I'LL CRACK OPEN ANY BASTARD WHO GETS IN MY WAY!'

Sadly for the noblewoman, I had a friend in need of a rematch. My spartoi murmuration had been patrolling the cathedral domes and spires. Now, it abandoned its post and flowed inside the temple chamber. The cloud darted around, between and over terrified warriors and Watch officers until it reached Link. Lady

Blez wisely abandoned her bodyguard's side, retreating towards her eldest son and his retinue.

Link popped open weapon hatches and began to fire off volleys, projectiles sparking against the defensive rotorheads' shields. Coin-shaped spartoi darted at random from the cloud, breaking free of the molten silver ring circling Link. They struck the ex-construction robot hard and fast, meteorites puncturing an unshielded space capsule. Metal debris spurted from each hole. Link twisted and turned, fiercely pouring fire against the murmuration surrounding him, violently punching and kicking out at the coiling spartoi.

Link was quickly left punching with more holes than hull in his hide, a veritable Swiss cheese. The robot slowed, growing clumsy as he shed vital motor functions. Link's counterfire grew erratic, weapons misfiring and losing tracking, my rotorheads mobbing him as they grew ever more confident.

'Oh dear — this is not how I predicted — the afternoon ending,' fizzed Link, jabbing and flailing. 'BURN YOUR—SODDING—WASP NEST—DOWN!'

A Frisbee formed from a hundred rotorheads before spinning out of the cloud, removing Link's head with the clean economy of a buzz-saw.

'Drlnkkkkks—on the—lawnnnnn, madam?' stuttered the decapitated robot skull as it tumbled across the floor. 'Aaahhhh—myssssself—againnnnnnn.'

Link's massive body collapsed to his knees, smoke leaking from the industrial strength battery pack inside his chest. What was left of the construction robot fell like a crane across the central well, propped there jerking while leaking black hydraulic fluid onto the mosaic floor.

Commander General Daylen, his retinue and mother were already halfway across the temple chamber, heading for one of the smaller exits.

'Whose Watch are you? Hers or the Four's'?' I shouted at the enforcers, my murmuration flowing towards the exit, cutting off the retinue's escape. 'And while you consider the answer to that question, ask yourself whether your necks are any better armoured than Link's was?'

'I hold a pardon!' cried Daylen Blez, showing contemptibly little loyalty towards his mother. 'I'm a free man.'

Nie Trabb jabbed an old twig-like finger at the boy. 'A pardon requires two signatures by the Four to be granted.'

'I *have* two!'

Lord Derechor shook his head. '*One*. A murderess cannot legally inherit her victim's titles or property.'

'Arrest them both!' barked Jenelle Cairo. 'Any officer who wants to wear the badge at the end of day will follow the word of the law.'

If that word was *expedience*, it seemed the warriors and Watch officers inside the temple chamber were all too eager to switch sides and obey. Daylen's retinue seized the struggling rebel leader. Lady Blez fell, bundled to the floor by her own fighters, many of whom needed to be restrained from revenging Uance Blez's murder under their watch. Was this to become a kangaroo court? Who am I to judge? Just a man with the threat of a Legion's wrath standing at his back, innocently waiting inside an abandoned temple that would also make a serviceable stopgap courtroom.

A trial by Alice's peers, at the very least, ensued. With her confession on record there was no alternative, not even for Alice's most ardent supporters and sucklers of her bounty. The grand assembly passed unanimous verdicts in record time on Lady Blez and her eldest son. Breaking by wheel for the crimes of multiple murder, sedition, treason, insurrection, and rebellion. The court's sentence to be carried out immediately.

And of course, the proposal for Hexator to petition the Melding for membership was tossed to the wind. All foreign forces commanded to depart the moon in haste. I suppose that included myself and my spartoi as well as all the filthy wurms on the world. Well, I would doubtless receive a warmer welcome in the Humanitum than the thwarted ambassador when she was recalled by the Melding. Failure wasn't an attribute the wurms bred for inside their gene-pool.

Finally, the motion passed for Rendor Blez to be married off to Nie Trabb's niece under the protectorship of Lord Derechor. A dividing of the Blez spoils which Solomon himself would have approved of. That Lady Blez's youngest son was deemed innocent of complicity in his mother's crimes seemed of little comfort to Alice. I watched Lady Blez pulled red-faced and trembling through the temple chamber, her destination the canals and death.

It took six large warriors to forcibly remove Daylen Blez, struggling every foot of the way. 'Blood on all existing social conditions! I don't recognise the authority of this fucking court! The axe's kiss will arrive for every noble leech's neck here!'

Alice threw her arms towards the retainers inside the chamber as she was dragged backward. 'I cared for the people! I'm the only one! I would have saved you all!'

There was more virtue in Lady Blez's signalling than her eldest son's, but her body would still be twisted apart and broken by the waterwheels.

Should I feel pity for Alice? A heathen-loving dreamer born into a position she'd abused to plot and subvert. I did feel compassion for my misguided lady, but perhaps I shouldn't. *Not for Simenon's killer. Not for a heretic wurm lover.* It was devolved idiocies such as Alice's which had collapsed this world's civilization in the first place. Ape Alpha barbarism causing darkness to descend until the very gods themselves had abandoned Hexator in despair. How many innocents had lived and died during that long night; sacrificed futures for their rulers' sins of pride, envy, and avarice? So easy to love the woman; so hard to love her schemes.

Sun of Clatch Rising slithered over to me, my three self-appointed spartoi bodyguards wobbling into position as they dipped kinetic gun heads at the disgusting creature. It wasn't going to try anything, though. I read its loathsome species' body language well enough to know that. *Thoroughly defeated, I should say.*

'Good game played by William Roxley,' hissed the wurm ambassador. 'Clever, clever.'

'Is that what you call what the two of us did to this damned world?' I asked angrily. 'A game? Tell that to the hundreds of dead we've left strewn across Hexator.'

The wurm reared up threateningly. 'How *humans* think.'

'The fallen here, perhaps. You might have visited the righteous inside the Humanitum for a fuller perspective on the race of man.'

It made a retching noise as though it was choking on its intestines. It seemed to physically deflate in front of my eyes, 'Such visits not for Sun of Clatch Rising. Sun of Clatch Rising must end her life.'

I shrugged. 'Yes, your kind's tradition. That's the trouble with summits, they're so often followed by a sharp cliff edge.'

'Sun of Clatch Rising glad for final ending. Corrupted mind, filthy deviant-form dirtied with human-DNA. Thinking like human filth. Sun of Clatch Rising fearing her own death *like* human filth!'

'You almost make me sad to see you go, madame ambassador. I'm sure the Melding will send another replacement soon enough to deal with the Empty. I'll be there to frustrate your replacement's evil heresies as long as I draw breath. Humble servant of Arius that I am.'

'Servant,' the wurm hissed raggedly in a foul mimicry of laughter. 'William Roxley acts as slave of cold machine monsters created by self-kind. Clever, clever slave, but William Roxley still vassal-slave.'

'Allow William Roxley to leave you to enjoy the freedom of your imminent euthanasia, then, madame ambassador.' I bowed to the foul thing and left.

I should have felt happy, victorious. But I found I couldn't. All I could think of was Alice and her fate.

Dark moon lost in the Empty; melancholy was her gift.

− 33 −
Sublime in the slime

Jenelle Cairo appeared outside the old cathedral to escort me to the port. Her honour guard of Watch thugs hung back at a discrete distance. I could almost imagine we were two old friends out for a stroll in the warm evening air. In a way, I suppose we were.

'What were you doing inside the hall?' Jenelle questioned me, an interrogator to the end.

'Clearing the central temple's well,' I said. 'It's state of repair bothered me, but I discovered it needs a better caretaker than I.'

'Is that all you've been doing, cleaning?'

'Of course, why do you ask?'

'My officers couldn't find Link's body or head after the grand assembly ended.'

I smiled at Jenelle. 'How very curious.'

'Also, Melding transports have been coming and going all day at the landing field,' said Jenelle. 'I haven't spotted your shore traffic, but—'

'—but the Legion seems to have disappeared anyway? They do that, you know, captain. They're a queer little crew.'

'Actually, it's commander general, now. I hope you're not disappointed by my promotion.'

'Why should I be, m'dear? I dropped a word on your behalf with Nie Trabb and the Lord Derechor.'

'*You?*' I enjoyed the confused look of shock crossing her face. 'But why?'

'Better to ask why hold grudges at my age? There's nothing wrong with wanting change for your people, Jenelle. What's the point of life, if not to strive for noble causes? To make your muddled moon a better place for those who'll walk it after you're gone. But such causes are preferably accomplished in deed and in truth.'

We turned a corner, heading down a lantern-lit shopping street. Hexatorians were out in numbers again inside their city. The storms had passed, both natural and sentient-stirred. There was shockingly little physical sign of the people's revolt against their rulers, the brief civil war's bloodletting or the Legion's brutal brush with the Melding forces. I wondered to myself what I was leaving behind, here. How much of an impact I had made and what it had cost me. The price Hexator had paid.

'And who decides on what's the truth…?' asked Jenelle.

I thought of the Legion's bizarre children eviscerating the hideous wurm commandos. Our eternal clash of cultures and worldviews. I gave the only answer I had. 'Evolution.'

Better to ride the tiger, even as fleas in its fur, than oversee the tiger's torment as zookeepers. How far we will travel and what glories might we see.

Jenelle seemed to accept my answer at face value. 'I sought you out first at your tavern lodgings. Your bag had packed itself. It ran off as I arrived, but these were inside your room.' She produced the marble-sized courier ball passed to me by Varnus Afrique, as well as my concert flute.

I noted there was a little green light flashing on the courier ball's shell. I had to smile. *Yes, I know, I am due a major pecking from Rena.* How irked would she be I had nominated her as Simenon's guardian and guide inside the Merge? Highly, was the best response to that. *Modd did answer and Rena will just have to get used to it.* Someone new in the afterlife for my dead wife Rena to fuss over and distract her from Sweet William's nag-time. Win-win was the ancient phrase for that, I believe. I am fairly sure I owed Simenon an apology, though, the first time we spoke through heaven's gate.

'Thank you,' I said. 'I was planning to leave the ball behind, but my flute almost has a mind of its own. I never know where I'm going to find it from one day to the next.'

'I owned a necklace like that, once,' said Jenelle.

Hah, I very much doubted it. I lifted the sphere and flute from her hands. The courier ball I slipped inside my carry bag for later. My flute had reappeared slightly burnished. I polished it with my sleeve until the maker's mark gleamed. Gemeinhardt Musical Instruments had been producing flutes back when humanity was confined to a single world and its *Die Zauberflöte* model was top-of-the-range.

'There is one small favour you can do me,' I said.

'A *bribe* in return for my new position, doctor?'

'You earned that job on your own merits.' I passed Jenelle a small canvas-wrapped package. 'Next time your airship calls at Hebateen, kindly make sure that this is passed into Master Arto Jagg's hands.'

Jenelle stared suspiciously at the package.

'Don't worry, nothing illegal. Your rulers are the drug dealers here, not me. It's a recording and projection orb containing Alice and Daylen Blez's execution. It's activation keyed to Arto's biometrics and I pray it brings the poor man some small vestige of peace.'

'You were at the execution?' Jenelle sounded surprised.

I nodded, sadly. No easy task to make the recording given the size of the mob turned out for the execution. Thousands of citizens sobbing, those grown-up saved by Alice's street sentries from drowning. There had nearly been a riot between would-be revolutionaries baying for blue blood and everyone fed and protected by Alice's charity. Even Daylen had looked shocked at that; how eagerly the revolution turned and ate its own. It had taken the angry threat of my Spartoi murmuration appearing, machine tornado of the gods, to lower the mob's boiling point.

You can't save everyone, doctor, you must have learned that. You shouldn't even try. Is that why Alice spat at me when I snuck past the Watch thugs strapping her to the waterwheel, fastening her limb chains. Is that why Alice rejected my offer to her for the Merge? Beautiful fire to the end. It was easy to love a woman like Alice Blez, even as she was torn apart. She found me there in her last moments, locked eyes with me in the crowd. I'm not sure why she did that. I had nothing left to offer her; certainly not salvation from my rejected gods. Yes, I had watched the damnable barbaric spectacle from start to end. A hypocrite's tears rolling down his irrational human cheeks as two murderers were ripped apart on the canals' waterwheels.

At least they were both executed together: Alice and her vicious eldest pup. Alice's false future for Hexator dying with my fair lady, as easily as Falt's foolish dreams of a perfect humanity.

Alice Blez had been wrong about so many things, yet right about at least one. *Kitten to my tiger, indeed.* Alice had murdered plenty. But me? I could pile all my victims up starting on Hexator's surface and not stop until I reached this system's star. I could fill the Empty with my sins and barbarities. Why the hell do you think my ship coos Sweet William at me? Did you also believe Little John was a midget, you dumb fuck?

As the two of us strolled to our destination I spotted something Jenelle hadn't noticed: a small street shrine built into a wall attracting a crowd on the opposite side of the street. Amazed peasants queued up to jostle around the shrine. I surmised that Goog, God of the Small Journey, had already starting interacting with supplicants. Not all the spartoi had returned to the soil. Repurposed as a seed crop, because the gods surely hate waste.

Jenelle served me with a heavy wax-sealed document roll as we reached the port complex. 'Doctor William Roxley, free citizen of the Humanitum, by order of the Grand Assembly your entry visa to Hexator is permanently cancelled. You are banned from conducting any and all trade here. You are barred without appeal from returning to this realm for the rest of your lives, both natural and synthetic. This order shall be breached upon pain of torture and execution.'

I kissed the commander general once on each cheek. 'Don't worry, Commander General Cairo, I'm rarely needed twice in the same place. May Modd's grace envelop and lift you in my absence.'

'What exactly is your Modd the god *of*, again?'

'God of Balance,' I said, 'Divine Justice and Shenanigans.'

I climbed the steps to the port building, halting to glance up at nebulae filling the night sky. I'll say this about Hexator, it gives a cursed fool a clear view over the constellations. Each of those spears of distant starlight far older than me; although I had travelled further. I was almost eager to see where the *You Can't Prove It Was Us* would carry me next. Exy had already sent me word that she had docked with the vast mothership, one among dozens of smaller merchant vessels, successful or otherwise, at the spore-spice auctions.

I left Jenelle Cairo standing there, scrupulously ensuring I departed, much as I had first encountered the woman. A dangerous vision; the promise of something rash and fresh.

I hadn't told Jenelle that Master Jagg's recording also contained details of who had had laid blasting charges to collapse his mine. I owed Arto Jagg the truth. Whether Jenelle survived her next trip home would depend on Master Jagg's feelings about matters of family, faith, flag and forgiveness. Where Arto stood in the feud and evils the Derechors had worked against Jenelle's clan. I prayed Arto might forgive Jenelle, as I could never forgive my son's butchers.

Billy Bones slipped past the legs of merchants and hustlers to join me as I approached the corridors feeding into the port. The hound had foreseen the generosity of the meat synthesizers on board the *Expected Ambush*. I foresaw Exy making me clean up every resulting turd pile sooner than deploying any of her maintenance drones.

No heavily armed harbour guards and shakedowns waited for me here. Anyone who could afford to leave Hexator was welcome to become someone else's problem.

'A profitable auction for you,' the elderly port official on the entry corridor peered inside my passport, 'Master Roxley?'

'I saved every soul on Hexator.' I pointed down at the bloodhound. 'My payment.'

The official took my words for a touch of parting horseplay. 'I dare say it could have been worse.'

I shrugged. 'You're undoubtedly right.'

Departing Hexator was easy. Only arriving was hard.

FINI

Reader's Universe offer

You can claim a complimentary copy of my sci-fi adventure novella *Sliding Void* by joining the free **Stephen Hunt Readers' Universe** group.

You'll be the first to know next time I have some cool stuff to give away (& you can unsubscribe at any time).

Get your free copy of Sliding Void at **http://www.StephenHunt.net/voidsliders.php**

Thanks

A big vote of thanks must go to my gallant crew of test readers who acted as the final set of eyes on the manuscript.

This includes (in the order of comments and typos returned):

Todd Rathier.
Joe Speranza.
Eva Sanchez.
Julian White.
Patrick Forhan.
Ron Olexsak.
Keith Hobman.
Stuart Robertson.